All the Things I Know

AUDREY RYAN

OYSTERVILLE, WA

ALL THE THINGS I KNOW

Copyright © 2017 by Audrey Ryan

All rights reserved, including the right to reproduce this book, or portions thereof, in any format whatsoever. For information: P.O. Box 34, Oysterville WA 98641

ISBN: 978-1-68131-021-3

Cover design by Zorylee Diaz-Lupitou
Image sources: pixaby.com, unsplash.com, iStock.com, 123RF.com, Alfonse Mucha
Layout by Ellen Pickels

This book is dedicated to the memory of my mom, who was the first champion of my writing, and to my aunt Naomi, who influenced my love of Jane Austen. I miss you both.

Chapter One

I t's seven in the morning, and I've just reached Portland's city limits. It's a Tuesday, and the traffic is starting to thicken with the morning commute. I will be in Seattle in around three hours if the traffic lets up. The air in my car is stale, and I need to brush my teeth. I've been driving for more than ten hours, and my hips ache from sitting too long.

My eyes zone out on the peeling bumper sticker on the car in front of me that reads "26.2." I think of Jane and wonder if she will run the Seattle marathon again as she has every other year. I can't wait to see her.

Jane recently passed the bar, and we're going to celebrate. She also found us a "darling apartment" in her favorite neighborhood, Ballard, where indie kids moved to have babies. Five years ago, it was affordable and still had a lot of parking. Now it's full of thirty-something internet geeks with tattoos and thick glasses, parents who hire babysitters so they can still drink PBR tallboys and catch a show on the weekend. The crowd that looks down with disdain on people my age because they figured it out first. The lucky ones who knew to buy a house when their Amazon jobs were still a novelty. My Uncle Eddie bought his five-bedroom house in Ballard in the nineties for just over $200K before his law practice was even successful. The house was recently appraised at over a million. Eddie's doing well these days.

I'm excited and apprehensive about the move to Seattle, but I'll be living with my best friend and sister. I have no doubt that our new apartment is as darling as she claims. When I get there, we will celebrate and talk until two in the morning about our hopes and fears for this new phase in life.

I pull up in front of the brick building close to noon and text Jane.

Here!

Where should I park?

A little bubble pops up under my text and blinks three dots. I can't contain my smile.

Yay!!!!

On my way!

Just pull into the alley and turn on your flashers. I'll help you unload!

I slide out of the driver's seat and brush crumbs off my lap. I know I look like shit. My teeth feel fuzzy, and I purse my lips together. I move to the pavement, stretch, and lean against the car. The cool breeze is a relief after hours in the stifling car.

Jane rushes out a moment later, eyes shining happily. I haven't seen her since Christmas, but I still marvel at how beautiful she is. Always have. Her hair is tied back in a scarf, her face free of makeup but scrubbed bright and dewy with the sheen of a perfectly balanced complexion. Radiant. She wears a casual black romper, a style only someone with long legs and a graceful shape can pull off. I try not to compare my sleepless complexion, dirty yoga pants, and haphazard bun to her effortless style.

"Lizzie!" She squeals as she pulls me into a fierce hug. "Did you drive all night? I've missed you sooooo much!"

I laugh and squeeze her back with the same amount of enthusiasm.

"Almost fifteen hours straight," I groan. "I'm exhausted. But *so* glad to see you!" I hug her again, and she laughs.

"C'mon, let's get your stuff upstairs and your car parked so you can rest and shower."

"Are you trying to tell me I smell?" I reply, my eyebrows raised. She laughs, shakes her head, and opens the back door.

Our apartment is a 1920s holdout in a four-story brick monument amongst the stretch of perfectly homogeneous eco-friendly townhouses. The chipped paint on the trim around the bathroom door reveals the layers that have built up over time. A picture window in the living room points north, and the shade of a large tree blocks our view of the neighborhood. We have to force the exhausted kitchen faucet handles to turn the water on, and then it doesn't shut off all the way. The scuffed hardwood floors are uneven yet buffed to precision. It's imperfectly perfect, and I feel immediately at home. And, thanks to Mom, I have two months to figure out how to support myself and keep living here.

After hauling my belongings up the three flights of stairs and finding street parking for my car, we settle together into a comfortable laziness. Jane makes coffee in a French press and cuts some apples for us. I am tired and ravenous. I can't wait to take a shower and nap.

I feel almost human again after a shower. I don't have any bedroom furniture yet, so instead I drape my towel on the doorknob inside my new room and wait for my air mattress to inflate. Fortunately, my pajamas from yesterday are at the top of my backpack.

My body sinks onto the mattress in exhaustion, yet my mind unwinds with the events of the last seventy-two hours. It all unfolded so quickly that I'm struggling to keep up with it. Last week, I feverishly pulled all-nighters while studying for finals and desperately putting the finishing touches on my senior thesis. Saturday, the morning of graduation, my roommate, Samantha, shook me awake. She was freshly out of the shower, wrapped in a robe and looking kind of annoyed.

"Your dads are here," she said as I shook off the haze of sleep.

"Huh?" I sat up and rubbed the heel of my hand against my eyes. I was half-undressed, wearing the same outfit as last night, and I felt the film of yesterday's make-up on my face.

"Your *dads*," Samantha emphasized.

I could barely make sense of the time. All I could think about was last night's party with the art department. My ex, Ian, was naturally celebrated for his visionary creations. I hung onto the sidelines and watched him laugh with my former friends. I drank too much, and I don't remember how I got home. What a way to end my college career.

I stumbled as I located a pair of sweats. Out in the living room sat my dad and his husband, Dave. They were neatly pressed and ready for the graduation ceremony. Dad watched me with a humorous gleam as I greeted them.

"Nice outfit, pumpkin," he said, trying not to laugh. "Did you forget about breakfast?"

"I think so," I moaned. "Can I have a few minutes?"

It took me a while to order my mind as I got ready. Dad and Dave had come early to take me to breakfast before the graduation ceremony. It was their way of having me to themselves before my mom arrived. I wondered, as I had countless times while we made plans for this weekend, if my parents would actually make the effort to interact. They didn't even try when Jane graduated. I wished she were there. But Jane was in a wedding for one of her law school friends and couldn't make the timing work.

After the ceremony, I found Mom. As always, she looked beautiful. She wore an elegant coral dress, and her hair was freshly styled. I hugged her while she congratulated me. I knew that Dad and Dave had arrived when I felt her stiffen.

"Hello, Nik," she said tightly.

"Barbie," he replied with a nod.

"Afternoon, Barbie!" Dave said cheerfully. "What do you think, should we toast our graduate with a glass of champagne?"

Mom glanced at Dave with discomfort. I smiled awkwardly. I hate this feeling that has lingered ever since my parents divorced. The way my mom doesn't understand why my dad married her in the first place. The way she doesn't try to understand him now. My dad's lingering guilt. The leftover resentment.

"I suppose," Mom replied coolly.

Dad agreed, and we met back at my apartment to drink the bottle of champagne Dad and Dave brought.

Conversation devolved after that. Mom had never liked my choice of major and jumped on this well-worn subject when Dad asked me about my plans in Seattle.

"What are you going to do with an art history degree, Lizzie?"

I shrugged my shoulders. "Curate?" I said nonchalantly.

"You should apply to law school like Jane," she replied.

"C'mon, Barbie, let Lizzie follow her dreams!" Dad replied, slinging his arm around me.

"*I* raised her by myself for eight years. *I* am helping her move to Seattle. Who are you to talk to me about supporting *my* daughter?"

"Mom, he only meant—"

"Of course you would defend your dad," she interrupted.

An awkward silence settled over us until Mom declared she should go.

"Lizzie, you'll stop by before you start your drive up north," she said as I walked her to the door.

"Stay, Mom," I pleaded, feeling both guilty and relieved.

"Tomorrow morning," she said, gathering her purse. "We can have some time on our *own*."

Sunday, I finished cleaning my apartment with my soon-to-be ex-roommate of two years. It was a strange feeling to suddenly be finished with the long list of tasks at the end of senior year as we stood there ready to drop our keys into our mailbox and say goodbye. Sam and I weren't that close, but we coexisted very well together. She was shy, serious, and paid everything on time. Our relationship was one of long mutual respect and a willingness not to judge each other's backgrounds. She never forced me to participate in her evangelical activities or complained when Ian stayed over. I made myself scarce during her Bible studies and kept quiet hours quiet. In short, she was exactly what I wanted in a college roommate: drama free.

Sam and I hugged awkwardly after we dropped off our keys. I imagined we would always remain cordial Facebook friends, but after college we would pursue different lifestyles as we always had. It will be nice to live with a friend again. I've always been closer to Jane than to anyone else, even with our age difference and the years we spent apart. It will be a relief on many levels, especially since my last semester at Stanford was so isolating.

I stopped and had breakfast with Mom before I started my drive up north. We lingered in the familiar sunny kitchen once we had finished, sipping coffee while Mom dispensed last-minute wisdom. "Join a club when you get there. That way you can meet a man with similar interests!" And, "Bake something for your neighbors. You never know who you might meet." She also gave me a large check and warned me not to waste it. "This is all you're getting, Lizzie," she said. "Try to find a good job, okay?"

It's surreal to realize what I left behind: California, Mom, my ex-boyfriend, and my ex-friends.

I've always been a social person. Though introverted, I make friends easily, and I pride myself on the ability to make others feel at ease. Last year I had the ultimate friend group. Ian and I were *the* couple, the kind that people liked to be around because we were so interesting. At least we thought we were. I loved the image we presented to the world: him, the talented artist, and me, the curator in training.

Then, after we returned from winter break, Ian dumped me out of the blue. True, we had been growing apart, but I hadn't let myself see it. Until then, I had imagined that we would move to New York together where he would pursue art and I would eventually apply to grad school. I would help him promote his work in the meantime. When he told me I had "lost my spark," it was as if the rug had been pulled from underneath me.

"What are you saying, Ian?" I had asked in disbelief.

"It's just that you used to have this vision and it was—I dunno—infectious. Now it's like there's nothing. You're just…there."

"I'm just 'there'?" I repeated.

"I think we need to find ourselves again. Apart."

Popular visionary Ian was on the prowl after that, looking for his next muse. It was painful and lonely. It's hard not to doubt my talents after an emotional blow like that. True, I'm at the point now that thinking of Ian's rejection no longer twists my heart, but it does make me doubt myself. And it pisses me off. Moments like this when I can't sleep, I dwell on how I'd like to tell him off. I gave everything to Ian and his vision. I guess that's why I was so ready to leave Stanford for my new life in a new city.

THE LIGHT HAS SHIFTED WHEN I WAKE UP, AND I'M NOT SURE WHAT TIME it is. I roll to my side, stretch, and check my phone. Six o'clock.

"Janey?" I call.

"Yeah?" she replies from the other room.

"When are we getting dinner?"

"What?"

"I'm hungry!"

"What? I can't hear you."

I groan and roll to my side so I can push myself to my feet. My back is stiff. I really will need a bed soon. I pad out to the living room. Jane sits on the couch, legs folded, furiously typing on her laptop.

"Sorry, Lizzie," she mutters with her eyes glued to the screen. "I'm just sending out my résumé to this firm. Give me a sec to finish the cover letter."

I shuffle into the kitchen and grab a banana while I wait. I hear the laptop snap shut a moment later.

"What were you saying?"

"Did you want to get dinner soon?"

Jane beams.

"Dinner and drinks! Let's get dressed up too! Oh Lizzie, I can't wait to celebrate with you; we've both worked so hard!"

Jane makes a reservation at Essex for eight o'clock and lends me a loose white V-neck sheath covered in bright flowers. It's a little too long, hitting my knees instead of resting above them, and it's tight around my hips and bust too, but still, I feel pretty. I cinch it with a belt and apply red lipstick as I study my reflection in the bathroom mirror. Jane comes in a moment later in a simple teal dress. She pulls her hair in a low ponytail and starts to apply eyeliner.

"Hey, good lookin'." I catch her eye in the mirror. "How do you make the plainest dresses look so gorgeous?"

Jane laughs. "It would look the same on you."

I snort and begin to tease the tangles out of my curly hair. "Doubtful," I reply. "But I appreciate your bias."

Anyone who compares our faces would know that Jane and I are sisters. We have the same cherub cheeks, our mother's perfectly shaped lips, and a small straight nose. But that's where the similarities end. Jane is tall like our mother and has the Gardiner eyes: huge, blue, and beautiful. Unlike my insanely curly hair, hers is straight and dusky blonde, like healthy strands of wheat. In many ways, it's as though our looks predetermined which parent would favor us.

It's still light when we wander down Market Street for dinner. Being with Jane is the perfect remedy for my last semester of hell. It's been too long since I've spent time with someone who understood me.

Moving here was the right decision, I determine confidently.

Jane recommends we try the whiskey sours with homemade sour mix at Assembly Hall when we're done eating. We're both giddy when we arrive, thrilled to be in each other's company and to actually be *living* out our plans.

"It's cute in here," I say approvingly, taking in the rustic wood and iron motif. Soft happy folk music plays, and I feel like we should be in Wyoming or Montana in the forties.

Jane nods toward a booth. "We're lucky we got here before ten. It can get pretty crazy!"

We settle down and order our drinks. I glance around and note the Skee-Ball on the far wall and the jukebox in the corner.

"Should we liven up the atmosphere?" I ask Jane, nodding at the jukebox.

"Go for it!" Jane replies as our drinks arrive.

I grab a five from my purse and hold my drink with my other hand while I weave through the growing crowd. The glass sweats in my hand when I flip through the songs. It's loud enough now that it's easy to overhear people's conversations.

"...vodka soda is the lowest-calorie drink you can get." I hear one girl say. "Don't let me drink anything else; I don't want to look like a whale in my bathing suit."

"Whatever," her friend replies. "What you really need is more cardio."

I remember these girls from school. *The vain perfectionists.* The type of girls who would stand on your shoulders and crush your head to get to the top. The ones who know they have it in them to "have it all," no matter what it takes.

"Oh my God. Look at her!"

"Who?"

"That girl over there at the booth. The one by herself!"

I glance over at two guys standing near the Skee-Ball. Unsurprisingly, they're both staring at Jane.

"She's the prettiest girl I've ever seen!" The guy who says this is the shorter of the two. His face is cheerful and attractive. He adjusts his Clark Kent glasses. "Should I go and talk to her?"

"Will *she* talk to *you*?" his friend replies. He glances at me, and we catch eyes. I haven't felt my pulse flutter like that since Ian asked me to be his study partner sophomore year. He looks away coolly like he's unimpressed. Not that I'm surprised—if he's anything like Ian, he thinks he's cooler than everyone else in the bar. I focus back on the jukebox, choose another song, and flip through the catalog again. I refuse to let hot guys like that intimidate me and select a song by the Pixies.

"She'd probably brush me off," the shorter guy continues. "You know, girls like that…" He turns his head, and I can't make out the rest of his sentence. But when he's done talking, his friend laughs.

I round out the last of my music selections with New Order. *I dare you to judge my musical taste*, I mentally challenge the tall one. I tap my fingers on the console and turn daringly toward the two. They seem surprised by my approach. I slide my empty glass to a nearby ledge and rest my hand on my hip.

"That girl," I state, clearly indicating Jane, "is my sister. If you want to talk to her, come and say hi. She is probably the nicest person you could ever meet."

The guys continue to stare at me in astonishment.

"Do you always eavesdrop on strangers' conversations?" the tall one asks.

"No, but in this case, you probably don't mind." I glance pointedly at the guy with glasses.

"You aren't from here," the tall friend remarks. "Haven't you heard of the Seattle Freeze? We don't like talking to strangers."

I shrug. "I'm from California."

He looks at me carefully, and I cock my head to the side. He's broad, but tall enough to still appear lanky. I look away.

"Whatever, dude," I scoff to the guy with glasses. "If you're really interested, Jane will talk to you. Although I can't promise anything more."

I turn and wander toward the bar to get another whiskey sour for Jane and myself. By the time I make it back to the table, the two guys are sitting comfortably and chatting with Jane. Mr. Glasses sits across from her, gazing at her in awe.

"Lizzie!" Jane says as I approach, "Chip told me that you told him to talk to me?"

"*Chip*?" I exclaim, sliding in next to Jane. I push her drink to her hand. "Is your sister named Buffy?"

"My sisters are Emmeline and Laurel," he replies in confusion. His friend laughs, and I chuckle. We catch eyes again, and my heart flutters uncomfortably. Just because he's good-looking doesn't mean he's a good guy. I'm not about to let my attraction to someone cloud my judgment again. I breathe out and look back at Chip and Jane.

Chip stares at Jane, and she smiles at him bashfully.

"Sisters' night out?" Chip asks with enthusiasm.

"Yes," Jane replies. "Lizzie just moved here—today, actually—and I just passed the bar. We're celebrating." She smiles at me fondly.

"You're a lawyer!" Chip exclaims. "Smart and beautiful—who knew women like you existed?"

"Easy there, champ," I snort. "She's only human."

"Lizzie just graduated from Stanford on Saturday," Jane diverts.

"Did you study law too?" Chip asks earnestly.

"Art history," I reply. "The major to kill all real career opportunities."

"I thought that was philosophy," the tall one remarks. I realize I haven't caught his name. I imagine it's something ridiculously hipster like Zane or Gunner—one of those stupid names that only work on a classically handsome face like his, an oval so perfectly symmetrical it could have been designed in a geometry class. An awkward, round-faced nerd with a patchy beard could not pull off Gunner.

"Art history may have more to offer than philosophy," I admit to Zane/Gunner. "But it isn't worth anything without a master's degree…" I pause and take a sip. "What's your name?"

"Call me Darcy," he replies.

"Darcy hates his first name," Chip explains.

"You would too if your first name was a last name."

"I don't know," I contribute helpfully, "Taylor isn't so bad."

"Or Thomas!" Jane supplies.

"Let me guess, your first name is Vanderberg. Vanderberg Darcy."

Chip guffaws and ribs Darcy.

"What are you drinking?" Darcy indicates our empty glasses and neatly changes the subject.

"Whiskey sours," Jane replies.

"Are they good?" Chip stares at her again. Jane's cheeks tinge, and her eyes are sparkling. I haven't seen her like this since before Joey broke her heart in eleventh grade.

"They live up to their reputation," she replies.

Darcy abandons the table for the bar. Chip and Jane lean over the table toward each other. It's hard to hear their conversation.

"I'll be right back," I call to Jane, indicating the bathroom.

"I'll go with you!"

"My sisters always go to the bathroom as a pair," Chip observes. "I never understood why."

"Mysteries of women," I reply, waiting for Jane to join me.

"Back in a minute." She smiles at him. Her cheeks are still pink. I grin at her as she follows me to the back.

"He's cute," I note.

"Did you really tell him to talk to me?" she asks in slight amazement.

There's a line to the ladies' room. I lean against the wall and give her a smug look. "Only because he was drooling over you from afar. I had to put the poor bastard out of his misery."

"He is really cute," Jane replies. "And he's nice. Did you know he's a project manager at Microsoft?"

"Gainfully employed—check." We shuffle forward as the line moves up, and Jane shakes her head at me.

"Our first night out together and we meet two cute guys. It's like…a good omen, or something."

We finally make our way back to the table. I can feel a happy anticipation emanating from Jane. Her optimism is contagious.

"…no way, Chip. Just ask her on a real date, and please don't leave me to babysit the kid sister."

I freeze.

Chip looks at us, startled. From behind me, I can feel Jane grip my arm.

Asshole. My chest stings even though I don't know the guy and I could care less if he thinks I'm immature. I suck in my breath, approach the table, and grab one of the cocktails. Jane slides into the booth across from Chip. I sit down next to her and take a gulp.

Darcy glances at me with some discomfort then looks away. I sigh. I've finished my drink already.

"Want another one?" Darcy asks. I glare at him and spin my empty glass on the table. I can feel my inhibitions lowering.

"You owe me ten of those, you pretentious dick. But since I'm old enough to know my limits, you can get me two more."

"All right," he mumbles.

"Whatever. My sister and your friend seem to really like each other. I can tolerate his douche friend if you can tolerate her kid sister."

Silently, Darcy leaves for the bar. Jane and Chip lean over the table again. Their conversation appears far too intimate for a loud bar. At one point, Chip passes Jane his phone, and she types in her number. She smiles at him. He smiles at her. My sister is on her way to perfectly achieving her next milestone right on schedule. Mom would be proud.

Darcy appears a few minutes later with another round of drinks. I grab mine gratefully and tell myself to sip slowly.

The crowd is impossibly loud for a Tuesday night. Is it because school is out now, or is it the promise of summer?

I'm pretty sure Chip is holding Jane's hand, but I'm more focused on my next drink. My head starts to swim in a happy buzz. Darcy glares at me.

"Make yourself useful and get me some water," I say to his intimidating stare. "You can't let the kid sister get shitfaced on your watch, can you?"

Darcy leaves the table without a word. I lean over and hug Jane.

"I'm so glad to be back with you!" I sloppily kiss her on the cheek.

"How much have you had to drink, Lizzie?"

"Enough to keep you safe." I glance at Chip. "She may like you, but she is going to her own place tonight. And you aren't invited. You have to earn that privilege!"

"Lizzie!"

Jane's blush deepens and Chip laughs with alarmed wonder. "I—I'm not the type to rush anything." He looks sincerely at Jane.

I can't find anything to criticize. Jane may be the nicest person in existence, but Chip seems to rival that title.

"Here you go, Sprout," Darcy says, pushing a glass of water toward me. I can't tell if he's joking or not.

"Took you long enough," I shoot back.

Chip and Darcy spend another hour at our table. I responsibly finish the evening with water so we can walk home relatively sober. Jane is quiet, but she manages to smile softly to herself the entire way.

I decide I will tolerate that shithead Darcy if it makes Jane happy. She deserves to fall in love.

Chapter Two

I didn't recognize it as broken at first. It was one of those truths that is slowly exposed as many childhood convictions are. Kind of like those expandable dinosaur eggs I bought at the corner store growing up. Brand new, it looked to be an innocuous marble, but as soon as it was immersed in water, its true form was revealed. All it takes is the introduction of a new element—or in our case, a family vacation and break from routine.

From an early age, Jane and I learned that choosing either Mom or Dad's side was normal. Jane and Mom liked going shopping or visiting with friends from the Berkeley Tennis Club. Dad and I preferred to go to the Sunday flea market and people watch. We happily functioned as separate yet parallel units. That isn't to say that Jane and I didn't spend our own time together. Away from our parents, Jane and I were inseparable. We were sent to stay with our aunt and uncle in Seattle together while our parents were in court. Every activity Jane would try, I would try. When one of us was scared, we would share a bed.

The Venetidis family was like a failed four of a kind. Sometimes there were pairs, but hardly ever anything else. I think that's why I'm close with my Dad and Jane (separately, of course), but my Mom and I hardly understand each other. Barbie and Lizzie Venetidis never were a pair.

The first time I noticed the dysfunction in my family was one summer when we uncharacteristically took a family road trip to Disneyland. The four of us packed up our '93 Volvo to make the eight-hour trek down the I-5. Jane and I were beside ourselves with excitement. She couldn't wait to see the Sleeping Beauty Castle, and I wanted to ride Splash Mountain. We planned to meet our aunt Penny and her family down in Anaheim where our cousin Lydia would join us.

The bickering started after we reached that long stretch of California highway before the Grapevine where there's nothing but miles of yellow grass, crops, and the occasional identical strip mall that appears each time you reach a new city limit. As driver, Dad wanted to control the radio. Mom complained that classical music did not give our trip the right "feel." He then suggested he pull over and switch with her so she could control the radio. This argument continued far too long for a pair of adults. I was nine, and Jane was twelve. We weren't ready to acknowledge the erosion of our parents' marriage. Instead, Jane put on her headphones, and I buried my nose in *Little House on the Prairie*.

Once arrived, we met Aunt Penny, Uncle Rob, and Lydia at a nearby Denny's after we checked in to our hotel room. Lydia, a year younger than me, could not contain her glee, though Aunt Penny often hovered over Lydia in a manner we came to accept as normal. Lydia had epilepsy, and we had witnessed seizures first hand. They were the scariest things I had seen in my young life. Uncle Rob thought Lydia would be okay on rides if she wore her helmet. Aunt Penny wasn't sure. She was only comfortable with Lydia slowly drifting through "It's a Small World." Earworms couldn't cause any lasting damage.

In a division that would continue the entire long weekend, Mom, Penny, and Rob grouped together to talk in low tones. Dad took us girls to a different booth where we could color or play word games. Lydia reveled in being just one of the kids, free from her parents' usual scrutiny. Jane quietly basked in the attention from our dad that she rarely got. I was happy that everyone was laughing and no one fought.

One evening after dinner while Lydia, Jane, and I watched cartoons on the TV in our room, Lydia said something I'll never forget: "I'm glad your mom and dad don't like to hang out. I usually never get a break from my parents."

IN THE FALL, LYDIA WILL START HER SENIOR YEAR AT SEATTLE UNIVERSITY. It wasn't a surprise she decided to go to school out of state. We all knew she was dying to get away from San Jose. Growing up with epilepsy and overprotective parents rarely lent her any freedom and Lydia desperately wanted to experience new things. Jane and I often talked about how our aunt and uncle's restrictions on Lydia were going to backfire someday. It's convenient for all of us, I guess, that we all ended up in Seattle where Uncle Eddie and Aunt Mai live; they give us a sense of family while we figure out how to be independent adults.

Lydia invited Jane and me out on Friday evening to help cheer up her friend Katrina, who was recently dumped and needed a girls' night out to drink and shit talk guys.

We meet at Linda's, a dive bar well known for being a favorite of Kurt Cobain. It's early still, just at the beginning of happy hour, so the crowds haven't started to descend. Jane spots Lydia at a table full of girls dressed in grunge-revival fashion: Doc Martens, floral skirts, plaid, and dirty hair. Lydia stood out among them by eschewing the androgynous trend with her girlish hippie dress, which was long and pastel pink with a plunging back. Jane and I make our way through the crowd of old crust punks and pseudo-punks-in-training to join the group.

"Lizzie! Jane!" Lydia squeals when we arrive. I know that Jane has seen her more recently in town, but I haven't seen Lydia in almost a year. She hugs me for a long time.

"I'm so glad you're here!" she exclaims, kissing my cheek. "It's been, like, forever!"

I laugh. Lydia's energy is infectious when it isn't overwhelming. When we were younger, it was easy to get annoyed at her enthusiasm when we spent long periods of time together. But right now, all I can think about is how much I've missed her.

Lydia drags us over to the table to find seats among her group of friends. I find a seat across from the girl I assume is Katrina. Her eyes are red-rimmed, and she holds a half-empty drink.

"Guys, these are my cousins, Jane and Lizzie," Lydia indicates us. Then she points out her group of friends. "This is Kayla, Rachel, Marianne, Alexis, and Katrina." Jane and I wave hello, and Katrina sniffs into her napkin.

"Thanks for coming…" Katrina's lips are trembling.

"Breakups are shit," I reply with understanding. "I was dumped in January, and I'm still bitter."

Katrina smiles bravely at me. She seems nice.

Katrina, I learn, is Lydia's roommate and closest friend. Aunt Penny taught her how to support Lydia's head during seizures, and I notice Katrina watching her unobtrusively but carefully as the evening progresses. There's a sort of co-dependence between the two. Katrina looks to Lydia for confidence, but she also gently tells her when she needs to take a break from alcohol. I learn during the course of the evening that she is originally from Hawaii and that she too moved to the Pacific Northwest to gain some independence from her family.

We leave Linda's after happy hour ends and stumble down the street to a karaoke bar. Even Jane is tipsy, which generally isn't like her, but it's easy to get caught up in the spirit of the night out. Katrina cheers up when she, Lydia, and Marianne sing "Single Ladies" together. At about three in the morning, we have all returned to Katrina and Lydia's apartment. Jane has passed out in Lydia's bed. Lydia is out on the small balcony, smoking weed with the other girls, while Katrina and I sit at the kitchen table, sobering up with glasses of water.

"I needed this," Katrina says after she takes a long gulp. "I mean, I don't think I was really *in love* with Ethan, but I really liked him, and I wasn't ready for it to end." She frowns down at her glass.

I hesitate and then ask her why he broke up with her. She exhales heavily. "He said he thought I felt too much for him."

"What a fucker." I can't help but bitterly recall Ian's insulting speech. Guys can be such bullshit.

Katrina smiles at me sadly, tears glimmering. "It's the rejection more than anything. Like, here I am opening myself up and then he shits on my heart."

"I get that. My ex gave a similar reason for dumping me. It's good that you have friends to lean on though. I lost all my friends in the breakup."

"Oh man, that sucks. At least you have friends here."

"I do." I feel a swell of accomplishment. I will not build my life around a guy here. I've learned my lesson.

IT ALMOST FEELS LIKE VACATION, HANGING OUT WITH JANE WHILE WE BOTH look for work. We stay out late and get up late. We scour the free section of Craigslist and go to the Antique Mall to decorate our apartment. I try not to be jealous when Jane starts dividing her time between Chip and me. I mean, I want her to find love. It's not her fault that I also want her to myself right now. At least I get along with Lydia and her friends and hang out with them when Jane's not available.

After I spend too many nights sleeping on an air mattress, I give in and call Mom to ask for help buying a bed. She agreed that adults shouldn't sleep on the floor and then informed me that Amazon, Microsoft, and Google are all excellent places to work in Seattle and that Jane could help me apply.

I thank her and apply to Café Longue where Katrina works.

The owner, Mary Long, used her life savings to model the coffee shop after The Factory, a place where creative geniuses could gather and conceive greatness. Seven years later, it's more or less a typical coffee shop with mid-century furniture, pop art posters, and informal artistic support groups. I applied here because it has some connection to art and I've been a barista before.

Right now, the walls are adorned with canvases showcasing pieces by some Banksy wannabe with no apparent message. I hope I can offer to scout better artists for them in the future so I can list myself on LinkedIn as a barista/art curator. It's all about the positive spin.

Charlotte, the manager, appreciates my barista experience and sympathizes with my higher education. She works at Café Longue full time, but her dream is to design and code the next indispensable cyber security software. We like to commiserate about our inability to matriculate into the job market.

Charlotte and I have almost nothing in common, but she laughs at my jokes, and I appreciate her pragmatic honesty. She trains me patiently, but really, the job is easy. I can imagine myself gliding through my impoverished life on a sea of coffee beans, the only stress a cranky person who needs their morning fix. I'd like to think I'm pretty good at soothing cranky people.

I ignore my niggling curator ambitions and settle for the comfort of a steady income. I have two months to figure out how to really pay my bills.

By eleven, the morning crowd has dwindled, and Café Longue buzzes quietly with the usual freelancers and aspiring novelists pecking away on their MacBooks. Charlotte wipes down the counters, and I switch the music to something more soothing. We are ready for the cozy afternoon hum of customers with few responsibilities. I can relate.

Jane rushes through the door excitedly and approaches me at the counter.

"I got a job!" She beams. "At a well-known firm too—I'm starting downtown on Wednesday!"

I shriek and hug her over the counter. "Congratulations! Not that I ever doubted you."

Jane shakes her head modestly. "I still can't believe it. It's too good to be true!"

"Of course it isn't," I admonish. "You worked hard, and you earned it. There isn't anyone who deserves it more."

"I don't know how you can have such a high opinion of me, but thank you."

"Coffee?" I ask.

"Chip is taking me to lunch. He took off the rest of the afternoon to celebrate with me." Jane shakes her head in bewilderment. If she wasn't so humble, kind, and so...*Jane*, it could be easy to resent her. But it's impossible. She is too good to think anything less.

"Have fun with your handsome man," I say with a wink. I give her a tall drip and wave away her five-dollar bill. "And let me know when you'll be home. I can make your favorite fajitas for dinner."

"You're the best," Jane says, beaming.

I get texts from Jane through the rest of the day. She sends me pictures of the view of the snow-capped Olympic Mountains from Golden Gardens Beach and relates to me how sweet Chip is.

He brought me daisies!

We're at this cute place called The Sweet Shoppe. They have the best fudge sundaes!

Did you know you can rent peddle boats at Green Lake?

The texts slow as the day progresses. At 9:00 p.m., my phone buzzes.

I'm so sorry Lizzie--looks like I'm going to miss dinner. I hope you didn't go to any trouble! Please don't hate me.

I could never hate you! I text back. *Have a great time with Chip.* I end the conversation with a kissy face for good measure.

Jane doesn't come home that night, and our apartment is quiet. I drown the silence with music and ignore the undercurrent of self-doubt. Jane is three years older than I am; of course, she's on her way to having her life all figured out.

Chapter Three

The summer when I was eight, Dad and I rode our bikes to the Sunday market. I remember he wore outrageous bike shorts with aggressively yellow zigzags up the side. Sometimes my dad would wear clothes I thought were kind of weird, but I was at that age when making fun of your parents wasn't really allowed yet. That was for the pre-teen years.

It was hot, and the back of my neck was tender from the sun by the time we arrived at the market. After locking up our bikes, we headed to our favorite bookstall to dig through overpriced antique tomes. Dad liked to read about a lot of bizarre things; I liked the musty smell of old pages when I flipped through the vintage Golden Classics.

The owner of The Literature Trove was an aging hippie named Stan. He had a long ponytail as thick as a frayed rope that hung to his waist. We liked Stan, but he took himself too seriously to the point that he would never barter. We had even witnessed him *raise* prices on a book if someone tried to talk him down. When I think about it now, I imagine he didn't care much what his books earned, just that they were sold to the right people.

One Sunday, Dad and I left the house after he and Mom had an argument. Mom took Jane to the mall, and Dad and I went out on our bikes to get away from the tension. I never liked that feeling: the emotional layers of hurt feelings, like an onion someone forces you to peel when you don't even like onions. The best thing I could think to do was cheer up Dad on my own.

Stan was in fine form that morning. Mrs. Pearlman, who had been volunteering at the Gold Rush Museum, was beefing up the museum library. She had found some books in Stan's stall and was trying to barter with him on the price "in the name of education." The more she tried, the more he dug his heels in. Dad and I pretended not to notice the escalating conversation as we filed through the selections.

He bent down close to me. "I wonder if Stan thinks those books are *made* of gold," he whispered.

I covered my mouth and giggled. "I think he's mistaking Mrs. Pearlman for a gold digger," I replied with mirth.

"She doesn't wear enough jewelry for that to be true," Dad snorted.

"She wears enough spray tan though," I remarked. Dad guffawed, and I felt immensely proud of myself for keeping up with him.

"You are a quick one, my little Lizzie," he said. I realized then that making adults laugh had power. Of course, I learned later that this could also go wrong. When I was mad at Mom, I would unleash my wit on her in a way that would make her cheeks darken in frustration. She would chastise Dad for teaching me to be mean.

"Your mother doesn't understand you," Dad said after one incident.

"I'm only saying what's true!" I replied defensively.

"And she doesn't want to hear it," Dad said with a wry smile.

It doesn't take long for me to fall into an early morning barista routine. Usually, I wake up before Jane and sleepwalk to the café. I get home in the early afternoon and have time to myself before Jane gets home. I wish I had more time with her, but I understand that a new job and a new boyfriend are time consuming.

On a Saturday morning, my alarm blares. The sun isn't up yet, and my eyes are heavy. I groan and roll over. I hate opening shifts.

I notice Winston, Chip's corgi, snoring on the couch when I make my way to the bathroom. I imagine my sister and her cute boyfriend waking up at a leisurely pace and wandering down to Portage Bay for brunch. They'll take Winston because, like so many places in this city, it's dog friendly. They'll sip coffee and gaze at each other. In two years, they'll be married and own a townhouse…right on schedule.

Thankfully, the weekend rush doesn't start till later in the morning. I drink two cups of coffee and arrange the pastries in the front display. I make a mocha with extra whip for an awkward patron wearing an ironic internet-themed T-shirt and a fedora. I draw a smiley face on his cup because the sun is out. He beams and thanks me. At least I'm good at my meaningless job.

"I'm so hungover," Katrina groans.

"Do you need ibuprofen?"

Katrina shakes her head and props her elbows on the counter. A few elderly customers read in the overstuffed chairs by the window. Fedora guy sips his mocha and types on a laptop.

"It's ridiculous that we open at five on Saturdays," Katrina grumbles. "I'm pretty sure I was still a little drunk when I got in this morning."

"Don't let Charlotte find out," I warn with a wink.

The slow trickle becomes a stream of customers as the morning progresses.

Mechanically, I take orders with cheer and scribble names on paper cups with a sharpie.

"What can I get you?" I repeat over and over.

"Hey, Lizzie."

It's Chip's friend Darcy. I haven't seen him since we met weeks ago. I'm surprised he remembers me. He is in running shorts and a sweat-soaked T-shirt. I can see the outline of his muscles under the fabric, and it makes me uncomfortable. People who try that hard to be in shape are usually vain—and usually assholes.

"Hey," I nod. "What can I get you?"

He looks at me carefully, unsmiling. "Grande Americano."

I nod and write on the cup. He hands me his credit card, and I glance at it.

"Your first name is Fitzwilliam?" I laugh.

"You can see why I don't use it," he says dryly.

"You had me thinking it was something really terrible, like Beauregard." I shake my head and give him his card back. Katrina passes him the Americano.

I don't watch him walk away.

"Who is *that*?" Katrina exhales when he's out of earshot. I roll my eyes.

"My sister's boyfriend's friend." I shrug.

"He's hot. Is he single?"

"I think so." I keep my voice neutral. "But I have to warn you that he's kind of a jerk."

"Really?" Katrina glances over at him alone at a table. He's reading the paper. Probably checking his stocks or catching up on the national news.

I shake my head at her and help the next customer.

Darcy comes up to the counter after the line has dwindled.

"Refill?" I ask casually.

"Actually, I was just wondering if you were coming out tonight. To meet Emmeline."

"Emmeline?"

"Chip's sister. Jane said she was going to invite you."

"When did you see Jane?" I feel a surge of jealousy. It's one thing if Chip is monopolizing Jane's time—but Darcy? He hardly even knows her.

"Oh, uh, yeah. Happy hour yesterday."

"Happy hour. The privilege of nine-to-five yuppies," I scoff, annoyed. "Honestly, I haven't seen her since yesterday morning," I admit. "Her love bubble with Chip is practically impenetrable."

Darcy leans against the counter. I don't understand his scrutiny. I start making Darcy another Americano—I need to do something with my hands. "At least when Chip comes over, I get Winston though," I say, placing the Americano in front of Darcy. He reaches for his wallet but, in a show of sisterly loyalty, I wave him away. "Perk of the job. Just don't make it a habit."

"Thanks," he replies. He stuffs a few dollars in the tip jar and studies me again.

"Anyway," he says abruptly, "Emmeline is in town doing PR for a winery in Woodinville. Chip and Jane decided to make a day of it, but I'm going up later for dinner. I thought we could go together."

I raise my eyebrows. "Really?"

"Sure." He takes a sip of the Americano.

"Is this you volunteering to be my manny?"

"Manny?"

"Male nanny."

"Listen, I'm sorry I said that." He shifts his feet. "We can get along, right? We should try for Chip and Jane at least."

"At least you're a good friend," I grumble. "All right, what time should we meet up?"

He smiles, and my stomach flips. God, why can't I make myself think he's ugly? I swallow and fidget with the pens near the register.

"I can come get you—at four?"

"Okay."

To my chagrin, I feel myself blushing at the thought of him in my apartment. So what if he's good looking? We're acquaintances at best. I tell myself to get over myself while fixing my eyes on the pen jar.

"What's your number? I can text you when I get there."

I feel odd typing my number into his phone. It feels too personal. I wonder what secrets he has in it.

I pass it back.

"See ya later."

I watch him go and don't notice my wistful sigh.

"You like him," Katrina says after he leaves.

"No, I don't," I shoot back. "Didn't I tell you he's kind of a jerk?"

"A hot jerk," she teases.

"I'm too young for him anyway," I reason. "I think he's, like, thirty, and besides, we're just going to get along for his friend and my sister's sake."

"Whatever you say, Lizzie."

I Google "wine-tasting outfit" when I get home. I have no idea what I'm doing. The only alcohol I'm a connoisseur of is cheap beer. I bet Darcy can tell the difference between merlot and pinot noir. He's probably never heard of Two-Buck Chuck.

I dig through my closet, but everything I own looks wrong. Desperately, I head to Jane's closet to see what she has.

Evidence of Chip is all over her room. His watch on the bedside table. His rolled socks on the armchair. We haven't known him a month, yet he and Jane have already braided their lives together. I wonder how they can be so trusting of each other. It only takes one stupid whim for someone to change his mind.

I spy a gauzy shirtdress and decide it will do. It looks like one of the dresses in my Google image search. I am ridiculous.

I'm untangling my hair after a shower when my phone dings.

Hey Lizzie, it's Darcy. Sorry I'm early.

Shit.

I quickly switch from towel to dress and reach for my phone.

No worries. I'm still getting ready though.

I pause.

You can come up and wait if you want.

The balloon with three dots pops up on my phone and disappears. It pops up again.

Be right there.

Darcy waits quietly on the couch and plays with his phone while I do my make-up.

"Just a few more minutes," I call apologetically.

Darcy stands when I finally emerge. "I like your dress."

"It's Jane's," I say by way of explanation.

"Are you ready?"

"Yep." I nod and lead Darcy out the door.

When we reach Darcy's car, I see he owns a goddamn Tesla. Of course he does. Although I had imagined he drove something more cliché like a BMW or Mercedes.

"What exactly do you do again?" I marvel. Who can afford a $70,000 Tesla?

Darcy shrugs. "Cog in the technology wheel," he says mildly.

He puts on The Cure as we cruise up I-5. Okay, so he has good music taste, I'll give him that. But he still hardly talks to me while we drive. I lean forward and clasp my hands around my knees. The evergreens streak past the window. Darcy is quiet. I reach for the first topic in my head.

"So, if I was going to apply to be a technology cog like you, what sort of responsibilities should I expect?"

"It depends," Darcy replies. He glances at me and back to the road. The sun frames his aquiline profile, and I blink.

"What do you mean?"

"Well, what do you want to do in tech?"

"Oh. I don't mean me, I mean you," I reply with an eye roll. "How does your cog...turn?"

I wince. Fucked up that analogy.

He laughs. "It's encouraging to know you don't get all your witticisms out perfectly."

"Yeah, well..." I smooth my palms over my thighs. My cheeks burn. "Anyway, why the mystery?"

"It's not really a mystery," he remarks. "It's just nice that you don't already know."

I watch him closely, intrigued, but don't reply.

"My father was George Darcy. You know...founder of PMB."

"Oh. Shit. So that's why you own a Tesla." I am mortified. Darcy. Of course. Why didn't I recognize the name? "Well, I feel like an idiot," I mumble.

Darcy glances at me again with a small smile and directs his attention back to the road.

"It's refreshing actually. I don't normally make friends without all that absurd clout."

He thinks we're friends? I laugh.

"I hope your friends are nicer to you than I am. And more in your age range."

He smiles again and shakes his head. "What are you—twenty-three? That's not *too* young."

"Twenty-two," I admit. "But I'm glad to know I convey an extra year of maturity."

We lapse into silence, and I begin to think that maybe Darcy isn't a jerk. Does he really think we're friends?

"So, George Darcy. I read that he passed away not long ago from cancer. I'm sorry."

"Yeah." Darcy frowns. "My sister and I have had the last two years to adjust, and they just hired a new CEO. PMB lives on."

"So you, what...own the company now?"

"Sort of," he replies uncomfortably. "My sister, Georgie, and I are now the major shareholders. She won't get control of anything till she's twenty-five, but since I was twenty-seven when my dad died..."

"When you said 'cog in the technology wheel,' what you really meant was owner of the wheel," I clarify. "But it sounds like you don't really do anything technological."

"No, not really." He changes lanes as the exit approaches. His eyebrows pinch.

"Well, I don't do anything either. Technological or otherwise."

"You give the world coffee," he says. He stops at the light and taps his thumbs against the steering wheel.

"Always the barista," I deprecate. "That is not a real job. It's a stopover till I figure out how I'm actually supposed to make money with an art history degree and no marketable passion." Of course, I know how to make my degree marketable. But the thought of going back to school right now is exhausting.

"The conundrum of every twenty-something," he remarks softly.

"Except Chip and Jane," I reply. Darcy laughs again. My shoulders relax.

"Your sister does seem to have a clear plan."

"As decided by Barbie Venetidis," I supply. "Our mother determined our life paths after she and my dad got divorced. Jane has followed her instructions faithfully. With Chip in the picture, she remains pretty much on schedule."

Darcy frowns but doesn't reply.

"Anyway," I say nervously, "Jane's perfect decision-making skills are a good way to distract our mom from my poor life choices."

I may not have been the golden child like Jane throughout school, but until recently, I had good friends and a vague idea of what I should decide next. I don't want to compare myself with my sister, but watching her life unfold while I'm still getting my head on straight is messing with my confidence.

Darcy pulls off the road to the front gates of Chateau St. Lucas. The wheels crunch over the gravel. I wonder if he's considering how aimless I am. I cross my arms and glare out the window, annoyed that he would judge me like that.

CHATEAU ST. LUCAS IS A QUIRKY TURN-OF-THE-CENTURY MANSION WITH a modern atrium jutting off the back. We are directed to a private tasting room where our group is. There are TVs on the wall flashing odd wine trivia, and smooth jazz drifts through the halls.

"Darcy!" a female voice exclaims when we enter the tasting room.

A well-dressed young woman pulls Darcy into a hug. She pulls back to kiss both of his cheeks. She isn't the type of girl you could call spectacularly pretty, but she is so well put together you almost don't notice.

Behind her, Chip rolls his eyes but maintains a pleasant expression. "Hey, Lizzie," he greets. His arm is draped around Jane's shoulder. "I'm glad Darcy was able to find you."

"Thanks for inviting me," I reply. I nod at the woman I assume is Emmeline. "Hey, I'm Jane's sister, Lizzie."

She examines me and asks, "Did you come up with Darcy?"

"It made sense to carpool," Darcy answers.

"Oh." Emmeline frowns. She gives me a look that makes me feel like somewhat of an interloper. Do they have a history? I smile at her. I could care less about Darcy.

"I'm glad you were able to make it," she says to Darcy. "I'm only in town for three days, and it's always great to catch up with old *friends*." The emphasis she puts on the word feels loaded.

"And you're also glad to meet my girlfriend and her sister, right?" Chip adds. His tone is good-natured, but I can tell he's annoyed. "Lizzie, this is Emmeline."

"I was going to get to that. God, Chip," she scoffs. She reaches out to shake my hand.

"So!" Emmeline exclaims. "I've finished all my meetings with Sir William, the sommelier. He's agreed to give us an exclusive tasting. Then we have reservations at The Lodge at seven."

"How thoughtful," Jane says. "You've arranged the royal treatment for us!"

"Jane, you're so sweet," Emmeline replies. "Darcy, don't you think Chip's girlfriend is the sweetest?"

"Ah, Miss Bishop!" A stout, middle-aged man bustles in. His neatly groomed goatee is so shockingly white that it looks like a ring of toothpaste around his mouth. "I see your group is assembled. I will have the pairing cheeses sent out directly."

We spend the next hour tasting, and I realize I never knew wine could taste so good. I feel warm and relaxed. Jane and I end up standing with each other, giggling.

"I like the pink wine," I declare. I swirl the glass and straighten my posture.

"You mean the rosé," Emmeline corrects. Of course, Darcy's friends know all about wine. I try not to let her comment sting.

"I assumed all pink wine tasted like Kool-Aid."

Emmeline sniffs. "That's to be expected if you shop from the bottom shelf."

"I appreciate the education, Emmeline," I downplay, ignoring my warm cheeks.

"Darcy, what's your favorite?" Emmeline places her hand on his arm comfortably, and he doesn't pull away.

"The Syrah is pretty good. And the rosé."

"I thought pink wine would be too girly for you," I say with the sudden need to tease him.

"I don't judge a wine by its color." He smiles.

"Do you want a bottle, Lizzie?" Jane asks.

"Don't worry about it," I reply, knowing it's not in my budget this month.

I divert the attention back to her. "What are you buying?"

We spend the next twenty minutes comparing the merits of everything we've tried and start purchasing full glasses. Occasionally, Emmeline pauses to study me or throw a disdainful remark in my direction. I reply with exaggerated cheer. Darcy is laughing and joking too, which seems out of character for him.

We're able to walk to The Lodge from the winery, which is fortunate since our entire group is tipsy. Emmeline giggles and stumbles along on Darcy's arm.

"Wow," I whisper to Jane and Chip from behind the pair.

"Oh yeah, Emmeline has had a thing for Darcy since high school," Chip whispers back.

Did that *thing* ever become something more?

We reach the restaurant, and Emmeline detaches herself from Darcy's arm to approach the host.

"How long have you guys been friends?" Jane asks.

"Fourteen years, I think," Chip replies, weaving his fingers together with Jane's.

"We met at lacrosse team tryouts," Darcy adds, "before the start of our freshman year at Lakeside."

"Is that when you started playing?" Jane gazes proudly at Chip.

"That was the first stop out of pee-wee league," Chip replies modestly.

"He was the star of our team," Darcy tells us. "Played in college too."

"Mom always says it's good for a boy to have a sport."

"Girls too!" I interject. "Jane was captain of the volleyball team!"

She shakes her head. "I didn't play past high school though."

"What about you?" Darcy asks me. "Did you have a sport?"

"Ready!" Emmeline calls to us and indicates the host.

We assemble at a comfortable half-moon booth. I pick up the menu and scan the array of gourmet comfort food. I don't want to answer Darcy's question. I started on JV volleyball when I was a freshman, but I was eventually cut after Jane graduated. I settled for team manager the next year, which only required toting uniforms and water bottles for the real players. Eventually, I gave up on sports and school spirit all together. I made more friends in drama club.

After dinner, Chip takes Jane and me back to our apartment but has to go home to check on Winston. Jane and I open a bottle of wine and talk about the evening. Jane sighs in optimism when we talk about Chip.

"He's exactly the type of man I've always looked for." She smiles tenderly.

My heart soars for her.

Chapter Four

Between Chip and her ever-increasing hours at work, Jane is rarely at home. I find myself more often in the company of the girls from Café Longue instead. I've learned that I prefer to hang out with Charlotte—except when she's glued to her gaming console. Katrina goes out almost every night with Lydia, and while I do enjoy a night out, I need to have some sober conversation once in a while.

The days stretch longer as June winds to a close. It's easy to lose track of an evening when the sun doesn't set till almost ten. My favorite nights are when I open the window at dusk and feel the warm breeze tickle my arms. The scent of flowers mingles with the chalky pavement dust. Seattleites stay out late to catch the last bit of sunlight, and their laughter hums along with the traffic.

I am clicking through discouraging job postings and listening to Jeopardy on the TV when Jane gets home. Her arms are weighed down with binders. I hurry to help her. I've never seen her look so tired.

"Thanks, Lizzie," she exhales.

"Busy day?"

"You could say that." Jane collapses on the sofa and kicks off her shoes. "I'm going to order Thai and finish this in my room."

"C'mon, Janey, take a weight off first!" I reach over to squeeze my big sister's shoulders.

"I wish." She sighs again. "One day I will figure out work/life balance. I miss spending time with you! And Chip," she adds wistfully.

"I thought you were spending all your time with Chip!"

Jane shrugs and leans her head back on the sofa. "I'm not seeing him much more than I am you. Last one hired gets all the time-consuming busywork and the clients no one else wants."

I pull her into a full hug. "I'm sorry, Jane."

The smile she returns is insincere and unlike my Jane. My heart clenches.

"At least take thirty minutes to relax," I instruct. "I'll get Thai and open a bottle of pink wine."

Jane and I eat takeout in the living room, though she does bring one of her binders out with her. I bookmark random jobs and think about applying for them; I can find no openings at galleries.

Jane is engrossed in her binder when her phone rings. She glances at the screen and picks up eagerly.

"Hey, you." She beams and pauses. "I miss you too."

She is silent for a while. I assume she is listening to Chip when she supplies the occasional "Oh really?" and "Mmmm" in agreement.

"I love that idea, baby. I'm sure I can get one day off, especially since it's a holiday." She pauses and glances at me. "I'll ask her." She smiles at me.

I raise my eyebrows in question.

"Okay," she continues. She stands up to stretch and walks into her room. I hear her talking but can no longer distinguish her words. I glance down at my laptop screen. I wonder if the curatorial internship at the art museum pays.

Jane emerges a moment later. Her expression is serene and more Jane-like than a moment ago.

"Chip's family owns a cabin in Westport. He wants to know if we want to come out for the Fourth of July weekend. Both his sisters will be in town."

"Me, your boyfriend, and two Emmelines for a whole weekend? Sign me up!"

"Lizzie," she admonishes. "Chip's other sister, Laurel, will bring her husband and their two kids. And Darcy is coming; you're friends with him."

"Kind of," I snort. "If you think three conversations and a rude comment makes a friendship."

"You've hung out more than that! He did drive you to Woodinville, and he stops in to see you at the coffee shop."

"He stops in to get coffee," I clarify.

"Anyway, Chip told me Darcy thought it would be more fun if you were there."

Well, Darcy and I did say we would get along for Chip and Jane.

"All right, I'll go," I agree. "Beats going to a bar with Katrina and Lydia or staying up all night playing *Street Fighter* with Charlotte."

Chip, Jane, and I arrive at the cabin early Friday afternoon. Jane is on the phone with her boss, pleading for more time on a case. Winston whines and trots after her. Chip guides her in through the front door, and I trail behind. He rubs her back in sympathy.

"... I understand, Steve, but if I'm taking this over from Nancy, I will need more than the holiday weekend to prepare ... Yes, of course I appreciate it. ... I understand. Wednesday is doable, I think ..."

The cabin is right on the beach. It's airy with an open kitchen and living room. Whoever decorated it must love Germany as Bavarian details litter the place. A cuckoo clock hangs above the wood-burning fireplace, and an ornately carved banister leads upstairs.

The faint smell of a grill drifts through the open sliding-glass door. I pause and take in the view. We're near Half Moon Bay, one of the nicer beaches in Washington State.

In the kitchen, a woman is chopping vegetables. Chip waves at her and then guides Jane up the stairs with Winston obediently following behind. I drop my bag, not sure where to go next.

"You must be Laurel." I walk over and extend my hand to the woman in the kitchen. "I'm Lizzie, Jane's sister."

"Pleasure," she replies with a limp handshake similar to Emmeline's.

Laurel is shorter and rounder than Emmeline but still taller than I am. Despite her slightly sleep-worn appearance, she has the same composed manner as Emmeline along with clear skin, a crisp white T-shirt, and a perfect manicure.

I offer to help her with the vegetables, and she passes me a bag of green beans to trim.

"Jane got a call from her boss," I comment in the absence of conversation. "It seems her new firm loves to delegate all the grunt work to her." I roll my eyes.

"I don't miss being at the bottom of the food chain," Laurel sympathizes.

"Tell me about it," I mutter. "What do you do?"

Laurel waves her hand lightly. "I *was* a marketing analyst, but I decided not to go back after maternity leave. My husband is a VP, thank God. I don't know what I would have done if I had to work and take care of my two little ones."

"Pay through the nose in child care?" I laugh.

"Oh, we still have an au pair," Laurel continues. "Otherwise, I would *never* have any time to myself! We did give Nadia this weekend off, even though she hardly cares about the Fourth of July." She laughs lightly, humbly, as if she can't believe how generous she and her husband are. I spy a baby monitor next to the salad bowl. I can't help the comparison I draw in my mind between her life and the life Mom wants for Jane and me. She had a good job she was able to leave when she married well and had babies. They're obviously well off enough to afford extra help on one income. I bet their house is nice too. I can't even fathom owning a house right now.

I suppress the impulse to roll my eyes. "I'm sure she appreciates it," I reply. "Anything else for me to chop?"

"Aren't you sweet?" Laurel says. "No, no, I'm almost done. Why don't you put your things away? I'm afraid you, Emmeline, and Darcy will have to decide who gets the last room. The other two beds are in the children's loft."

I shrug. "I'll sleep in the loft."

"I hope my Sadie doesn't keep you up!" she smiles. "You'll appreciate that we'll keep Asher in our room since he's too fussy to sleep through the night."

"Which way am I going?"

Laurel gives me directions, and I climb two flights of stairs to the open top floor. There are four twin beds along the eaves of each side of the sloping roof. I wonder how they expect Darcy to fit in one of those beds; his feet would hang off the end. Maybe Emmeline will be nice enough to volunteer the extra room to him—that is, if she doesn't try to share it with him.

I drop my bag beside a bed and plug in my phone. I plop down on the mattress and pick at the faded quilt. Best to take a breather before I join the rest of the household. Reaching into my backpack, I retrieve a sketchpad and lean against the pillows.

My bed faces a large picture window, and I watch the peaceful waves roll in and out as sunlight catches the peaks in the water. I start to sketch. It's nothing spectacular, but I like to have something to occupy my hands. I am so engrossed that I barely register footsteps coming up the stairs.

I glance up to see Darcy. My stomach jolts in surprise; I thought Emmeline would offer him the room to impress him.

"Hey, Darcy." I lay my sketchpad on my knees. "You got exiled up here too?"

"Hey!" He drops his bag on an empty bed. "Damage control," he says. "Emmeline isn't here yet."

"I hope she'll appreciate it," I reply. I'm a little bothered, but I can't really say why. Maybe because Emmeline seems like the type to always get what she wants as most spoiled rich girls do.

"I'm sure she will," Darcy says.

EMMELINE ARRIVES BY THE TIME WE SIT DOWN FOR LUNCH. I SIT NEXT TO Laurel's husband, Matt, at the end of the table and feel a bit like an outsider among Chip's family and Darcy and their easy familiarity. Jane makes a brief, gracious appearance but has to leave after getting a small amount of food before a Skype meeting. Chip watches her go and shakes his head.

"I forgot what it's like to pay your dues." He frowns and leans down to scratch Winston's ears.

"I'm so glad to have gotten past that phase in my career," Emmeline says. "What a nightmare—the endless hours and compromise."

"I remember my first position at Google," adds Laurel. "I wouldn't go back there for the world."

"Poor Jane," Emmeline continues. "She's really lovely, Laurel. I hope she can free herself enough this weekend so you can get to know her."

Laurel smiles at Chip. "We haven't met a new girl in a few years, Chip."

"It's disappointing she's so overworked," adds Emmeline before Chip can reply. "Remember how much of a slave I was before my last promotion?"

"At least, we can all indulge this weekend," Laurel says.

"Did you book Ida?" Emmeline asks excitedly. "You guys, Ida is *magic*, and she only charges ninety dollars for an hour!"

"Only ninety dollars?" I cough as I try to swallow my water.

"Yep," Emmeline replies. "It's a bargain considering she sets up a station right in our front yard. You'd enjoy one of her massages, Darcy." Emmeline smiles knowingly at him.

"Totally worth it," Laurel agrees.

"Sounds like it," I say, trying to hide my sarcasm. Darcy and I catch eyes, but I can't read his expression. It bothers me that I can't tell if he's into Emmeline or not. Maybe he is, but it won't work because it would be long distance? She does seem like the "perfect" sort of woman: well groomed, good job, worldly… Of course, she's also kind of a snob, but that's neither here nor there.

Matt picks up his tablet and starts scrolling, apparently unable to socialize without it.

"There are lots of other things to do around here," Chip jumps in. "We have the sailboat and the badminton net. And there are some hikes nearby too."

"You have a sailboat?" I reply, grateful for the change in subject.

"Just our old Hobie Cat, but we keep her in good shape," Chip replies enthusiastically.

"Ugh, that thing is older than you are," Emmeline criticizes.

"But she still does the job," Chip says.

"Well," Laurel cuts in, "you can all go on the dangerous sailboat, and I will let Ida work all my tension out. Motherhood can be so tiring."

The sisters continue to chat with Darcy, and I let my attention wander. "The salmon was really good," I offer to Matt.

"It's because my new grill has a ProSear burner," he replies. "It's good on the fish, but you can really taste the magic with steak."

"Oh, I don't eat red meat," I apologize.

"That's too bad," Matt replies. He doesn't continue the conversation.

To my relief, Jane appears a few minutes later. She slumps in the chair next to Chip.

"I need a glass of wine and to forget work exists for the next two hours."

"Oh, Jane," I console.

Chip puts his arm around her shoulders and draws her near. He kisses her head and murmurs into her hair. I look away.

"Can I help with the dishes?" I ask Laurel with more cheer than I feel.

MOM WAS ALWAYS THE EPITOME OF THE PERFECT WOMAN, AT LEAST IN terms of her looks. She is tall, blonde, and fit. Jane, who favors her, gets much of this same praise. My looks, while never degraded, were really never spoken of at home unless my mom was complaining about my hair. My curls were often a rat's nest growing up to the point where brushing it resulted in tears.

The one thing my mom lacked was a certain awareness in the world. Perhaps that's why she didn't see the warning signs with my dad. I know that's why she didn't mind that she dropped out of college to get married.

Now she regrets that decision, but she has Jane to make up for her failings: Jane has both the looks and the smarts.

I know that she has good intentions, I really do, but I can't agree with Mom that the only thing that makes a perfect job perfect is that it's lucrative. It's like believing that any guy is good enough to marry as long as he's well off and straight. I'd like to enjoy my job and love my future spouse, if I'm lucky enough to meet one. From what I can tell, Mom doesn't understand that life is more than making money and looking attractive. Nevertheless, we've been taught as a certain truth that a happy life is the type of life that photographs well. Intellectually, I know this isn't necessarily true, but it's hard not to think this way. I've internalized it.

THE REMAINDER OF THE AFTERNOON IS QUIET. JANE AND CHIP TAKE THE dog for a walk, and I end up playing dolls with Sadie after she wakes up from her nap. Laurel relieves me, and I decide to take my own long walk along the beach.

When I return, the entire group, apart from Jane, is playing poker at the dining room table. Chip invites me to join, but I say I don't know how to play. It looks like they're using real money, and I don't want to admit how strapped for cash I really am right now.

"You never learned?" Matt replies in amazement. "I thought everyone knew how to play."

"Lizzie spends her free time mastering the art of coffee. She doesn't have time for anything else," Emmeline says derisively. I'm starting to grow tired of her subtle jabs. It's not as if I'm a threat or anything.

"I have time for plenty of other interests," I say wearily.

"We could teach you," offers Chip, "or we could play something else when we're done."

I thank him and reassure the group that I'm happy to sit and sketch.

"Our mother used to paint out here." Chip gestures toward my drawing pad. "I wish we had some of her supplies here for you to use."

"I bet you're overflowing with art supplies with Georgie's talent and all," Emmeline says, redirecting the conversation to Darcy.

"She has a good collection," he agrees.

"And you are always buying interesting art."

He shrugs. "I might as well get what I like."

"You make it sound like you only have a few original pieces! Your office could be a gallery. Chip, when you get your next bonus, you should get me a piece by an artist Darcy recommends."

He laughs in disbelief. "For what occasion?"

"Oh, I don't know. Labor Day, my birthday…you can figure something out."

He rolls his eyes. "I will get something Darcy suggests that I can afford for your birthday."

I wonder what sort of art Darcy likes. What kind of artist is his sister? My curiosity piqued, I set aside my sketchpad and draw up a chair between Chip and Laurel.

"How is Georgie doing?" asks Emmeline. "Is she starting college this fall?"

"She is. She'll be abandoning me to the other coast. Brown."

"I'm not surprised! Your sister is so intelligent. And talented! So accomplished at the violin. Doesn't she volunteer at the animal shelter too?"

"It's amazing," notes Chip, "all the hoops high school students need to jump through these days in order to get into a good college."

"Some people do what they like for fun, no matter if it gets them into a good school or not," Emmeline argues.

"Well, yeah, they probably like their activities in order to pursue them. But I bet they wouldn't do half as many extracurriculars if it wasn't required for admissions," Chip says.

"I agree," said Darcy, "But a passion for the activity makes it more impressive, I think."

"Exactly!" exclaims Emmeline.

"Then," I observe, "you probably believe an occupation is worthless without passion."

"For the activity to be fulfilling, yes," Darcy says seriously.

"Nothing is more motivating than doing what you love!" Emmeline supports with animation. "The most accomplished people can't help but work hard because they love what they do, wouldn't you all say? And you can tell when someone really loves their work by their air. People who love their jobs are happy people."

"But all that achievement comes to nothing if you can't balance it with family and friends," adds Darcy.

"The ultimate goal of Having It All," I remark to him. "Do you know someone who has actually achieved this?"

"I know several!" declares Emmeline.

"So do I," echoes Laurel.

"I appear to know all the wrong people then." I shake my head and reach for my sketchbook while the rest of the group finishes their game.

Chapter Five

By the time I go to bed, Sadie is already snoring softly in the loft. I am reading my worn paperback copy of *The Agony and the Ecstasy* when Darcy makes his way up. He gives me a slight nod, and I place my fingers against my lips and indicate the sleeping child.

We go to bed without speaking, and when I wake up the next morning, his bed is neatly made as if he never slept in it.

It's warm today, almost eighty degrees. I throw on my swimsuit and decide to join the group on the beach.

I find Laurel sheltered under a large rainbow umbrella with Asher in her lap. Matt is building a sandcastle with Sadie, and Laurel calls to him to check her daughter's sunscreen.

Emmeline suns herself and flips through a *Harper's Bazaar*.

Jane and Chip are on another walk with Winston. Darcy returns from a jog up the shoreline and Emmeline watches him with interest. He wipes his face with the back of his arm and jumps in the water.

I sit on my towel and begin to apply sunscreen.

"Sadie slept well last night," I tell Laurel.

"That's what Darcy said," she replies. She leans forward and tickles Asher's tummy. He gurgles.

Sadie giggles at Matt and jumps in excitement in the distance. Darcy walks up toward us. Emmeline passes him a towel.

"You're so diligent," she compliments Darcy as she hands him a water bottle.

"Just burning off steam." He takes a swig of water. I am struggling to reach my back with sunscreen when Darcy offers to help.

His touch is cold on my back, and I shiver.

"You have a tattoo," he notices, indicating my right ribs. "Is that Mucha?"

"It is," I reply. "It's *Painting* from 'The Arts' series. I got it after I spent a semester in Prague."

"I could never get a tattoo," Emmeline says. "It's so *permanent*."

Darcy gives the bottle of sunscreen back to me and moves to an empty chair.

"I consider my time in Prague a defining life moment. I did a study on Mucha, and I wanted to commemorate my time there."

"Most people make a scrapbook for memories," Darcy observes.

"*Some* people," I correct. "But what makes a stronger memory than six hours of unbearable pain?" I quip.

Winston bounds toward our group, and I laugh. "Hey, buddy," I croon. Chip and Jane wander up from the shore hand-in-hand.

"I'm so happy you're not working!" I exclaim as Jane approaches.

"Almost," she sighs. "I have a few more things to finish up and email to my boss. Then I'm finally free for the rest of the weekend."

"Thank God!" I laugh. "I thought I had imagined your presence here."

"We can't wait to have you to ourselves," Chip agrees. He kisses Jane's temple.

She sighs again and kisses his cheek. "I'll try to finish by lunch time."

"Poor Jane," Laurel says as we watch her go. "It's not easy to have a demanding job. This is our last family weekend before Matt has to go to Geneva for two weeks." She glances fondly at Matt while Sadie buries him in sand.

"I hate traveling for work," Chip groans in commiseration. He sits on a clean towel and stretches his legs out. Winston rolls onto his back, and Chip scratches the dog's belly.

"Really?" I say in surprise. "I would love any opportunity to travel on someone else's dime."

"If I got to decide what I could do, it would be great," he explains, "but it's such a pain to fly nine hours only to see the inside of a hotel and conference room for a week."

I prop my chin in my hands and squint at him. "Where would you go if you got to plan your trip?"

"I'm not sure." He pauses thoughtfully. "When I travel on my own, my plans tend to be spur of the moment. I'm happy as long as there are things to do and this guy is taken care of!" He illustrates his point by rubbing Winston on the head.

"That sounds about right." I laugh.

"Does it?" Chip raises his eyebrows.

"I wouldn't expect anything less than spontaneous from you."

"Thanks…I think." He chuckles. "Although, you make me sound more predictable than adventurous."

"No, not predictable at all. I think you are someone who faithfully follows your heart, no matter where it leads."

"Do you always analyze people so closely? Or should I feel self-conscious?"

I laugh. "People are fascinating. And I did minor in sociology, so maybe I'm meant to be a student of personalities,"

"Art history and sociology?" Darcy asks. "So you're interested in art as a means of self-expression?"

"Kind of. I like the self-expression part of it, for sure. But also the message, technique, and nuances. There's always more to a painting than we realize."

Sadie runs up the beach toward us laughing.

"Lizzie, Lizzie!" she cries. She stops in front of me and drops to her bottom.

"Uhhhhhmmmm, we havda go over dis way for jus' girls! It's okay to jus' be wid girls over here and play Once Upon a Time Princess Dolls! Mommy wants you and me to play be-because Nadia izzn't here."

Chip presses his lips together to suppress his mirth.

"You are being summoned," Emmeline clarifies helpfully.

"Why can't Uncle Chip be a princess doll?" I tease Sadie.

"Boys can't be pretty princess dolls!" she huffs.

"Anyone can be a pretty princess doll!" I exclaim dramatically. "All you have to do is believe you are pretty!"

"I'm not sure Chip has the natural beauty Sadie is looking for." Darcy chuckles.

"Does that mean you want to the prettiest princess doll?" I retort.

Sadie giggles. "Nooooo!" she declares. "Darcy iz too tall. He can't be a doll or a girl!"

Chip finally does laugh, and Darcy smiles.

An awkward silence settles over our group, and I wonder if I should say something else but can't think of anything.

I rise to my feet and offer my hand to Sadie. "Let's go play dolls, Lady Sadie."

JANE "ONLY HAS AN HOUR TO GO" BY THE TIME LUNCH ROLLS AROUND. WE eat turkey dogs and coleslaw on the back deck. Sadie feeds Winston bits of her hot dog bun, and Chip turns on Bob Marley.

Emmeline rolls her eyes. "You have no taste, Chip!"

"It goes with the atmosphere," he argues.

Darcy picks up his tablet, and Emmeline leans over his shoulder.

"That reminds me, I need to check on my fantasy baseball team," Matt says, pulling out his own tablet.

I pull my knees to my chest and rest my chin on them. Laurel flips through a magazine while Sadie draws around her on the deck using sidewalk chalk. Matt starts to explain his lineup to Chip, and Emmeline perches on the arm of Darcy's chair.

"I can't imagine how you keep track of so many investments." She pauses but he doesn't answer. "You are so organized."

"Not more than anyone else," he remarks mildly.

"You must buy and trade *so* many stocks throughout the year! And you manage the ones from your father too—it must be so difficult to try to tell them all apart," she says.

"You're lucky you don't have your own portfolio to manage then." He frowns at the screen.

"I have been meaning to learn. You should give me advice on how to start."

"If you're really interested—"

"Where do you find your tips?" She leans close his shoulder.

He doesn't reply. I'm still trying to puzzle out their dynamic. Is it one-sided? Does he like her? He seems to be brushing her off right now, but they did spend most of the morning talking.

"I think if I were to invest, I would choose a retail or technology company before it becomes too popular. Like Starbucks or Apple when they were new. Do you know of any good startups?"

"Nothing promising at the moment in those fields," he replies without looking at her.

"Oh well, I'll have to wait then. You'll have to let me know if some new and interesting business does come to the market."

"I will keep my eyes open."

He rises to put his tablet away and returns to a different chair.

"I have noticed that financially successful people always have a healthy stock portfolio," Emmeline declares to the group.

"How is that a compliment to Darcy?" Chip asks laughingly. "He inherited most of his investments, right, Darcy?"

Emmeline scowls and slides from the arm to the seat of the chair.

"My major shares are from my father," Darcy says.

"Who are you to talk!" exclaims Emmeline. "You don't even have a 401(k)!"

"I'm using my salary to enjoy my twenties while I'm still young. I'll turn on my 401(k) on my thirtieth birthday."

"Your priorities are consistent," I tease. "The impulsive traveler investing in his memories."

"You really should prepare for the future, Chip." Darcy admonishes.

"I prepare for my future by indulging in great experiences."

"Just as long as you can retire someday."

"You make it sound like he can't do anything!" I protest, bothered that Darcy seems to be lording his "togetherness" over everyone—like his standards are the best for everyone. "Better to have currency in adventure instead of sitting on your pile of money!"

Chip shakes his head. "Thanks, Lizzie. That's one way to put me in the best light. But Darcy is right: I should be more responsible with my money."

"I'm sure you are," I insist. I nod at Darcy. "Your friend here just needs to learn a lesson in leisure."

"I don't think he understands the concept." Chip snorts.

Darcy catches my eye. "You can still save for retirement while indulging in other experiences," he contends.

I drop my feet to the deck and lean toward him. "True, but once you learn to relax, you could use your piles of money for fun, not just savings."

"What makes you think I don't have fun?"

I tap my chin in mock seriousness. "I'm not sure. It may be your stoicism. Or your serious face."

"I'm not serious right now." His smile smoothes the crease in his brow, and the dimple in his cheek insists he is not a solemn man at all.

"A smile is a start," I concede.

JANE APPEARS AT DINNER LOOKING TRIUMPHANT. "IT'S DONE! NO MORE work till I'm back in the office on Tuesday!"

Chip whoops and hugs her till he lifts her feet off the ground.

I grin. "I'm so relieved for you, Janey."

"Oh, me too. I keep reminding myself that these hours won't last forever." She drops down into an empty chair, and Chip sits next to her. She smiles and rubs her forehead. Even sleep deprived, Jane looks beautiful. Chip gazes at her affectionately.

He smiles at her. "We should celebrate tonight. We could go to Nichols?" He looks around at the group.

"I could go for a beer," Matt agrees.

"You wouldn't dare abandon me to watch the kids!" Laurel swats his arm. Matt grumbles and slouches.

"Well, the rest of us could go," Emmeline says with a meaningful look at Darcy.

"Lizzie?" Jane asks.

"Only if I get to buy your first shot," I say.

The five of us take Chip's jeep to Nichols, a local dive bar. The bar itself is moderately occupied with weekenders, despite the homely decor. The air smells faintly of stale cigarettes even though smoking in bars has been outlawed for the last twenty years. The dingy carpet is covered with dull splatters, and I try not to imagine what a black light would disclose. Emmeline finds a table.

"Over here," she waves. "Darcy?" She indicates the seat next to herself.

Darcy nods at her but walks over to the jukebox. I detect a little desperation and start to feel a little sorry for Emmeline.

Jane stands with Chip at the bar. I walk up to them and loop my arm through hers.

"What'll it be, sis? Tequila?"

"You were serious?" Jane asks. "Please save your money. There will be enough time for you to treat me all you want when you get out of the coffee shop."

"Jane, let me get this!" I exclaim. "Just one shot. I can handle the six dollars."

"Fine, just a shot." She laughs. "Then you save your money."

"Cross my heart," I promise, gesturing over my chest. I approach the bar and order two shots of tequila with limes.

"Here's to kicking legal ass," I declare and clink my glass against hers.

We down our shots and bite into the limes. I shudder and throw my arms happily around Jane.

"You got a good one, Chip," I announce with my arms hooked around Jane's neck. "If you break her heart though, you'll have to answer to me."

"Lizzie!" Jane flushes.

"I only tell the truth. And you would do the same for me."

"She's right," Jane tells Chip.

"You're lucky to be so close," Chip notes. He glances at Emmeline, sitting at the table by herself drumming her fingers.

"Never underestimate the Venetidis bond," I respond. I order another drink and head over to keep Emmeline company.

"It's not too lonely over here, is it?" I pull up a chair next to her.

Emmeline sniffs. "I hope Chip remembers to get me something." She eyes Darcy as he lingers by the jukebox and then wanders to our table.

Hall and Oates comes on, and I praise his choice as he approaches. "Hell yes! 'Rich Girl' is a dive bar anthem!"

"When did you have time to learn that?" Emmeline laughs. "Didn't you just turn twenty-one?"

"Twenty-two! I'm not that young!"

I push my empty glass away from myself. "I am so happy to see Jane out in the wild. I feel like I haven't seen her in months, and we *live* together!"

Jane and Chip approach our table with a round of margaritas "to go with our tequila shots," Jane reasons.

I lose track of the number of drinks we consume. I vaguely recollect Chip cutting himself off so he can be the designated driver.

Emmeline and I become friends at some point in the night, and we dance to "Twist and Shout" in front of the jukebox. Jane and Chip make out at the table, and Darcy awkwardly pretends they aren't there while he watches us dance. Emmeline invites him to dance with us.

"He doesn't seem like the dancing type," I taunt in his direction.

"I wouldn't want to embarrass you," he calls back.

"You could never embarrass us!" Emmeline declares. Darcy shakes his and scoots his chair away from the enthusiastic couple.

We arrive back at the cabin around two in the morning. I feel a little silly as Darcy and I stumble up the stairs and shush each other.

"You'll wake the child, sir!" I whisper loudly.

Without thinking, I strip off my dress and reach for my shorts and camisole. I stumble and snort at myself when I put both feet through one of the legs.

"Are you okay?" Darcy whispers laughingly.

"Don't judge me!"

I straighten after my pajamas are on and freeze.

Behind me, Darcy's palms press my hips. He turns me around. The hairs on my arm stand on end, and I shiver.

"What are you doing?" I whisper. I blink and stare at his unfocused eyes, my mind whirling. Doesn't he like Emmeline? What does this mean? Does he hit on random girls when he's drunk?

"I don't know," he whispers back.

His breath is on my face, and I'm not sure if I should pull away or close my eyes.

Instead, I say I'm drunk.

His hands slide from my hips, and his arms drop to his sides.

"Me too."

I step back from him and sit on the bed. He stares down at me, and my brain is too impaired to make sense of it.

"Good night, Darcy," I whisper.

"Good night."

He backs away and finds his own bed in the other corner. I fall backward against my pillow and quickly slip into an alcohol-soaked sleep.

EMMELINE BREEZES INTO THE KITCHEN AND PAUSES ABRUPTLY IN FRONT of Darcy and me miserably drinking coffee in awkward silence. What's worse is we woke up at the same time and met eyes across the loft. He immediately looked away. God, how embarrassing. Needless to say, we've avoided eye contact since then. I can't decide if he's embarrassed because he hit on someone *not* his type or because I turned him down. Probably the former. Good Lord, Sadie was even in the room with us.

"Someone woke up on the wrong side of the bed this morning," Emmeline observes with a raised brow.

Darcy glares at his coffee cup but doesn't reply.

I rub my temples. "How are you not hungover, Emmeline?"

"With enough experience, you learn to alternate between water and alcohol," she says imperiously. "Would you like a Bloody Mary, Darcy? Hair of the rabbit, you know."

"You mean hair of the dog?" I snort and wince at the effort.

"Dog, cat, rabbit, whatever…" She waves her perfectly manicured hand at me dismissively.

"I'll stick with the coffee, thanks," Darcy replies. His voice is still gravelly with sleep.

Darcy gazes absently into space, and I bury my head in my arms to block out the morning light.

Last night was fun.

Last night was weird.

What the hell was Darcy doing?

I can't make sense of it. Darcy isn't interested in the aimless kid sister. Not that I care *what* he thinks, but, Jesus, am I confused.

But…even through an alcoholic haze, I remember the pressure of his hands and the shock of his touch. I think I changed in front of him too, and I inwardly cringe. Well, I guess he knows for sure I'm not some classy girl like Emmeline. I firmly tell myself not to be embarrassed since we were all confused by alcohol. Not even Emmeline was herself last night; she acted like my friend.

"You both should really get your act together," Emmeline states. "We only have one day left, you know."

I lift my head from the nest of my arms. Emmeline smiles at Darcy, and he shrugs.

"Maybe after I hook up an IV of this stuff." He indicates his mug.

"I'm going to pass out on the beach." I push my chair back purposefully. "I'll bounce back in a few hours."

I walk through the beach grass by myself and revel in the feeling of sand between my toes as I make my way to the surf. The water is freezing and clears my head for a moment.

I imagine Jane and Chip are still in their room, making up for the quality time they lost while she worked. Laurel and Matt must have taken the kids to the playground since their car is gone. Emmeline is probably relieved I left her alone with Darcy. I wonder what will happen when she leaves town again.

Jane and Chip join me on the beach after I've made myself comfortable. Chip is very careful with Jane, who seems to be recovering from the same kind of hangover that I am, though Chip seems perfectly content.

"Do you Bishops even get hangovers?" I grumble.

"You probably don't remember, but I was the designated driver." He laughs.

"You are a responsible man," I reply. I sit up on my towel, and Jane exclaims I need more sunscreen.

Darcy joins the group not long after; Emmeline follows. Darcy looks better than I feel, and Emmeline sits near him smugly.

"...you remember Taylor?" she's saying as they approach the group.

"Sure," Darcy replies as he nods hello at the group.

"She's been repping these novelty books. You know the kind I mean?" She notices the rest of the group is listening to her and smiles at the attention. "I was just telling Darcy about the Proust Questionnaire. It's our new favorite party icebreaker," she says to us. "Here," she says, reaching into her bag to retrieve a paperback. "It's an advanced reader copy. We should fill it out!" she says enthusiastically.

She hands it to Darcy, and he flips through it quickly before passing it back.

"Looks interesting," he comments.

Emmeline frowns and looks around at our group. She fixes her eyes on me and leans in to offer me the book.

"Have you ever done the Questionnaire, Lizzie?"

"I've never heard of it."

"It's a famous questionnaire Marcel Proust created," she states knowingly. "He used it to interview people about their personalities. *Vanity Fair* prints celebrity versions every month. My client is marketing it to the everyday person. You should try your hand at one; it's very thought-provoking."

I frown and flip through the pages. "Looks like a listicle for pseudo-intellectuals. Are you sure you're interested in...'the fault I find easiest to tolerate'?"

Emmeline glances at me slyly. "My guess would be naïveté. Am I right?"

"I wouldn't call naïveté a fault. More like a symptom...but if you're asking, I'm really not sure. Maybe lack of ambition?"

"Lack of ambition is a quality everyone your age has—it's probably easy for you to overlook."

"Some people don't lack ambition, just direction. But it can appear as lack of ambition," Darcy remarks.

"Isn't that just as bad? How can someone who lacks direction have any real goals?" Emmeline asks keenly.

He shakes his head and glances my way for the first time since this morning. My face is hot. How did my life decisions suddenly come under the microscope?

"Did *you* have your dream job your first summer after college?" I challenge Emmeline.

"I had an internship," she replies smugly. "They hired me on after a year."

"Lucky for you," I reply tartly.

"It wasn't luck," Emmeline replies. "I worked hard for it."

"There's something to be said for starting at ground zero," Darcy cuts in. He glances at me and back to Emmeline. I can't tell what he means. Does he approve of Emmeline's method of likely living off her parents for a year?

"Some people have to take shitty jobs to start out," I challenge. "Not everyone can live off no pay."

"*You* didn't start from ground zero," Emmeline says to Darcy.

Darcy shrugs. "Lucky for me too, I guess. Thanks to my dad, I was able to jump right into the business."

Emmeline fixes her gaze on me in challenge. I'm barely able to keep myself from rolling my eyes. "Thank God for that," she says.

I look between the two of them, annoyed and feeling somewhat ganged up on. So what if I'm not where they were at twenty-two? Between this conversation and that weird interaction with Darcy last night…I don't know what to feel. I want to brush them off and change the subject. I wish Emmeline would let up. I opt to appear unruffled.

"Well, I have lots to learn from you two, I guess. Thank you, Emmeline, for explaining to me how to be successful."

Emmeline smiles back at me warily as if she can't tell if I'm sincere or not.

"What is your dream job, Lizzie?" Darcy asks after a pause. I feel his attention on me like a weight of judgment. I shrug breezily.

"That's a complicated question," I reply nonchalantly. "The short answer is I studied to be a curator." I'm not in the mood to think about Ian and those lingering doubts about my abilities. I squint over the horizon and watch the breeze whisper over the beach grass. Darcy and Emmeline are still watching me. I glance at Emmeline, who looks smug, and raise my eyebrow.

"I'm not lucky like you," I say. "Paying my dues has to come with income. Maybe, in a few years, I can look to your example to see if I've made the right choices—even if I am starting out making coffee at minimum wage."

"It would be better for your career if your coffee shop showed art," Emmeline replies. "At least then you would be doing *something* related to your field."

I don't reply but smile to myself. She really thinks she knows everything, doesn't she? I decide not to draw attention to the fact that Café Longue in fact does show art and that's why I applied there. I would rather not spur on her jealousy.

"Anyway!" I change the topic. "What's the weather report for today?"

"Sunny and perfect," Emmeline replies pleasantly. I can't help but feel she's happy making me uncomfortable. I lean back on my elbows and try not to look at her and Darcy, though when I glance over my shoulder, I see he's watching me. He looks away quickly.

"We should set up a badminton game!" Emmeline's declaration slices through the silent tension. "Chip, Jane, would you like to play? Darcy?"

Darcy agrees and goes off with the other three to set up the net; he and Emmeline don't even look at me when they walk away. I debate watching them play, but decide against it.

It's easier, as the day wears on, to distance myself from Darcy and Emmeline. I almost feel guilty for monopolizing Jane's attention, but I decide Chip doesn't mind. He's had most of her non-working attention all weekend.

We spend that evening on the beach around a bonfire. Matt lights off fireworks, and Laurel continues to call out that he needs to be careful. Jane nestles against Chip's chest and gazes at the sky. I sit cross-legged and toast marshmallows. Emmeline mentions how much fun she is having and how she isn't looking forward to returning to New York.

Darcy sits next to me, subdued. We barely talk except to share the s'more supplies. I try not to mind that I feel weird around him. He's made me uncomfortable since we first met anyway. I imagine after we go home tomorrow, we won't see each other that often unless it's with Chip and Jane. The thought is a relief.

Chip takes Jane and me home on Monday morning, and our apartment is a welcome sight. I'm glad for my own bed, the privacy of my room, and getting back to normal—whatever that is.

Chapter Six

I open Café Longue with Charlotte the next morning. I welcome her company even if I'm not awake yet.

After the morning rush, we dawdle behind the counter.

"So I have a proposition for us," Charlotte tells me.

"Close the café and day drink at Gasworks Park?"

"A *responsible* proposition," Charlotte berates me with an amused smile.

"That's right, we are supposed to be playing the part of adults." I sigh dramatically. "What do you propose?"

"You know Rose & Hunts?"

"The online luxury store?"

"The very one. I heard they are hiring a bunch of contractors for a three-month project. Really easy stuff—digitally cataloging new inventory for the home goods branch they'll be launching soon. I think we should apply."

"Where did you hear about that?"

"One of our regulars works there. Anyway, we should do it. Break out of retail hell and into the real job market."

I shrug. "Why not?" I would probably make more at a job like that. Even if it's a temporary position, it's worth the risk, I reason.

My shift ends at lunchtime, and Katrina comes in to replace me.

"We're all meeting at Bright Bay at eight for drinks," she says while I clock out. "Want to join us?"

"Some other time. I'm still recovering from my weekend away, and I open again tomorrow."

Charlotte comes over later that evening for dinner, and we submit our résumés to Rose & Hunts. I go to bed early to prepare for another 5:00 a.m. shift.

THE NEXT FEW DAYS SETTLE INTO A COMFORTABLE PATTERN OF COFFEE, THE occasional night out with Katrina and Lydia, and waiting to hear back about the contract job. Charlotte gets more and more nervous as time wears on. I feel pessimistic.

I receive an unknown call a week and a half later while wiping down counters. I motion to Charlotte that I'm going to take it outside. I step out back among the smokers and lean against the brick wall.

"Hello?"

"Hello, I'm looking for Elizabeth Venetidis."

"This is she."

"Hi, Elizabeth. My name is Frederick Fitzwilliam from Rose & Hunts. We received your application for associate catalog editor, and we would like to bring you in for an interview if you're still interested."

"That would be great! I *am* still interested!" My relief bubbles to a grin.

"Great! How does next Tuesday work for you?"

I have next Tuesday off. I grin wider at my luck.

"Anytime on Tuesday is perfect."

When I re-enter the cafe, I am beaming. Charlotte gives me a questioning look.

"Looks like I have an interview next week!"

"That's great, Lizzie," Charlotte says. She isn't as enthusiastic as I would expect her to be, but maybe it's because she hasn't received a call yet. Her phone vibrates a moment later, and she smiles at me in relief. "Wish me luck."

She takes the call outside. I let optimism take hold.

THE NEXT MORNING, CHARLOTTE AND I OPEN TOGETHER AGAIN. WE ARE both unbearably happy for the hour.

"We should interview-prep together, Lizzie," Charlotte buzzes as we juggle the morning rush.

"Let's do it! After our shifts are done?"

"Okay! I found some helpful blog articles we can go over. And we should research the company."

I laugh. "You are really taking this seriously." I scribble another order on a cup and draw a sun next to it.

"Aren't you?" Charlotte retorts. "But let's go to my place. I hate using your unsecured Wi-Fi."

"It's not bad," I claim. "Plus, Jane and I don't really know how to work our router."

"You really should secure your Wi-Fi," one of our regulars adds to our conversation. I glance at him. It's Grande Mocha with Extra Whip. Today his shaggy, sandy-colored hair is stuffed under a newsboy cap. His T-shirt, adorned with a drawing of a cartoon steak, reads "This Is Why I'm Not Vegan" and strains against his heavyset frame. He squints at me from behind his transition lenses.

"See, Lizzie, Colin thinks I'm right!" Charlotte insists.

Colin. I can never remember his name.

He ogles me and leans across the counter a little too closely. "You know, someone could hack your personal information or steal your identity through an unsecured connection," he continues. "One of the reasons I was hired at my job is because I know about these things. How to secure a connection and protect against viruses. Rose & Hunts is like a fortress thanks to my efforts. The CEO even told me that my work has helped defend against fraudulent transactions. Imagine, the CEO!"

"Colin is the one who told me about the contract jobs," Charlotte explains, glancing at him with interest.

"I see." I pass Colin his mocha over the partition.

"I could secure your connection for you if you'd like," Colin suggests. Even though I've stepped back from him, I can hear him breathing audibly. He raises his mocha and taps the side. "I like your doodles."

"Thanks. And, uh, I'll ask my sister's boyfriend about the secure connection thing," I deflect. "Enjoy your mocha! We'll see you next time!" I dismiss him cheerfully.

Colin beams back at me. "Yes, I will definitely see you soon."

I look over to make a face at Charlotte, but she is staring at the espresso machine with flushed cheeks and a frown.

Colin appears at the coffee shop again Saturday afternoon when I'm working with Katrina. He's on his laptop in the corner and keeps looking over at me.

"Dammit," I mutter to myself. I try to ignore him and wipe down the espresso machine.

"That guy is staring at you," Katrina whispers.

"I know," I mutter back at her. "If I ignore him, maybe he'll stop?"

Katrina giggles and takes an order for another customer.

Colin approaches us a moment later to order another mocha. He lingers after he pays and leans against the counter.

"Did you get your Wi-Fi sorted?" He squints at me.

"We did," I lie. "Thanks for the tip!" I keep my tone cheerful and distant. If he weren't a customer, I would kill the conversation more quickly.

"Good, good. I'm glad you took my advice to heart." He smiles smugly. "Did you hear about the National Retro Gaming Convention this coming Saturday? It's the first time it's being held in Seattle. I myself plan to buy some rare SNES games I haven't been able to find anywhere except eBay. And there's the Pong tournament. Last year, when the convention was in San Francisco, I won the entire thing. I have to defend my legacy this year!"

"I think Charlotte mentioned it."

"It sounds like fun, don't you think? You should go. I mean, with me—we should go. You could cheer me on!"

"Oh, um…" I can hear Katrina laughing into her fist behind me. My blush is warm.

"Sorry, I have a thing—a birthday party that day." Thank God for Chip. I exhale in relief. He's chartered a boat for his thirtieth birthday party. That's a bulletproof excuse.

"All day? I'm sure you could spare some of the day to meet up. You won't regret it. Maybe before your party?"

"Really, I can't," I apologize almost sincerely. "I work in the morning, and the party is on a boat, and it will take up the rest of the day. It's not the sort of thing someone can pop in and out of unless you have a canoe!"

Colin laughs a little too enthusiastically at my joke.

"If the party wasn't so inaccessible, then I could run into you."

"A shame," I concede cheerfully. "There's no way to get onto this boat unless you know someone."

Colin watches me and rotates his coffee cup thoughtfully. "Like a date?"

"Or something." I look over at Katrina helplessly, and she pretends not to notice. I can see she is still laughing at me though. My friends are the worst.

"Thanks for the mocha." Colin touches my arm to regain my attention. I try not to be too obvious as I pull it away.

"Thanks for coming in! Have a great day!" I can feel a headache start behind my eyes. This is why customer service sucks.

"See you soon," he replies. I stifle my groan; I wonder if he's memorized my schedule.

"Someone likes you," Katrina sings after he leaves.

"I don't want to deal with this," I gripe. "I just want to focus on my interview and making rent."

"Then you need to have a talk with him outside of work," she replies knowledgeably. "That guy seems like the persistent type."

"I should have said I have a boyfriend," I grumble.

"Except lies don't come easily to you," Katrina points out. "It's better that you set him straight."

"But I don't want to see him outside the coffee shop," I whine.

Katrina gives me a look, and I roll my eyes. "Fine," I concede. "Later. After Chip's party and stuff."

I wish I didn't have to deal with this, but I have some time to come up with a plan.

Chapter Seven

've met the greatest guy."

I'm out on a Tuesday night with Lydia and Katrina. Jane is with Chip, and Charlotte generally doesn't go out that often, so I've spent a lot of my free time with these two. They're fun, sometimes a little crazy for my taste, but I can deal. At least Katrina reins in Lydia when necessary.

"Details!" I grin back at Lydia.

"You'll like him," Katrina adds. "He's an artist."

I raise my eyebrows at Lydia in expectation.

"He's so hot," Lydia gushes. "His name is Geoff, and his art is up at Café Longue right now; I'm sure you've noticed it. He also DJs and bartends at Bright Bay. He is the *best* kisser—"

"So jealous." Katrina sighs.

"We met him after Katrina's shift the other night, and we all went out. His friends are *so* cool. They share this art studio in Pioneer Square. So bohemian. I bet you would like them," Lydia finishes.

"I bet I would," I reply with interest. I would love to meet more artists out here. Maybe I would feel less like I was floundering if I got more connected to the arts scene.

"I'll introduce you!" Lydia declares. "Next time I see him, I'll mention you and that you like making friends with artists."

"Thanks, Lyd!" I say. She smiles back at me, clearly pleased by my response. Sometimes I forget that my younger cousin likes to have my approval.

Lydia makes eyes across the bar at a group of guys. This is her strategy for drinking on a low budget. Flirt, get free drinks, move on. Sometimes that means that we have to hang out a little too long with randos she's picked up, but it is nice not to spend the money.

I'm almost done with my drink. I glance at Lydia, who's still throwing flirty looks at the guy across the room. He looks a little sketch to me, so I nudge her with my foot.

"Can we go somewhere else?"

Lydia shrugs and looks at Katrina.

"Let's get out of here," Katrina agrees.

We start to gather our purses, but then Lydia whines she has to pee.

"Go at the next bar," Katrina says.

Once outside, Katrina and I walk arm-in-arm, chatting happily until we realize Lydia is no longer with us. We turn around, scanning for her. Katrina starts giggling.

"What is it?" I ask.

"Look by that apartment," she points, laughing.

Lydia is squatting under a window. "Is she peeing?" I ask incredulously.

"I guess she couldn't wait."

Lydia finishes and saunters toward us.

"Where to next, ladies?" she says, waggling her eyebrows.

"Gross," I say when she laughs at me. "That's my dress."

"I'll wash it, don't worry," she says laughingly. "Let's go to the Redwood! I want to flirt with some lumberjack hipster boys."

The Redwood is the type of bar where you expect to see dudes with mighty beards wearing flannel and playing the banjo. The floor is littered with peanut shells, and they serve drinks out of mason jars. The three of us find a table, and Lydia instantly surveys the crowd.

"That guy is checking you out," she says to Katrina. She nods her chin at a baby-faced guy in cut-off jorts and horn-rimmed glasses. He looks like the human embodiment of craft beer. Katrina glances his way and looks back quickly.

"You think?" she asks nervously.

"Totallllly," Lydia replies with a giggle.

"Should I get drinks?" I ask, starting to rise. "What do you want?"

"Someone will get them for us," Lydia says airily.

I sink back down in my seat and shrug. Lydia continues to survey the room and seems to catch someone's eye. She beams back at us.

"Here we go," she says triumphantly.

A large guy with a gnarly beard approaches us. He punches his fists onto the table aggressively enough that we all jump in surprise.

"What are you drinking?" he asks. Somewhat startled by his manner, we all stare at each other. It takes a while, but Lydia finally replies slowly.

"Uh, we were planning to get Rainer's." She glances at us for confirmation.

"Nah, that's nothing," the dude replies. "What kind of shots?"

"Sorry, man," I reply. "We're not trying to get shit-faced."

"Then why are you even out?" he asks belligerently.

"Move along," I say with a dismissive laugh. I feel Katrina shift uncomfortably next to me.

"Naw, sss'ok," the guy replies. "You want beers?"

"No thanks," I reply firmly. "Not interested,"

He tries to scoot into the booth next to Lydia.

"Hey!" she exclaims.

"Do you want me to get someone to throw you out?" I ask angrily.

"Okay, okay," the guy replies, standing up and raising his arms in surrender. I hear him mutter an expletive about me under his breath. Lydia almost goes after him, but I shake my head. We just need to get this creeper away.

He does leave us alone, but it seems he's taken the spirit of fun with him. We look around, sobered, until Katrina suggests we pick up some bottles of wine and head back to their place.

"We'll go out with Geoff and his friends next time," Lydia assures us. "They'll keep the douches away."

For all the fuss building up to it, the interview at Rose & Hunts was practically effortless. Charlotte and I were brought into a group interview and were both extended offers within twenty minutes. They must really need people. The pay is double what I make at Café Longue. I feel guilty when Charlotte and I give our two weeks to Mary at the same time.

Colin continues to come in during my shifts and suggests we get lunch after I start at Rose & Hunts. I mention he should invite Charlotte too.

Early Saturday during my shift, Mary tells us that the artist we are currently hanging will be removing his art.

"If Geoff Whitney comes around," she explains, "he's free to remove everything. I've marked what we've sold and have checks for him too. Make sure to give him contact information so he can arrange pickup or delivery."

I admit I'm curious to meet this dream guy of Lydia's. His art may be mediocre now, but he could have some talent. And I would love to get connected to the community somehow.

"Hey guys!" Lydia saunters in looking way better rested then Katrina. But then, Katrina opened with me, and Lydia probably slept in. Aunt Penny doesn't think she needs a job while at school. She looks happy, almost glowing.

"Are you here to see Geoff?" I ask knowingly.

"Mayyyybe," she says happily. She fidgets with the ends of her hair. She is wearing a flower crown and a maxi dress—very boho-faux-hippie-chic. "BRB—gotta take a selfie."

Lydia poses in front of one of Geoff Whitney's creations. It's a spray paint stencil of a rocket ship and an orange. It looks flat.

A guy swaggers to the counter. "What's up, Kitty Kat? Who's your friend?"

He's tall, not as tall as Darcy, but a good height with a structured round face, perfectly messed blonde hair, and piercing blue eyes. He has the quality of the clean-cut sort of boy next door you would bring home, but with an air of mischievous apathy. Like the type of boy who could get you to do his homework for him in high school.

"This is Lizzie, Lydia's cousin," Katrina says.

"Hiya, Liz," he raises his chin in greeting. "I wonder why I've never seen you around before."

"Maybe you have?"

"I don't think so. I would remember you."

He shoots me a knowing smile, and I feel myself flush. I avert my gaze and reach for a manila envelope. "Mary tells me you're here to collect your money and art."

"Hafta pay the bills somehow." He smirks as he takes the envelope.

"I'm guessing you're a Banksy fan?" I lean on my elbows.

"Who? Oh, that guy and the kissing cops. Yeah, I guess, but I like to think my art is more spontaneous. I'm a present-minded person, ya know?"

I try not to snort. He's clearly full of hot air, but I know Lydia likes him, so I decide to give him a chance.

"Does that mean you I should look for your tags around town?"

"Nah. Too busy for that. My hustle is too unpredictable."

It doesn't escape me that Geoff and I are monopolizing conversation at the expense of Katrina and Lydia. Lydia joins our group from her selfie photo shoot, pouts, and twists her hair.

I feel kind of disloyal for stealing his attention. *Sisters before misters*, I remind myself.

Geoff Whitney though—what a charming bullshitter. There's something about him—a hidden potential. I bet I can figure it out.

"Can I get you a coffee while you work?" I offer.

"Aren't you the treasure? Venti hemp milk latte with a pump of hazelnut, please."

I make Geoff's coffee and watch him absentmindedly. He teases Lydia, and she giggles, touching his arm. He touches her arm back. Katrina sighs beside me.

"Hey, Lizzie!"

"Chip!" I reply cheerfully. "Happy Birthday!" He approaches the counter, and I spot Darcy hanging back behind him.

"Thanks!" he says genuinely.

"You get a special birthday drink, but your friend can pay for his Americano," I tease back.

Darcy consents with a shrug but doesn't say anything. He looks away from me around the coffee shop. His eyes fall on Geoff, and he starts.

Geoff and Darcy lock eyes.

Geoff looks like he wants to barf, as if he can't believe Darcy's here. Darcy looks like he could punch Geoff in the face. I try to catch Chip's eye, but he is fixated on his phone, oblivious to the exchange. Probably checking all his Facebook birthday wishes.

They glare at each other a moment longer than is comfortable until Geoff approaches us and greets "Hey, man." Darcy's reply is a curt nod. He snatches his coffee and leaves abruptly. I can hear the door slam behind him.

Chip looks after him and back to me uncomfortably. "Um, see you tonight at my party?"

"I'll be there," I reply warmly.

"Thanks for the coffee." He follows after his friend, looking concerned. *What the fuck?*

GEOFF HAS LOADED THE LAST OF HIS ART INTO HIS VAN BY THE TIME I clock out. He suggests I get lunch with him and Lydia.

I still have to get ready for Chip's party, but that isn't for hours.

Why not?

The three of us walk a few doors down to the Gouldings' for vegan BLTs. Lydia, in the middle of the group, hooks her arms through both of ours.

Lydia brags at how the unseasonably warm summer has been great for her tan. I joke that it makes old non-air-conditioned buildings miserable. We are all laughs and smiles as we settle at our table, despite the meaningless topics of conversation.

Lydia is as talkative as ever as we eat our sandwiches. I long to ask Geoff about what that look with Darcy meant, but it's hard to get a word in edgewise.

The opportunity presents itself when Lydia's friend Dennis joins our table and distracts her.

"So, you're going to Chip Bishop's birthday party tonight?" Geoff asks while Lydia is chattering away with Dennis.

"Chip is dating my sister," I explain. "Apparently, he's chartered a boat for his thirtieth."

"*Extravagant,*" he comments wistfully.

"My guess is it was one of his sister's ideas." I laugh.

Geoff chuckles and hesitates before asking, "And Darcy? Have you known him long?"

"A couple of months. I hear his dad was George Darcy. PMB George Darcy," I add, my curiosity increasing.

"The one and only," Geoff says. "I could tell you more about that family than anyone else, you know. I've known the Darcys my entire life."

"Seriously?" I blurt out. Unable to stop myself, I continue, "Because when you saw each other earlier today—"

"We have a complicated history. Do you know him well?"

"Well enough. I spent the Fourth of July at Chip's cabin, and he was there. He can be..." *Unreadable? Confusing? Frustrating?* "...standoffish."

"I have no right to give my opinion on his personality. We've known each other too long for me to be unbiased. Most people I know would be surprised to hear anything other than praise about him...but we're among friends." He pauses. "Does he come to Café Longue often?"

"From time to time. I'm sure only if he's in the area. I hope that doesn't stop you from coming back."

"Darcy doesn't bother me," he says confidently. "If *he* wants to avoid *me*, he can be the one to stop going there. Our history makes it awkward, but there isn't any other reason for me to avoid him. We used to be good friends, but I'm still pretty pissed at the way he treated me, especially considering… well, you know that George Darcy became my guardian when I was fourteen? He was my godfather, and both my parents died in a car accident."

"I'm sorry to hear that." I lightly touch his arm. He acknowledges it with sad eyes. He's starting to make more sense to me now. An orphan finding a way to express himself.

"The thing is, George Darcy favored me over his own son. Who knows why. Maybe because I wasn't so goddamn serious. I couldn't help it that we got along. Darcy was always jealous, trying to steal his attention from me." He swallows and peers off in the distance at nothing but his memories. "George loved my art and supported me while I took my portfolio around the country. After he died…well, his son cut off the support. Said my work was meaningless and I needed to get a real job."

"He did?" I exclaim. "I heard Darcy supports new artists."

"New artists who aren't me," Geoff clarifies. "He doesn't want to see me succeed."

"I wonder why you didn't inherit stock like Darcy and his sister. That would help you along."

Geoff shrugs. "Wasn't in the will."

He taps my nose and straightens his posture. "Enough of my sad story! You should come out with the girls." He indicates Lydia as she rejoins us. "I DJ at Bright Bay Friday nights. I'm planning an electro-psychedelic set. It should be sick."

"Channeling Burning Man?" I tease.

Geoff grins. "I'll have the mushrooms ready."

"He really will," Lydia adds. "Last time he DJ'd was wild."

I laugh. "I'll think about it." Geoff seems like just the sort of blowhard who could easily get under a girl's skin. But there's just enough pain underneath his carefree façade to squeeze my heart in sympathy.

Chapter Eight

Jane and I plan to take an Uber to Pier 55 in the evening. I am dressed, make-up done, and taming my curls a half-hour before the boat is supposed to leave. Jane still isn't home, and I wonder why she went to the office on a Saturday. My phone buzzes.

Finishing up a few things. Will meet you there. Sorry I can't split the Uber!

I wonder if I really want a real job if it means being chained to my desk like Jane.

The dry August evening settles warmly over me. The sun, still bright, prickles my skin while I wait by the curb. My neighbors pass by me without acknowledgement, and I feel as insignificant as the sidewalk dust that has yet to be washed away by rain.

The drive to the pier is quick. I wander up the metal ramp toward the entrance. Music strains from inside. I look around for Jane. Turning the corner, I almost bowl over a person.

"I'm so sorry!" I exclaim. I regain my balance and, shocked, look straight into Colin's round face.

"I was wondering when you'd get here." He leers at me and begins rubbing my back. I shudder.

"What are you doing here?" I blurt out rudely.

Colin continues to smile and rubs my arms up and down like a cheese grater. I step backwards, out of his grasp.

"Meeting you for our date, m'lady," he says as if it's the most obvious thing in the world.

"Bu…I didn't—how did you know…Jesus, Colin, I was just being friendly!"

He scowls. "Friend-zoning me already? And here I thought you were giving me a chance!"

"Oh my God. I don't have time for this; the boat will leave soon."

I go to brush past him when I hear Laurel call my name.

"Lizzie! How are you? Who is this young man you brought to my brother's birthday?"

She hugs me, and Colin shakes her hand in greeting. He is ushered in alongside Matt, and I groan to myself. This is not the way I wanted this evening—or any evening—to start.

The main cabin swells with guests and music. Chintzy casino-themed decor glitters around us as I listen to Frank Sinatra crooning "Luck Be A Lady." I allow distance to stretch between Colin and myself and slink over to the bar to order a whiskey ginger. Hard alcohol may not be the best way to deal with Colin, but dammit if the guy didn't stalk me here.

Chip joins me a moment later, beams a greeting, and asks if Jane arrived with me.

"She was finishing some things in the office," I offer apologetically.

"On a Saturday?" He frowns.

"I promise she's on her way!"

Colin sidles up to me a moment later, and Chip raises his eyebrows. I roll my eyes and sip my drink.

"Chip, this is Colin. He's a regular at Café Longue."

"Nice to meet you." Colin smiles smugly. I roll my eyes.

"Colin is your...date?" Chip surmises.

"Well—"

"Yes! It's a first date, actually," Colin replies presumptuously. I press my fingers to my temple and take another drink.

"Colin, please," I groan. "This isn't—"

"But you said you would give me a chance!" he whines. He looks at Chip seriously. "Nice guys never get a break, do they?"

"I need some air," I say abruptly. Colin starts to follow me, but I beg off to use the ladies' room. When I enter, Jane is touching up her make-up in the mirror.

"Janey!" I cry. "I was wondering if you would make it!"

"Of course I made it," she says. She runs her finger over her teeth to shine them and looks at me. "Am I presentable?"

"You always are. Chip is looking for you."

"I should find him." She picks up her purse, but I stop her with my hand.

"I should warn you, one the regulars from the coffee shop followed me here and thinks we're on a date."

Jane's eyes widen. "Did you explain?"

"Sort of," I admit. "He doesn't really let me talk. If you have any spare moments, can you find it in your heart to protect your poor sister?"

"Is he really that bad?"

"I didn't actually tell him where the party was; he just showed up. And he's already accused me of friend-zoning him."

"Ugh. I'm sorry, Lizzie."

I grimace and shake my head. "Someone needs a talk about boundaries and soon."

We exit the bathroom and find that the boat has already left the port. Jane finds Chip, and he wraps his arm around her waist. I sigh. They are in couple-land; I won't see them for the rest of the evening. I decide to take a moment outside on the deck.

"Who's your friend?" I turn to find Darcy sitting on a bench, drinking a beer. Surprised, I sigh and lean against the wall. Explaining myself to Darcy is not what I need right now.

He stares at me in question, and I sink down to an opposite bench.

"He's not my friend," I explain. "He followed me here."

"He *followed* you?" Darcy examines me as if he can't tell if I'm joking or not. I can't tell either.

"Kind of. I mean, he's a regular at Café Longue, and he asked me on a date, but I said I was busy because of this party, and he was just…here when I arrived. I don't even know how he knew where it was!"

Darcy glances through the window at him and scowls. "That's a bold move."

"Tell me about it." I groan and rub my temples. "And I was looking forward to having fun tonight too."

Darcy frowns. "Who says you can't still have fun?"

"Colin does," I grumble.

"Well, I can help you with him."

"You don't want to do that." I laugh.

He shrugs. "I know what it's like to be imposed upon."

"Fighting off all the Emmelines of the world with a stick?" I tease.

"You could say that. But if you told him no, he shouldn't be bothering you," he says soberly.

"Thanks…" I play with the hem of my skirt. Darcy drinks his beer quietly and squints out over the Sound. Wind plays over the waves and is almost as loud is the music inside.

I wish I hadn't forgotten my drink inside. I could use the crutch.

"Do you—?" He pauses but doesn't look at me.

"Do I what?"

"We could go play a game? I could teach you poker."

"I already know how to play."

"But, I thought at Chip's cabin—"

"I lied. Didn't want everyone to know I was too poor to play." I look at him, daring him to judge me. He catches my eye briefly and looks away.

"I see."

I recall the conversation on the beach with him and Emmeline. "Not everyone is fortunate enough to have their way paved financially," I reply grumpily.

"I didn't mean—"

"I'm not going to work at a coffee shop forever! I only graduated three months ago—"

"I'm sure you won't—"

"—so you can wipe the judgmental look off your face!" I finish, crossing my arms.

"Lizzie, I know you will find your way."

Our eyes meet; his are intent and deep brown. There's no way he really believes this; he and Emmeline were so judgy about my lack of an appropriate job. I avert my gaze quickly and rise and glance back at the party. The wind whips my hair into what I'm sure is a frizzy mess.

"If you want to play poker with fake money, though, I promise to beat you," I dare him with a challenge in my voice.

Darcy rises and grasps my hand. I feel a familiar jolt.

"Deal," he says.

I release his hand quickly.

I PEER AT THE GIRL ACROSS FROM ME AND CHEW MY LIP. NEXT TO HER,

Darcy gazes at his hand blankly. The girl can barely contain her grin. I push chips toward the center of the table.

"Call."

The guy next to me lays his cards down. "I fold."

The girl beams and adds to the pile. "Raise you a dollar."

Darcy narrows his eyes and glances between us.

"Call," he says lazily.

I stare at my hand and tap my thumb against the table. Darcy watches me closely. I lock eyes with him and inhale sharply. His expression is flat, and I huff in frustration. Damn him and his mystery.

"I fold," I mutter.

The girl is giddy and continues to raise the bet until she lays down a full house.

"Tough luck," Darcy says and shows his four of a kind.

The girl's face falls. "I was so close!" she exclaims. Her friend consoles her.

"Don't gloat," I admonish Darcy. He smiles sheepishly.

"Do you want another drink?"

"Sure."

We thank our friends for the game and make our way toward the bar. In line, Colin accosts me. I had almost forgotten he was here.

"I've been looking for you everywhere!" he exclaims.

I fold my arms. "Colin, look, this isn't a date. We can be friends or whatever, but you know I didn't invite you here."

He blinks at me and reaches for my hand. "I know you're shy, but I really did want to come out tonight. I picked up your hint."

I pull away abruptly. "I think you need to work on your listening skills."

"We haven't met," Darcy interrupts. He inserts himself between Colin and me. I smile gratefully.

"Colin Williams," he says proudly.

"How do you know Chip?" Darcy asks closely.

"Oh, I don't know him. I'm here with Lizzie."

"Oh my God," I groan in frustration.

"You should just enjoy our date!" he exclaims. "After all, you owe me!"

"I *owe* you?" I laugh in disbelief. "What's this imaginary debt you've decided I hold?"

"I got you your new job," he retorts. "And you flirt with me all the time."

"I *flirt* with you?" I start to yell, and Darcy places his hand on my arm.

"That doesn't mean she owes you anything," he says sternly.

"This isn't your business," Colin snaps.

"Want to go play roulette?" Darcy says to me, ignoring Colin.

"Gladly."

Colin trails after us.

"Look, Lizzie, I'm sorry. Let's start over, okay? I know you like spending time with me, and you always draw those cute doodles on my coffee cup. And we'll be co-workers soon!"

I turn around and cross my arms. "Charlotte and I both appreciate the job lead, and I'm glad you like the doodles I draw on everyone's coffee cups, but this"—I motion between us—"isn't going anywhere. Please give me some space, and *maybe* we can *eventually* be friends."

Colin stares at me, crestfallen. Then his face morphs to anger. "You're such a tease," he chides.

Darcy grips Colin's shoulder and steers him away from me.

"It's time for you to go somewhere else," I hear him say.

I exhale shakily.

Darcy shakes his head when he returns to me sans Colin.

"That guy can't take a hint," he remarks.

"He's an idiot," I grumble.

We wander away from the gaming tables aimlessly. The sunset glows neon against the sparse clouds. We both walk out into the cooling air. I lean against the railing and peer out.

Darcy leans next to me.

"Thanks for the help," I say softly.

"Anytime," he replies.

We don't look at each other. Chip's friends mull around the deck sociably. I stare at the Sound, hypnotized by the rush and motion.

"I didn't know you had a new job," Darcy's voice breaks through the roar of the waves.

"Oh, yeah, just a dumb contract job. But it's something…better."

"Where at?" Darcy leans on his arms and turns toward me. The wind rustles his hair.

"Rose & Hunts. I'll be an associate catalog editor along with thirty others." I push my hair behind my ears and try not to fidget.

"Ah. My aunt works there."

"Seriously?"

"Yeah…uh…she's the CEO."

I laugh out loud. "Does your entire family own the internet?"

Darcy looks embarrassed and turns back toward the view of the water. "Do you think you'll miss making coffee?"

"Maybe. I enjoy meeting new people."

We fall into another stretch of silence.

"I was hoping to convince the owner to let me start curating art there, but I never got around to it."

"Yeah?" He looks back at me, interested.

And suddenly I can't help myself. "That artist who was just hanging, Geoff Whitney—you know him, right? Well, the café could do better."

Darcy scowls at the water but doesn't reply.

"I mean, I guess he likes that street art aesthetic, but he isn't quite there. Maybe in a few years?"

"I guess," Darcy mutters.

"Maybe he needs the right inspiration," I press. "He has a lot of life tragedy to tap into; he could be too afraid to use it."

Darcy looks at me sharply. "What did he tell you?"

I cross my arms. "About his parents and your dad taking him in. And that you guys don't talk anymore."

"You should stay away from Geoff," he says darkly.

"But why? If he feels the need to create, shouldn't we encourage him to find his voice?"

"Why are you so interested in him?"

"I don't know. He seems…sad, behind it all. Why did you stop support-ing his art?"

"I can't…it's not something I can talk about," he replies roughly.

"I think he misses you," I say softly.

"You should stay away from him," Darcy says forcefully. "I'm seri-ous, Lizzie."

I step back from him. "Well, excuse me! Sorry for butting in!"

I turn on my heel and re-enter the party. He doesn't follow after me, but I'm glad for it.

Darcy and I avoid each other for the remainder of the evening, and I know it's better this way. I seem to have offended him, and from what he says, once on his shit list, it's hard to redeem yourself.

The boat docks around eleven, and I find Jane to see where she's spending the night. She and I take an Uber home without Chip, and I wonder why, but she's strangely silent. I decide not to push it tonight.

I WAKE UP THE NEXT MORNING WITH A SLIGHT HEADACHE.

I grimace and roll over. The dull light of early morning fills my room. This is the last week I'll have to open the coffee shop. I roll over with the intention of sleeping in.

I finally emerge by late morning. The closed blinds darken the apartment. Jane is stretched out on the couch, stomach down, staring aimlessly at the TV. Next to her are crumpled candy bar wrappers.

"Janey?"

"Morning, Lizzie," she says hoarsely.

"Are you okay?"

Jane takes a shuddering breath and shifts to a sitting position. She looks exhausted.

She frowns and rubs her eyes with the heels of her hands.

"I couldn't sleep. Chip and I...we got in a big fight last night." She frowns and gazes fixedly at the TV. A girl twirls in a wedding dress on screen and declares it's the one. Everyone cheers and cries.

"All couples fight," I encourage. I pull Jane into a hug and she drops her head on my shoulder.

"He—he was upset that I almost missed the boat," she muffles.

"You're just busy and just starting out. Your job won't be this demanding forever."

She pulls back and blinks but doesn't cry. "He thinks I would rather work than spend time with him."

"He can't really believe that! He sees you more than anyone else does!"

"I've never seen that side of him before. He was upset anytime I had a conversation with one of his guy friends. I was trying to impress them, but...I guess I made the wrong impression."

Jane sniffs and blinks quickly. She reaches down to a paper bag next to the couch and pulls out a Butterfinger. She must have stocked up while I was sleeping.

Jane became addicted to cheap candy bars while our parents were going through their divorce. It was a nasty affair. Amidst the lawyer battles and Mom's rants about Dad's 'defect,' Jane started eating several candy bars a day. It's the only time in our lives when she wasn't slender. Once the dust had settled, Mom made her attend the spin classes she taught to work off the weight. I haven't seen Jane touch a candy bar since then.

"You guys will work it out," I hug her again, and she sniffs.

"I really feel like we're falling in love, you know?" She stares at me earnestly. Tears pool in her eyes. She blinks, and one streaks down her cheek.

"Falling in love is scary. You should call him and talk it out."

Jane nods and focuses on the television screen. "I'm just going to stay here a little longer," she says dejectedly.

"Put your feet in my lap then. And give me a KitKat."

Jane smiles at me gratefully and passes me the bag of candy. I fish out a KitKat as she stretches on her back and I take her feet in my lap.

The next episode of *Say Yes to the Dress* starts, and we watch without speaking. Every once in a while, Jane contemplates her phone but then places it next to the candy bag with a sigh.

We are several episodes in when her phone dings. She picks it up and frowns.

"Excuse me," she whispers and goes to her bedroom.

Ten minutes later, she emerges. I look up in anticipation.

"It's over," she says numbly.

I can hardly believe my ears. "It can't be! I've never seen two people more smitten."

"He doesn't think I have time for a relationship right now."

Then she bursts into tears. I rock her in my arms while she sobs. I hold her until she pulls away, sniffing, her eyes swollen and red.

"I hope you don't mind, but I need to be alone right now."

"Whatever you need, Jane." I hug her again, and then she fetches her candy bar bag.

Her bedroom door slams, and I hear her crying on the other side of the door.

My heart aches for her.

THE REST OF THE WEEK STRETCHES OUT PAINFULLY. I WANT TO BE EXCITED that Charlotte and I will start our new jobs soon, but I don't have the heart to feel truly happy with Jane so miserable.

My last shift at the coffee shop is early Friday morning. Charlotte has already handed in her keys. Katrina convinces me to come out with her and Lydia that evening to celebrate.

"One last hurrah before you become an office zombie." She laughs. "Bring Charlotte too. The more the merrier!"

Charlotte is apprehensive about going out with the girls but agrees. I feel bad for leaving Jane behind, but she isn't in the mood. I left her at home binging on *The Bachelor* and eating potato chips. Sadness clings to her like stale junk food crumbs.

Strawberry Alarm Clock strains through the open door at Bright Bay. The bouncer, positioned like a boulder, examines our IDs closely. Lydia flirts and teases him. He tries to suppress his amusement and lets us through.

Geoff stands in the back on a raised platform, leaning over a turntable and laptop. He wears a tie-dyed shirt and a puka shell necklace.

"He's so talented," Lydia breathes adoringly.

White girls with dreads dance badly in an open space near Geoff's station. It's humid and smells like BO and cultural appropriation. I feel entirely too prep school in my cotton skirt and Keds. Geoff catches my eye and gives me a nod. I acknowledge him, and Katrina grabs my arm.

"Let's get drunk," she giggles. She and Lydia scan the crowd until they locate Geoff's friends, Dennis and Carter.

They buy us a round of tall boys, and we drink. Charlotte hangs by my side and grimaces with each sip of cheap beer.

"You don't have to drink that," I mutter to her.

"But they bought it for me!"

"Just leave it on the ledge and get something you like."

Charlotte wears cut-off shorts and a cat T-shirt that's baggy enough to make her figure look insignificant. Her outfit, along with her Wednesday Addams braids, makes her almost look fourteen. Next to Lydia with her backless hippie dress, she seems to blend into the woodwork.

"Let's find a table," I call to the girls and their friends.

We wedge together in a booth like incompatible puzzle pieces forming a confused picture—a well-intentioned, lazy attempt at something enjoyable.

After ten minutes, Charlotte and I are left alone.

"Bright Bay is losing its luster," I remark to Charlotte.

"Should we ditch them?"

I shrug and sip the last dregs of my now-tepid beer. "Maybe. Chances are they'll be high on mushrooms soon."

Charlotte wrinkles her nose. "I'd rather be at Gameworks with an Electric Lemonade and a full game card."

I stand up and pull Charlotte to her feet.

"Let's go to The Apothecary. They won't miss us. I'll text Katrina and let her know."

We move in slow motion through the dusky warm night. Bros yell out the windows of their out-of-place SUVs at the people on the sidewalk. We push through the drunken meat market and feel a sudden relief once we reach the corner. Charlotte heaves a sigh.

"I'm not cut out for partying," she says.

I smile in encouragement. "The Apothecary is much tamer. I'll get you a fancy cocktail."

Inside the dark bar, we locate a small table and scan the limited drink menu.

"Fifteen dollars for a cocktail?" Charlotte exclaims.

"It's artisan, didn't you know?"

Charlotte laughs. "I don't know what half these ingredients are."

"Let's pick some random drinks then and order them confidently. No one will ever know." I wink.

"I think I'll get Palm Beach Punch," Charlotte remarks. "Anything with 'punch' in the name must be fruity."

"And I'm getting the Socialist," I reply. "I can't resist the most controversial drink on the menu."

True to form, the bartender—with suspenders, sleeves rolled to the elbows, and a bowtie—makes our drinks with artful gusto.

Charlotte makes a face at the ridiculous glass her "punch" comes in. I raise my pinky when I sip from my martini glass.

"Lizzie?" Charlotte hesitates and looks over my shoulder.

"What is it?"

"I have something I've been meaning to tell you all week. But with our opposite shifts and you spending all your free time with Jane…"

She glances at me nervously and plays with the pineapple on the edge of her glass.

"What's going on?" I try to catch her eye.

"I hope you can be happy for me. I—I've started seeing someone. Colin, actually."

I nearly choke on my drink. "Colin?" I swallow the liquid painfully to keep from spitting it out. "But, he just tried to date me last weekend!"

"I know," Charlotte says defensively. "We talked about it, actually. He was really upset until I helped him see that you weren't really suited for each other. He thought you had been flirting with him at the coffee shop."

I huff and cross my arms. "He stalked me to Chip's birthday party!"

"He thought you had asked him."

"He didn't even know where it was!"

Charlotte frowns. "He knew. He has coworkers who were invited, and they told him about it."

"But, he's so...so..." I wrinkle my nose.

"What, a nerd? Socially awkward? I'm those things too, Lizzie!"

"No, you aren't!"

"Of course I am! All I do when I'm not working is play video games. I spend more time talking to people online than in real life. The difference is that I had to make myself less awkward because I worked in customer service. Colin has the luxury to be himself."

"He was so sexist to me, Charlotte! He called me a tease and told me I owed him."

"That was in poor taste," Charlotte admits. "But he also has his good traits. He got our foot in the door at Rose & Hunts and he *knows* people too. He really thinks my software can go somewhere." She pauses and looks at me pleadingly. "Please be happy for me. I really do like him."

I raise my eyebrow skeptically.

"Please?"

"Give me some time and I'll try to come around. I promise."

Charlotte is the closest friend I've made since moving to Seattle, but I don't see a way to maintain our level of friendship now. Colin makes me uncomfortable, and I doubt his motives. But I really do want Charlotte to be happy. I hope she's dating him for the right reasons.

We finish our drinks silently and leave the bar. We pass by Bright Bay, and Geoff is outside smoking.

"Heya, Liz," he calls. Charlotte and I walk up to greet him. "Did you like my set?"

"Not as much as your groupies with the dreads did," I remark.

Geoff's eyes dance with mischief. He indicates his half-smoked joint and offers me a drag. Charlotte shifts uncomfortably and crosses her arms around her stomach.

"Not this time," I say. "We're turning in for the night."

"What a shame," Geoff smirks. He touches my hair lightly. "I hope I run into you again soon."

My stomach jolts uncomfortably, and I step back to add some distance between us.

"Have a good night," I call, looping my arm through Charlotte's.

When I get home, Jane is asleep on the couch. Wads of candy bar wrappers litter the floor, and the Kardashians drone on the TV.

I decide not to disturb her.

Chapter Nine

It was a shock when Mom and Dad took us to a family counselor to explain why they were getting divorced. I was ten and Jane was thirteen.

"It's nothing you girls did," Mom explained. "None of us could have predicted that your father would reject us."

"Barbara, that's not fair!" Dad interrupted angrily. "I'm not rejecting them. And you know we've raised the girls to be open-minded!"

The furious expression on Mom's face is forever branded in my memory.

"You would think it would occur to a man to admit the truth to himself before marrying a woman and having two children."

Jane held my hand during this argument, and I remember my confusion. The truth about what? Was Dad sick? What was wrong with him?

I was always taught that it was okay when men love women and men love men. At that point in my life, it didn't occur to me that you could go from one to the other. I didn't understand till I was much older that it was difficult for a Greek Orthodox man to admit he was gay, especially after a religious upbringing.

Mom never did get over it. She would wax eloquently about Dad's lying to her and convincing her to drop out of school to marry him. She would bemoan the good years she wasted keeping herself attractive for a man who never cared.

After divorce proceedings started, Jane and I were sent to Seattle to spend time with Uncle Eddie, Mom's younger brother. His girlfriend Mai had just moved in with him after finishing grad school. It's the only thing I remember Mom and Dad agreeing on since that fateful visit to the family counselor. Uncle Eddie and Mai would be a good distraction for Jane and me.

I always loved Uncle Eddie, but that summer drew Jane and me closer than ever to our uncle and future aunt. Mai knew just how to distract us from our confused, hurt feelings. She would take us to the beach or for ice cream. She found all the free concerts at the park, which made thirteen-year-old Jane feel especially cool. Eddie, who was getting his career in family law off the ground, was our rock. We took comfort in the fact that he knew how everything worked throughout the divorce proceedings and he was on our side. Though she's never said so, I'm almost certain Uncle Eddie's support is what inspired Jane to follow the same career path. She's told me so many times that her priority as a lawyer is to be an ally for kids.

Best of all, both Mai and Eddie listened to us. One night, when I was feeling homesick and like I would never have a normal home to go back to, Mai found me crying in the guest bedroom.

She snuggled with me on the bed and let me bury my face in her arm.

"I know it's hard to understand, but sometimes, even though changes hurt, they turn out for the better. It wasn't easy for your dad to tell you all that he loves men instead of women. That doesn't mean he will stop loving you and Janey as his daughters. It means he's being honest with you both. You're lucky he trusts you that much."

After that time in Seattle, we returned home to California, but it was less serene than before. Dad had moved to Chicago to take care of his mother, our Yiayia. Mom, still full of bitterness, was remodeling the house. I tried to stay out of her way, and Jane tried to help.

Dad faithfully called us every Sunday to catch up. The "sad dad" days were the worst. When he called, I felt like I was pulling him out of a depression with every conversation. Yiayia passed away when I was fourteen. A year later, after Jane's graduation, he asked me if I wanted to live with him in Chicago.

It was a hard choice. I didn't revel in the thought of spending three years of just Mom and me, but I was fifteen and didn't want to leave my friends. I had never lived anywhere besides California, and I wasn't ready to leave.

"What if I visit more?" I compromised, hoping he wouldn't feel it as a slight.

"If that's what you want," he replied thickly.

I still always wonder how my life would have changed if I moved to

Chicago with Dad. I don't think I'll ever stop feeling guilty that I didn't choose him.

AFTER RESCHEDULING NUMEROUS TIMES, JANE AND I REALIZE THAT WE'VE been neglecting Uncle Eddie and Aunt Mai. I moved to Seattle almost three months ago and have yet to take them up on their offers of dinner.

We arrange for Sunday evening, the night before my first day at Rose & Hunts, and bring Lydia along. On the car ride over, she animatedly chatters about her burgeoning relationship with Geoff.

"I can really tell he wants to be exclusive with me," she enthuses. "I mean, when we went out the other night, he didn't even *look* at another girl, and I went home with him!"

I have mixed feelings about this assessment. Last time I saw Geoff, I felt like he was sort of hitting on me, but then again, he could be just a flirt. I don't want to burst Lydia's bubble just yet.

"When will you see him next?" I ask.

"Whenever," Lydia replies dreamily. "We don't make solid plans, ya know? We just always want to be around each other."

Jane doesn't contribute much to the conversation, but I'm not surprised. I can tell she's still sad even though she tries to hide it. I wish I could have predicted Chip would turn out to be an ass.

Despite the fact that she's obviously miserable, Jane does think to bring fresh flowers for our aunt and uncle. Even sadness can't conquer her thoughtfulness. Aunt Mai greets us all at the door. It's the first time we've seen her since she announced her pregnancy, and there's a small baby bump visible on her petite frame. We hug, and it's instantly like we've never been apart.

After dinner, Uncle Eddie and Jane get caught up in a discussion about family law while Lydia looks bored and plays on her phone. Aunt Mai pulls me aside discreetly.

"Is everything okay with Jane?"

"Kind of. I think the break-up is hitting her pretty hard."

"Ah. The infamous Chip. I'm sorry to hear it didn't work out."

"Me too. They really seemed to be getting along."

Aunt Mai sighs. "That's the way of life, unfortunately. It's hard to predict how things will go in a new relationship."

Aunt Mai watches Jane and Uncle Eddie in earnest conversation. "I wonder…do you suppose Jane would be up to helping Eddie at the family law conference next month? He's a keynote speaker. I know she's busy, but it might help distract her—"

"It wouldn't hurt to ask," I cut in. "She needs an outlet."

"It could backfire," my aunt warns. "Didn't Chip end things because she worked too much? I wouldn't want to rehash any hurt feelings."

"Maybe," I reply thoughtfully. "I think it's worth a try though. And maybe it would help her climb the ladder at work."

Turns out, Uncle Eddie had suggested the very same thing to Jane while Aunt Mai and I were talking. It was the first glimmer of enthusiasm I've seen from her since the break-up. It means she'll be gone over Labor Day weekend, but I imagine it would be nice to avoid socializing over a holiday. I wouldn't want her to be reminded of the Fourth of July.

I WAKE UP THE NEXT MORNING OPTIMISTIC: FIRST DAY AT THE NEW JOB, A plan to help Jane, and the promise of change. I love change. Mom always attributed my restlessness to being a Pisces. I guess that may be true, but once I find something I belong to, I cling to it obsessively. A part of me will never give up on my curatorial dreams, even if I do procrastinate at fully pursuing it.

The office at Rose & Hunts is located in one of the older buildings in Pioneer Square, and it's ridiculously lavish. The pristine furnishings look as if they belong in New York high society, and fresh flowers liberally adorn gilded side tables. The pretty receptionist is dressed as if she should be working at a fashion magazine instead of an online retailer. I hardly feel like I'm in Seattle.

I approach the reception desk and put on a confident face.

"Can I help you?" the girl asks lazily.

"Yes, I'm starting today."

"Right, one of our catalog editors. Name?"

"Elizabeth Venetidis."

She gives me a "Visitor" badge and a clipboard of paperwork.

"Go to conference room 102 and fill this out. Freddy will meet you and the rest of your group shortly."

The conference room is sparsely occupied. I keep my expression pleasant but don't talk to the other people in the room while I fill out the packet.

Everyone in the room looks young and scared. I'm glad I'm not alone.

Charlotte comes in and claims the seat next to mine. The room is as quiet as a library, and I feel like I should whisper, even as the rest of our new team gathers.

Freddy Fitzwilliam enters the room thirty minutes later. When he interviewed us, he seemed friendly if slightly intimidating. The intimidation factor is all but erased in his demeanor now—maybe because he's twenty minutes late and doesn't seem to care.

He plugs his laptop into a projector and leans back in a chair.

"Free coffee is in the kitchen if any of you need it before we start," he calls to the room.

I need a caffeine fix, so I go make myself a cup. Freddy smiles at me when I return from the kitchen. "Elizabeth, right? Brace yourself for eight hours of computer screen time."

"Can't be worse than eight hours on your feet covered in coffee grounds!"

"Maybe," he says. "I always recommend a full playlist of music and podcasts for all my contractors though. I did warn you in the interview that this job is dry."

Once Freddy finishes the hour of training and we get to work, I am almost immediately bored. I have no headphones, and all I hear are the keyboards tapping around me. This job pays double what I get paid to make coffee? The tedium makes me want to scream.

The only relief is that Charlotte and I have seats next to each other, and we occasionally make snarky comments on the items we're tagging.

AFTER THREE DAYS OF MIND-NUMBING WORK, A GROUP OF US START GATHering for a regular happy hour to remind ourselves that human interaction is a real thing.

Unfortunately, Charlotte starts bringing Colin along. I mention it to Freddy offhandedly at the coffee machine one morning.

"Colin and Charlotte are dating?" he asks thoughtfully.

"Yeah, he's the one who told us about the contract positions. He was a regular at the coffee shop where we worked."

"Maybe I should tag along with your group today…keep an eye on the metadata misfits."

"So you can give them detention?" I tease.

"Or something to do." He grins back.

I walk with Freddy to the bar across the street from Rose & Hunts. It's a dirty knockoff of an old English pub with random menu items like Scotch eggs and totchos. I like Freddy; we have a similar sense of humor, and he seems to follow all of the seemingly non-sequitur observations I make.

"I think Todd and Julie feel weird that their boss is drinking with them," I murmur before we enter the pub.

"Todd and Julie could use a little discomfort," he mutters back. "I found Todd sleeping on his desk this morning, and Julie was texting instead of working."

I snort. "Will your omnipresence help them grow a conscience?"

"Not likely. But if they're going to be lazy, I can at least make their lives miserable."

I laugh. "What a good boss you are, Freddy."

He chuckles. "I have no illusions about our contract jobs; they are dull résumé padding. As long as you have a brain in your head and get the job done, I can't complain."

"Glad to know you hold us to such a high standard."

He shrugs and holds the door open for me. "I do what I have to."

Colin leads Charlotte to a booth, and I hesitate to join them.

"What are you waiting for?" Freddy asks.

"I'm bracing myself," I admit. "That relationship makes me feel…awkward."

"Can't handle nerd love?" Freddy laughs. I elbow his arm.

"Be nice! But, no, it's not that…it's…well, Colin tried to date me only a week before he and Charlotte got together—"

"—and you're jealous," Freddy concludes knowingly.

I make a face. "Not jealous, just…weirded out. I'm not sure if Colin is really a nice guy."

Freddy looks at me sincerely and nods. He's not what I would call the best-looking guy around, but his presence is so comfortable that it's easy to forget. I loop my arm through his and pull him forward.

"C'mon, we can't loiter here forever."

Freddy starts joining us for happy hour more frequently. He and I occasionally get lunch together too. It's a friendship I didn't anticipate, but we get each other. He was dumped as unceremoniously as I was, though he seems to be nursing the wound a little more than I am. Still, it's nice to commiserate with someone who's been through it, especially since Jane has been tight-lipped about guys since Chip dumped her. I wonder if it's strange for me to be friends with my boss like this, but then I decide I don't care. I have two months left at this job, and then we won't have the awkward boss/employee divide.

Cathy de Boer, CEO of Rose & Hunts, strikes me as the type of woman who idolizes Anna Wintour. She deigned to observe our sad little group one time, and I immediately noticed the red soles of her Louboutins.

Nothing, apparently, is below her notice at the small internet empire, including the work of thirty wide-eyed catalog editors. Her executive assistant sends daily pearls of wisdom to the company she calls "Quotes by Cathy."

This morning's: "Remember that you will never refine your skill without practice. Work hard during the day and practice at night, and you will present yourself in the best light."

Today our inspirational email is followed by an all-company invitation to a Labor Day barbecue at her house. Charlotte IMs me after the invite comes through.

We have to go to this - it would be a great way to network.

I glance over at her, and she nods in encouragement. I shrug and click "Accept" on the invite. I have no plans, and Jane will be out of town that day anyway.

Chapter Ten

I t's unseasonably hot the night of Cathy's party. My old Toyota Corolla won't start, and I resign myself to taking the bus to Cathy's McMansion.

The party is called a barbecue, but there isn't a grill in sight. Instead, fancy cups of potato salad and cocktail weenies are passed around by servers.

I feel too casual in my faded sundress and scan the crowd for someone to say hi to. Freddy comes over after I catch his eye.

"Lizzie, glad you could make it!"

"Thanks. This is the fanciest backyard barbecue I've ever attended."

He smiles warmly. "Cathy doesn't believe in casual. Take advantage of the open bar though." He indicates a bartender to my right.

I laugh and wink. "I'll try to keep it moderate."

Freddy looks over my shoulder and nods a greeting to someone. "So, I hear we have a mutual acquaintance."

"Aside from our thirty associate catalog editor friends?"

Freddy laughs. "My cousin said he knows you." He nods behind me.

I turn around, bewildered, to see Darcy approaching. He offers me a glass of pink wine.

"You two are cousins?" I grip the wine glass, my mind devoid of pleasantries.

"Hey, Lizzie," Darcy greets. "I haven't seen you in a while."

"Not since Chip's birthday." I peer at him. "But with all the changes since then, it probably would have been awkward to socialize."

Darcy rubs the back of his neck and looks at his shoes. "It's rough when things don't work out," he mutters.

"Especially when such deep feelings are involved," I stress.

"Lizzie's sister dated Chip this summer," Darcy explains to Freddy.

"Small world," Freddy remarks.

"If you two are cousins, does that mean you're also Cathy's—"

"Nephew, yes," Freddy interrupts. "But I try not to advertise it."

"Is that your strategy to keep a modicum of respectability?" I tease.

Freddy laughs. "My only strategy at present." I can feel Darcy watching us closely.

"So, Freddy is your boss?" Darcy says abruptly.

"For the time being. Sorry, Freddy, I don't know how much longer I can take all of this mindless cataloging."

"Should I expense all the happy hours to keep you motivated?" He winks.

I laugh. "We may have to change bars in that case. Cathy may find the Owl 'N Thistle too unrefined."

"She won't know if we don't invite her," he jests.

"Do you go out to happy hour with your employees frequently?" Darcy interrupts, scowling at Freddy.

Freddy shrugs. "I guess, but they won't be my employees very long. It's not as if we can extend permanent offers to anyone in this group. Sorry, Lizzie," he adds with a small smile.

I sigh dramatically. "Whatever will I ever do with my life if not offered the chance to stare at endless pages of schmancy knick-knacks forever?"

"Are you still looking at galleries?" Darcy looks at me intently. I let my gaze flicker from Freddy and back to him. A tension settles over our group that I don't quite understand.

"I should be," I admit. "I guess steady income has made me complacent."

"I hope you don't give up on it." Darcy smiles at me openly in a manner I don't remember seeing before. I take a gulp of my wine and look around the crowd.

"Looks like Colin and Charlotte made it," I say, raising my chin in their direction.

Darcy's expression darkens. "That guy," he mutters.

"He's dating my friend now."

"Are you serious?" Darcy looks to Freddy for confirmation, and Freddy shrugs.

"For the past month, I believe," he says.

"That takes a lot of nerve."

"At least I don't have to worry about him stalking me anymore," I joke.

Freddy almost chokes on his drink. "*Stalking* you? I thought he just asked you out and you said no."

I brush off the comment. "Charlotte says he's just socially awkward, and I'm giving him the benefit of the doubt for her sake."

Freddy and Darcy both stare at me as if I'm crazy, and I look away from them.

"Sometimes one has to suck it up for the sake of the friendship. Colin is basically harmless."

I keep my drinking moderate despite the open bar that evening. I awkwardly mingle with Charlotte and Colin while he proudly leads her around by the waist.

"Did I tell you that I was able to introduce Charlotte to Cathy?" he brags to me. "It pays to know the right people."

"She offered some very helpful career advice," Charlotte says placidly. I can't tell if she's sincere.

"I think she's giving her toast," Colin adds. A glass tings a moment later, and Cathy stands in front of us with a microphone.

"Before I start," Cathy begins, "I would like to acknowledge that this evening could not take place without the excellent hard work of my executive assistant, Annalise Metcalfe. I insist you all take a moment to thank her before the evening is out."

A smattering of applause follows this statement. Cathy clears her throat.

"Thank you all for taking a weekend night away from your lives to celebrate the launch of our new home goods line. Rose & Hunts exceeds at outfitting elegant but busy ladies and gentlemen of refinement. Now we will supply these same high-end customers with the fine goods to reflect their high taste in decor. We should all be proud of the standard of class we promote." She pauses and surveys us with a superior air. "It is my hope that this evening of luxury will motivate you all in pursuit of our vision. Let's all raise a glass to new ventures!"

The group murmurs around me. Colin calls "hear, hear" a little too loudly, and Charlotte tries to cover her wince.

As the evening draws to an end, I stand on the curb outside of Cathy's house and scroll through my phone. I think I have enough money to take an Uber home. I click on the app for a fare estimate.

"Are you waiting for a ride?" Darcy asks from behind me. I spin around. "Just calling an Uber."

"I can take you home," he offers.

"I, uh—" The fare estimate is forty dollars, and I really don't want to spend that much. Can I overlook this discomfort for the sake of my bank account? "Sure. Um, thanks."

Darcy leads me toward his Tesla. I wipe my palms against the front of my dress. I imagine my apartment will be stifling when I get home.

I slide into the passenger seat, and Darcy starts the engine. The AC is heavenly.

"I'm actually glad I ran into you," Darcy says as he pulls away from the curb.

"Really?" I shift. The leather seat pulls against the back of my thighs like a dull Band-Aid. I grimace.

"Yeah. I mean, we had fun this past summer, don't you think? I sometimes have a hard time making friends with new people. But, it was…fun. The Fourth of July and everything."

My mind immediately races to our shared loft at Chip's cabin. His soft snores. The press of his hands against my hips. His breath on my face. The mystery of him.

"It was fun," I drawl, rebelling against my quickening pulse. "If not a little awkward at times."

Darcy laughs. "Emmeline is persistent. I've gotten used to it since I've known the Bishops for so long. And I only see her a few times a year."

"I see…" I wonder why he is explaining this to me. I look over at him as the Tesla rolls to a stop at a light. He holds my gaze and abruptly clears his throat.

"Freddy says you're one of the best people on his team," he says lightly.

"Freddy is exaggerating." I roll my eyes. "Typing metadata for eight hours a day isn't a task that requires much skill."

"Maybe you're the fastest typist?"

I laugh uncomfortably. "Maybe. I don't know. I'm glad this job is temporary; I've never done anything so *boring*."

"And then you'll go back to latte art?"

I shrug. "Maybe. I'm actually thinking of cold calling all the art galleries in the city. Maybe there's an admin job or something available like that. I need to work in my field, I think."

"I understand. Any job is easier to tolerate if it's related to what you like."

"Exactly."

A silence settles heavily over us; the sound of the blinker is amplified. I wonder why he doesn't turn on the music.

"You think you'll miss working for Freddy?" Darcy interrupts the silence.

I shrug. "I'm not sure. I think we're better as friends instead of colleagues."

Darcy pauses for a moment before asking softly: "Just friends?"

I try not to feel offended. Does Darcy think I'm not good enough for his cousin?

"I hadn't actually considered anything else," I mutter, momentarily annoyed.

Darcy pulls up to the alley behind my apartment, and I unbuckle my seatbelt.

He turns toward me with some sort of foreign expectation in his expression.

"Thanks again for the ride."

Unthinking, I lean across the parking brake to give him a hug. His palms slide to my back, and I shiver.

I pull back, and he holds eye contact with me. "I didn't mean anything rude by asking you about Freddy," he says. "I just had to know."

His gaze is clear and steady, the opposite of that night at Chip's cabin. I think I should say something, but I can't speak. My heart thrums wildly.

It's as if I'm disconnected from my body when he leans in to touch his lips against mine. I haven't kissed anyone since Ian. And kissing Ian was nice, but it was nothing like this.

Darcy cups my cheeks, and I part his lips with my tongue. Our breathing mingles rapidly, and I can't tell who gasps. I'm dizzy.

I pull back, panting. What the hell just happened?

"I can't tell you how long I've been wanting to do that," Darcy admits. His thumbs stroke my cheeks.

"I—I had no idea."

I don't know how to justify this…this…whatever *this* is. Darcy has wanted to kiss me for a long time? I thought he found me annoying. But the chemistry, I admit to myself, is amazing. He leans down to kiss me again, and I shift awkwardly and stretch over the center console. God, he's good at this. His fingers tangle in my hair, pressing into my scalp. I attempt to pull myself closer. His mouth is soft, decisive, and perfect. The realization hits me with alarming clarity: I want him. Should I? I don't even really like him that much, I think. But when he moves from my lips to my jaw, I feel again the flutter of desire and tell my brain to turn off.

"Jane is out of town," I murmur impulsively. "Do you want to come up?"

He follows me up the stairs to my apartment. I can feel his gaze, and my pulse races. Am I really doing this? He runs his fingers up and down my arm, and I tremble as I unlock the door. He kisses the side of my cheek near my ear, and I feel that sudden whoosh of attraction. It reminds me of the free fall on a roller coaster at the county fair. I have to steady myself to get the door open.

I step inside and boldly grab a handful of his shirt. The hot air is oppressive. He walks me backward toward the couch.

"Sorry I don't have AC," I say breathlessly.

"It doesn't matter," he replies. He pushes me onto the couch, and we continue kissing. His fingers drift up my ribs to my shoulders, and he toys with the strap of my sundress.

I slide my hands under his shirt. All I can think about is his body, my body, sweat, heat, and our skin pressed together. I meet his gaze and flick the first button open on his shirt. He smiles, and I undo the second and slowly make my way down till his shirt gapes open. I push it from his shoulders.

He leans me back against the couch cushions, and his chest flattens over me. His erection feels insistent against my leg and I move my hand to cup him.

"Oh God," he moans, pushing against my palm. Then he pushes the straps of my dress off my shoulders until he can roll the top of my dress down my torso. He kisses the top of my breasts. My palm lingers on his erection, and I rhythmically rub him.

He continues to kiss down my body, over my strapless bra, and down my stomach to my hips. He pushes the skirt of my dress up and kisses my thigh then slides his thumb over my damp panties. I'm lost to the sensations. I want him to touch me so badly *right there*. I've never felt so passionate.

"Jesus, Darcy," I groan. He bites the skin of my hipbone and applies pressure to my apex. I strain toward him, panting.

He slides his hands under my ass and squeezes. I lift my hips and he pulls off my panties. He presses his lips against my hipbone, over my thigh, and then glides his tongue over my labia. I push my pelvis toward him, and his tongue caresses my clit. My legs tremble.

His tongue flutters against me, and he clenches the flesh of my ass. I grip his forearm and cry out softly. My head spins. He closes his lips around my clit and sucks. I rise forward, belly clenched, and a hot frisson jolts through me.

"Oh fuck, oh God," I cry, pressing against his mouth till I am too sensitive to handle the pressure. I convulse, and I reach down to draw his head away. He crawls up my body and places a salty kiss against my lips.

"I need a moment." I sag under his weight and inhale. Exhale. My thoughts are still hazy, and I can't believe what I just gave in to. I've never done anything like this before. With Ian, we dated for a month before we first had sex. Even so, I don't regret what just happened. I didn't know passion like this existed.

He pulls me close to him and kisses my cheek. I can feel the shape of a smile.

"Aren't you proud of yourself?" I tease breathlessly.

"You're beautiful."

It's too hot for him to feel my blush. I push myself to a sitting position and grab my panties off the floor. I stand up, weave my fingers with his, and tug him up off the couch.

He follows me wordlessly.

Inside my room, I pull my dress over my head and unhook my bra. He stares at me and undoes his belt buckle. I push back my comforter and we slide into the sheets, naked. He rolls me on my back and palms my breast. Our skin sticks together.

"Let me get a condom," I exhale.

We have sex urgently. His strokes are needy, and I touch myself in sync with our rhythm and can feel myself approaching the pinnacle again. When he comes, I pull him close, and he collapses against me. Our foreheads touch, damp and warm.

I get up from the bed and switch on my oscillating fan while he disposes of the condom. Dusk paints the sky. I push the window open and get back into bed.

Darcy settles me into the crook of his arm and drifts his fingers up and down my back. I glance at the clock on my wall. We parked forty-five minutes ago. An hour ago, I had no idea I would sleep with Darcy.

What did I just do?

Chapter Eleven

I haven't heard from Darcy in two days, and I can't bring myself to text him. I wonder if he regrets what happened that night.

Jane comes home from the conference in good spirits with a healthy dose of optimism. She asks me if I did anything interesting over the long weekend, and I say no. I can't admit I'm mortified.

It's one thing to sleep with someone casually who you don't know. It's another to drag your sister's ex-boyfriend's best friend back into your lives. I hate to keep anything from Jane, but I also don't want to hurt her by reminding her of Chip.

I'm ashamed of myself for acting so impulsively. I'm annoyed that he hasn't said a word since he left that evening. A small part of me wonders how much he likes me and if this is going to be the beginning of something more, but I dismiss the thought. Relationships start with a declaration and a date, not casual hookups. And I'm not the kind of girl Darcy would want a relationship with; I'm too young, too poor, too aimless, and too underemployed.

I can't help the unsettled throbbing in my chest when I think about him. He said he had wanted to kiss me for a while. How long? But I'm sure he also thinks I'm not his usual type, and he always seems to be judging my decisions. Is he really the kind of guy who messes around with girls for fun?

Could I be that kind of girl?

Because, God, the things he did to my body...

No, I decide. *I choose self-respect.*

I join Jane in the living room, feeling newly confident in my decision.

We talk about ordering pizza and bingeing Netflix. I whine about returning to the office tomorrow.

My phone dings, and I glance at it. Just like that, my bubble of resolve pops.

I can't stop thinking about you.

I stare at the phone in disbelief. Is this a line?

I vaguely recall my dad's advice to me about boys when I was thirteen. *No matter what, remember that all guys really want is to get their rocks off. Even the good ones are ruled by their lizard brain.*

What about my nature? Am I not a sexual being? Could I not just enjoy our purely physical rendezvous?

I thought I had scared you off, I text back.

I watch the text bubble stop and restart numerous times.

Of course not. Can I see you again?

I realize I'm holding my breath. I glance at Jane who is scrolling through TV shows on Netflix. She looks over and smiles at me. Should I ask her advice? I hesitate before texting back.

Jane is home. Tomorrow?

Okay, he replies. *Should I meet you after work?*

I can't have Freddy knowing about this. Or Charlotte for that matter. And Jane? I can't help but picture my heartbroken sister moping on the couch. No. I can't do that to her. I can't remind her of Chip.

I think of a nondescript dive bar in a different neighborhood.

Streamline Tavern at 6?

I WEAR A LACY UNDERWEAR SET TO WORK THE NEXT DAY EVEN THOUGH MY outward appearance is casual. I know I'm not nearly as attentive as I should be at the computer, and I feel vaguely guilty for letting Freddy down. The excitement of my attraction to Darcy is only tempered by the niggling thought that I am allowing myself to be used for sex.

I am doing this for me, I affirm to myself. *I am in control of my decisions.*

The Streamline Tavern is sparsely populated by construction workers drinking cheap beer. I slide into a booth, drum my fingers against the table, and will my pulse to slow down.

Darcy spies me immediately upon entering the tavern and heads to the table.

"Do you want a drink?" he asks.

"No," I reply breathily. "Let's go to your place."

He raises his eyebrows and stares at me. "Are you sure?"

"Definitely."

Darcy parks in the driveway of a newish townhouse on upper Queen Anne. I'm surprised; I had assumed he lived in my neighborhood since he frequented Café Longue.

He leads me up the stairs to the living room. It's tastefully modern and pristinely clean, like a West Elm showroom. A large abstract painting in browns and blues hangs above the couch, taking up half the wall. I stare at it. "Is that a Guy Anderson?" I ask.

"My mother bought it in the seventies," Darcy replies.

A cat slinks around the corner, and he leans down to scratch behind its ears. I didn't peg Darcy as an animal person.

I perch on the couch and wonder how we should start.

"Do you want something to drink?"

I shake my head. He sits next to me on the couch awkwardly, and I edge closer. He reaches up and lightly runs his fingers over my frizzy curls.

"The humidity," I explain.

"I like your hair," he says.

And then we start kissing.

With our intention in mind, it's easier to take our time.

I REVEL IN THE FEELING OF HIS SOFT SHEETS AGAINST MY SKIN AND STRETCH. My legs are still weak from my orgasm. I absently wonder what the thread count is. Are they Egyptian cotton?

Darcy leans against the doorway to the bathroom, framed for a moment like a painting hung on the wall of some art savant's bedroom.

He smiles at me and approaches the bed. I sit up. He sits across from me, cups my breast, and runs this thumb across my nipple.

"Ready for round two already?"

He grins and shakes his head. "Your breasts are perfect."

The compliment makes me uncomfortable. Most likely, he appreciates my body and nothing more. I distract myself by kissing him again.

He pushes me back on the pillows and touches the slick spot between my legs.

"I think you're ready," he murmurs roughly in my ear. I shudder.

Darcy spoons me from behind. I glance at the clock and see it's getting late.

I shift and roll to my other side so we are face to face.

"I should get home," I say.

"Stay the night." His fingertips trace my cheek.

"I don't have anything here for tomorrow, and Jane will worry."

He kisses me and rests his hand on my bare hip.

"Can I see you again?"

"Yes," I breathe.

I can see this thing between us becoming an addiction, and I wonder how wise it is to keep indulging.

As long as I stay in control, I tell myself.

Darcy drives me home, and we carry on a trivial conversation while I set up ground rules in my head.

No staying the night.

Jane can't know.

No alcohol-induced sex.

I wonder if I should mention my rules to him but then decide not to. I am a self-possessed person. I have control of this situation. I feel a pang at my decision to keep this from Jane. But it isn't a serious thing, and I don't want to dredge up Chip again for her.

Darcy kisses me when he pulls up to the alley behind our apartment.

"Until next time," he says.

September in the Pacific Northwest settles in, and the weather moves from the unbearable last days of summer heat into clear skies and temperate weather. The smattering of deciduous trees among the evergreens is tinged in reds and oranges. I've never been here during this time of year, but I immediately decide it's the most beautiful.

Within a few weeks, my rendezvous with Darcy have become a regular habit. His cat, Misty, likes to curl up on a corner of the bed with one eye open while we fool around. Misty is unconcerned with multiple orgasms. The only thing she doesn't like is when our feet accidentally push her off the bed.

Sometimes, after sex, Darcy orders take-out and we stay in bed and watch the *PBS Newshour* because it's "the most accurate and unbiased." I don't admit to him that it doesn't hold my attention. Instead, I trace the cords of his muscles with my eyes and wonder what we're doing.

Somehow, I know if we define it, it will end.

I know Darcy doesn't seriously choose girls like me. He prefers women like Emmeline with a career and regular manicures and fancy designer handbags. Someone worldly and not grasping for direction. Maybe I'll be ready for him in a few years, but by then it will probably be too late.

"Do you want to watch something?" Darcy asks one evening, passing me the remote.

I can tell what he's trying to do and look up at him playfully.

"Is this a test so you can judge my taste? It won't work, you know. I'm too stubborn to be intimated."

I pull the top sheet across my breasts and cross my arms.

"I would contradict you," he says, "but I know you don't really think I'm trying to judge you. We've spent enough time together for me to know you enjoy making up thoughts for people."

I laugh at this view of myself and shake my head. "Are you trying to make me retaliate?"

He smiles. "I'm not afraid of you."

"What about when we first met? You judged me then. Kid sister, remember?"

"That was before I knew you."

"And you couldn't have suspended your judgment until you got to know me?"

"I should have," Darcy admits, "but you have to admit most people your age are—"

"Are what?" I interrupt. "You were once my age if you can remember back that far."

"Very funny," Darcy says. "And I happen to know I was obnoxious when I was twenty-two. I've learned a lot since then."

"A person can experience a lot in life by twenty-two," I retaliate. "And I'm sure you wouldn't claim your sister is obnoxious."

"Point taken. I should be thankful you didn't judge me harshly when we first met. I would hate to have missed out on this."

We abandon thoughts of watching TV.

It's a lazy Saturday afternoon, and I decide to bake and crank up my music as I gather the ingredients. It's so loud I barely hear the apartment buzzer.

I click the intercom, puzzled. "Hello?"

"Hey, it's, uh, Darcy."

Surprised, I buzz him in.

"Did you run out of Saturday activities?" I joke as I answer the door.

"I felt like seeing you." He smiles.

I wipe my flour-covered hands on my apron and indicate he should follow me to the kitchen.

"Jane could be home at any moment," I warn.

"How is she doing?" he asks, apparently unconcerned.

"Okay," I reply casually. "She's talking about joining a dating website."

"I have friends who've met their partners that way."

"Yeah, I'm sure it's a decent option. I'm not sure about Jane though. I think she's probably just tired of waiting for some people to change their minds."

"I see," Darcy replies. He approaches me and indicates the lump of dough on the counter.

"What are you making?"

"My Yiayia's butter cookies. I usually just make them for the holidays, but I felt inspired today."

"Are you close to your family or just Jane?"

"I love my dad, but he lives in Chicago, and I don't see him enough to be close to him. My mom is another subject altogether. But my aunt and uncle, my mom's brother, live out here. That's what motivated Jane and me to move to Seattle."

"Are your aunt and uncle Greek too?"

"You're full of questions today!"

Darcy shrugs. "Shouldn't I be?"

"I guess," I say dismissively. I start rolling the dough into a cylinder. I change the subject. "You've caught me in a rare domestic mood. I'm also doing laundry."

"I've never actually done my own laundry."

I start slicing the dough. "Are you serious? And I thought I had things to learn!"

"My parents didn't think it was important."

"I guess we're all susceptible to our parents' priorities." If it weren't for my mom, I never would have learned Pilates. Or Jazzercise.

Darcy draws closer to me. "At some point, we eventually have to break away from those expectations."

A memory tickles my brain. Darcy's frown that day we drove to the winery when I said Jane followed our mom's life course.

Would he have encouraged Chip to dump Jane?

I dismiss the thought and start spreading the slices of dough across a cookie sheet. "Are you saying you need a laundry lesson?" I quip. He laughs.

We continue to chat while I wait for the oven to preheat when we hear the front door open.

"Darcy!" Jane exclaims in surprise when she enters the kitchen. She looks between us in question. I try not to grimace in guilt and force a look that says Darcy's appearance is normal and expected. I wish I didn't have to stretch the truth with her.

"Oh, hey, Jane." Darcy shifts his feet and looks at me anxiously.

"Darcy was just returning my jacket," I fib. "He gave me a ride home after that barbecue for Rose & Hunts I told you about."

I'm thankful it's not in Jane's nature to be suspicious.

"Well, you have to take home some of Lizzie's cookies. No one can make them like her except our late Yiayia." She smiles at me sweetly, and my guilt intensifies. I feel like I'm cheating on her.

The oven beeps to indicate it's preheated, and I almost jump.

"They'll be ready soon!" I say overly cheerfully.

"Your *jacket*?" Darcy asks in confusion after Jane has left. I flinch.

"I don't want to hurt Jane."

Darcy stares me down incredulously. "How would our relationship hurt Jane?"

"How wouldn't it?" I exclaim back. I glance back toward her room and lower my voice. "Can't you see she's still heartbroken?"

Darcy stares at me. "I thought—" He glances back toward Jane's room before catching my eye again. "Have you told *anyone* about us?"

I shrug and place the cookies in the oven. "I'm just, you know, going with the flow."

Darcy considers me for a while and sighs. "Sometimes I don't understand you at all."

"That makes two of us," I mutter.

I'm not sure if I mean him or myself.

My thoughts on our benefriendship run together like the layers of a failed watercolor painting—each new idea seeping into the next till it's a puddle of muddy color with a vague idea behind it. If I squint at him, maybe he'll make sense.

I send Darcy home with a Tupperware of cookies and a discreet, uncertain kiss.

Chapter Twelve

nitially, I went into art history because all the art I tried to produce was mediocre. My love for it grew when I spent a semester in Prague and became obsessed with Mucha. From there, my tastes expanded to Pollock and Calder and political graffiti art.

I met Ian in Prague. He was an art major and an insomniac. Ian was constantly inspired, and he would brag that the dark circles under his eyes were the equivalent of battle scars. His poor sleep habits also left him edgy and argumentative.

I thought we represented the ultimate artistic couple. He had the talent, but I was the undisputed connoisseur of the Art History department. For a while, we reigned supreme: I uncovered jewels and he created them. That's probably why we were together for so long. Now that we've broken up, I can admit to myself that I was more attracted to his art than I was to him. Yes, he did break my heart, and there is lingering bitterness over how callously he dumped me, but the rejection of our friend group wounded my ego the deepest.

My last year of school was an odd mixture of extreme focus and senioritis. I had an internship at a neighborhood gallery as part of my thesis and, perhaps because my social life was shit, spent more time at the gallery than on campus. I half-assed my final paper for American Architecture 428 but got nearly a perfect score on my thesis. Both ready and afraid to launch myself into the unknown, I would daydream about how my life would change for the better once I was settled in Seattle with Jane.

I never would have predicted that the current state of my professional endeavors would consist of endlessly tagging pictures of throw pillows while trying not to burst from the tedium.

Maybe that's why the sex with Darcy is so good; I have too much pent-up energy.

FREDDY IMs ME AT WORK TUESDAY MORNING.

Bored out of your eyeballs yet?

Not yet. That means you only have yourself to blame if I don't make it through my queue today.

I can take a hint, he types back. Then he sends an emoji of a beer glass. *Later?* he writes.

I send him a thumbs-up emoji in reply.

"THANKS FOR COMING OUT WITH ME," FREDDY SAYS. HE NURSES AN IPA and gives me a fleeting smile.

"Of course," I reply. "What's on your mind?" I ask, raising an eyebrow.

Freddy takes a swallow of beer and zones out for a moment.

"Well…I guess I could just use a friendly ear. Rumor is my ex is moving back to Seattle."

"Seriously?"

"Yeah." Freddy stares down at his pint glass, frowning. "She really drop-kicked my heart, you know? I don't know how I'm supposed to not think of how I could run into her."

"I get that," I reply in empathy. "My last semester in college was hell. But, then again, I couldn't get away from Ian's presence on campus. Do you still have mutual friends?"

"Not really," he says. "Just interested mutual acquaintances."

"It's a big city. You probably won't even see her!" I conclude positively. "And if you do, it's been *years*, right? I have faith in your ability to move on."

"*You* haven't moved on," he accuses me.

"Have too!" I argue. "You just don't see it because you only see me during office-ish hours."

"So, what, you have a boyfriend?" he teases.

I laugh. "No, just a person I'm hanging out with."

"Oh, one of *those*," he says knowingly. "Is it someone I know?"

"Freddy!" I laugh, feeling embarrassed.

"It is!" he goads.

"Stop—"

"Is it Todd?" he asks and I shake my head. He raises his eyebrows, "Julie?" I laugh and shake my head again. "I know it's not Colin—"

"God, no," I exclaim.

We catch eyes, and his brow furrows. I can tell the name is on the tip of his tongue, but he hesitates.

"It's Darcy, isn't it?"

I nod and look away. My face is hot.

"But if you're seeing my cousin," he says, "how is it not serious?"

I look at him in confusion. "Not everyone is trying to trick rich dudes into relationships. We're just…having fun. I'm not the type of girl he takes seriously anyway."

Freddy stares at me incredulously.

"Are you kidding me?" he finally exclaims. "Darcy takes everything seriously!"

"Apparently not everything."

Freddy sighs. "You really should talk to Darcy if that's what you think. Never in my life have I known him to have a fling. My cousin is a serial monogamist."

"No," I say defensively. "Not with me. He's never suggested that what we're doing is anything more than physical—" Freddy winces. "Sorry." I pat his arm in sympathy. "But, seriously, he didn't ask me out or anything. He just—"

"I don't need to hear the details," Freddy interrupts. "Let me just say that my idiot cousin probably has a different idea than you do."

I shake my head. "You're wrong about this."

My phone dings a moment later, and I see it's Darcy.

What are you doing tonight?

I look up at Freddy with a streak of rebellion.

You, I text back.

I know for a fact that Darcy and I are friends with benefits. That's why I made sure to remain in control of our relationship.

HALF AN HOUR LATER, I ARRIVE AT DARCY'S.

He opens the door and greets me with a grin. I smile flirtatiously back at him and follow him up to the living room.

"How was your day?" he asks.

I shrug and lean against the kitchen counter. "Nothing special. I'm glad to be here." I look at him boldly.

"I missed you too," he replies tenderly.

"Do you want to go upstairs?" I reach out and trace my finger up his arm till I see the hairs stand on end.

He laughs. "Always. But let's hang out a bit first."

He pulls me close and kisses the top of my head. My heart races. *"Never in my life have I known him to have a fling. My cousin is a serial monogamist."*

I glance up into his eyes, but suddenly the expression doesn't make sense. There's lust there, certainly, and something else—something I don't understand. He tips my chin up and kisses me softly, and I sigh.

He doesn't move to deepen the kiss, just continues soft chaste touches against my lips. His tenderness makes me tremble. This isn't a relationship. We never talked about it. We hardly talk about anything. I haven't told anyone about us, and since Freddy didn't know we have a...thing, well, he probably hasn't either. It's just physical. Just sex. He's nearly thirty and has his life together, and I'm not ready to settle down yet.

I press my lips back to his firmly and run my tongue across the seam. His hands move down to squeeze my ass, and I smile.

This, I understand. This was the agreement.

I run my hands up under the hem of his T-shirt.

"How can I never get enough of you?" he says roughly.

"Animal magnetism," I reply huskily and pull his shirt over his head.

I drag my palms up his chest then push him back to sit on the couch and climb over him. I can feel his erection through the thickness of our jeans when I press down on him. He draws my shirt over my head, and I unhook my bra and shimmy it off. He gazes at my breasts with appreciation in a way that makes me feel powerful. I push my pelvis against his again.

We catch eyes. His gaze is tender, and he touches my cheek. My pulse jumps, and I slide off his lap to my knees in front of him and start tugging his jeans off. He lifts his hips, and I push them to his ankles. His erection springs toward me, and I grasp it. He closes his eyes, and his head falls back against the couch.

I have control of this situation.

I slide my lips around him, and he pushes toward me.

"Lizzie," he groans.

I trace circles with my tongue and slide my mouth over him again and hum. His fingers dig into my scalp and urge me forward. I pull back slowly and stand.

He opens his eyes while I shed my jeans. I climb over him again and rub my wetness over him. He grips my hips to guide me, but I draw his hands up to my chest.

"I'm calling the shots this time," I whisper. He breathes rapidly and kneads my breasts. I push my pelvis against him again.

"You're driving me crazy," he pants.

"How do you want me?"

I expect to slide him inside me at that moment—to ride him on the couch. Instead, he turns me in his arms, almost cradling me, and kisses me softly, softly, softly until the pressure increases and I realize I'm pinned below him with my arms over my head and my fingers intertwined with his.

My heart starts racing as he enters me, and I cry out in both pleasure and confusion. How did he take control of the situation? He reaches down between us and touches me, and I can feel it building—the fear and ecstasy. He grunts above me, and his skin erupts in goose bumps when he comes.

"Are you okay?"

That's when I realize I'm crying.

"I'm fine," I whisper.

He pulls out of me and drags me into an embrace.

"Do you want to talk about it?" he asks quietly.

I shake my head and shift. My thighs stick together where his sperm trickles down my leg. I pull back.

"Darcy," I say urgently. "We didn't use a condom."

He stares back at me in disbelief.

I start to cry again, this time frantically. "I'm not on the pill or anything."

"You're not?" he replies weakly.

I jump up quickly and reach for my clothes.

"I—I have to go to the pharmacy. What's open? Oh God. How much does Plan B cost?"

He starts to pull on his clothes too.

"I'll go with you. Please let me pay; this is my fault."

"How is it your fault?" I cry. "I practically mounted you when I walked through your door!"

"I should know better," he replies, almost too calmly.

"Like I shouldn't." I rub the heel of my hand against my eye, and he touches my arm. I shrug it off and step away from him, wrapping my arms around my stomach.

"When was the last time you were tested?" I sniff.

"Last April."

"And you don't have...anything?"

"No."

"Me either. I was tested over the summer."

He reaches around me, and I press my face to his shoulder.

"It will be okay. I promise."

I nod into him, and I can still feel myself shaking. How did this evening spiral so out of control?

It's 3:00 a.m.

Darcy and I had unprotected sex eight hours ago.

I have sixty-four hours to take the pill.

I could have taken it right away. If I had, I probably wouldn't still be up. I guess I'm holding onto the last threads of this affair with Darcy. It's been fun—*too* fun—and now it's become real. We won't survive it.

The clock ticks on the bedside table. Darcy hugs around my middle, softly snoring. Despite the stillness, my mind won't shut off.

I try to will myself to sleep, but it doesn't work.

I shift away from Darcy, and he rolls over in his sleep. His expression is serene and youthful. I sit up and pull the T-shirt I'm borrowing over my knees. Darcy sleeps on, ignorant of my watchful gaze. I lightly run my fingers over his beautiful face, and his eyelashes flutter as he dreams.

I can't help but imagine what we will talk about in the morning. I hope it's amicable. At least we aren't in love.

Earlier this evening Darcy comforted me in the pharmacy. He held me close and stroked my back. Then he took me back to his place where we watched dumb action movies and drank milkshakes from Dick's Drive-In. It was a good distraction.

I didn't expect him to be so attentive. I didn't expect *anything* from him.

It occurs to me how little I know about Darcy. Yes, his dad was a tech mogul, he went to prep school in the area, and he likes Americanos, but what else? Where did he go to college and what did he study? What does he do in his spare time? What are his passions and priorities?

The majority of the time I've known him, I've challenged his judgments against me or made assumptions about him. How could I not be more inquisitive?

What would happen if I got pregnant?

I shudder at the thought. I would be repeating my mom's mistakes. She hardly knew my dad when they got married, and look how that turned out. I can't imagine tethering my life to someone I hardly know. More importantly, I've barely started out. The thought is sad and scary at the same time. I don't want a baby right now. Some deep part of me latches on to the craving of what could be, though—my traitorous maternal nature.

It doesn't matter. I will take the pill in the morning. It's early enough that we won't have to worry. I wonder fleetingly if we can go back to the way we were before. Passionate meaningless sex.

No.

We can't.

Not after this.

We've ruined it.

My eyes crack open, and I realize I finally did fall asleep. It's early; the morning air is still cool with new sunshine. I shift and roll over to my side.

Darcy is watching me. He smiles softly.

"Morning. How are you feeling?"

"Okay." I nudge closer to him, and he wraps his arms around me. I love the comfort, but I hate the vulnerability.

"I know we had a hard night, but I'm glad you finally stayed over."

I can hear his heart thrum wildly. I understand the anxiety. I imagine he is dreading our imminent conversation as much as I am.

I breathe in and out. Should I bring it up first? Should I bring it up *now*?

On the nightstand sits the Plan B box, signifying the end of our self-imposed illusion. I want to get it over with so I can move on with my life. I also want to stay where I am, pressing my cheek against Darcy's chest while his breath stirs my hair and his heartbeat is close.

He brushes away a tear from my cheek with his thumb. His heart still races.

"Why don't you—um, what I mean is, I think you shouldn't—"

I glance up at him and meet his eyes. He looks concerned. I guess he's decided it's time to talk.

He reaches for my free hand and seems to come to a decision.

"Lizzie," he murmurs tenderly. "Last night may have been unexpected, but I want you to know that I'm crazy about you. And...I was wondering... why haven't you taken the Plan B yet? You don't have to if you don't want. Maybe we just see what happens?"

My stomach drops and I sit up abruptly.

"What do you mean?"

He sits up as well. "I'm crazy about you," he repeats with a warm expression.

"And you want me to get pregnant? Are you insane?"

"I know the timing isn't the best, but we work so well together. Don't you think? We could be happy with a kid. We wouldn't have to get married right away or anything, but you could move in here, and you wouldn't have to worry about finding a job. I know you're still young, but you seem mature enough to settle down. I've always wanted kids—why not now?"

I stare at Darcy in disbelief. Freddy's words from the night before haunt me.

"Never in my life have I known him to have a fling. My cousin is a serial monogamist."

Holy fuck.

"Darcy," I exclaim with alarm, "think about what you're asking me."

He places his hands on either side of my arms. "I'm in love with you," he declares earnestly.

His proclamation is more than I can handle. Were we that out of sync this entire time? What I thought was casual sex, he thought was one step closer to starting a family?

He *can't* be in love with me. We don't really know each other.

I throw off the covers and quickly get out of bed.

"What are you doing?" he asks while I locate my clothes.

"Why are you complicating this?" I know my tone is shrill, but I can't control it.

"I don't understand—"

"What are you doing asking me to have a kid with you? We haven't even been on a real date—I mean, you've never even asked me out! And I'm only twenty-two! I thought we were just hooking up."

I grab the Plan B box off the nightstand, and he grasps my wrist.

"Stop. Slow down, Lizzie."

"I need to go home," I assert firmly. I tug my arm, but he doesn't release my wrist.

"Don't leave yet."

He searches my face, and I see his distress. I sink onto the bed with the Plan B box squished in my grasp.

"I'm taking this pill," I say in a dull voice.

He stares back at me, his lips pressed in a thin line.

"Please respect my decision."

His nod is nearly imperceptible. Gently, I tug my arm away from him and open the box. He watches me swallow the pill dry. I blink and look away. I can feel his disappointment in me.

Then comprehension dawns. The person he really wants is an illusion, not me. He may think he knows me, but what does he know? Hardly anything. Besides, he has revealed a future that is so far from the direction I'm heading. I'm not some put-together woman ready to start a family. My life goal isn't to be a Lululemon-wearing stay-at-home mom with a Mercedes SUV. If I was with Darcy—like, *really* with him—would he try to make me into that?

I stand up again and start searching for my shoes. Darcy is out of bed in an instant, gripping my shoulders.

"Wait—"

"This is too much—I—I can't handle..." I gesture vaguely toward the rumpled, unmade bed with the empty pillbox on the pillows.

He pulls me close and presses his forehead to mine. I've never seen so much emotion from him. I start to tremble.

"Please," he implores. "I'm sorry I mentioned it."

I exhale shakily and pull myself from his grasp. "Darcy," I state in a firm voice, "go find a woman who's ready for you. We both know I'm not her. Not yet at least, and I'm okay with that. So, please, go and be happy."

"You make me happy," he replies in a soft voice.

I step back and stare at his pained expression. I shake my head and swallow my urge to cry. "I don't think we want the same things." My voice cracks.

"Please don't leave," he pleads while I locate the rest of my things.

I push my hair behind my ears and smooth my palms down my thighs. "I'm really sorry," I nearly whisper. "If it's easier, you can hate me."

He doesn't reply, just watches me while I grab my bag and leave his bedroom. He doesn't follow me to the door, and I close it softly behind me. My throat burns. What did I just do?

Chapter Thirteen

I don't want to go to work Monday morning, but I force myself to get up and go through the motions.

On Wednesday, my period starts. I use it as an excuse for my mood. It isn't helping; all my symptoms are worse than usual, which is apparently a typical side effect of Plan B. And even though I'm happy not to be pregnant, I can't help but think of my argument with Darcy.

I feel sick when I recall the details.

He was pleading with me not to leave, but I did anyway.

But he was moving so fast. Way too fast. I needed him to ask me on a date, introduce me to his family, and spend time outside of the bedroom to feel comfortable enough to think about a future.

No. What he asked of me wasn't fair. He should go for someone like Emmeline, who would be more than willing to give him the life he wants.

I have to stop thinking about this. I made the right decision.

It's the first Thursday in October and I decide to wander the galleries during the monthly Art Walk in Pioneer Square after work. I don't ask anyone along. I need some time to think.

I spend a long time at D.B. Shaw Gallery, staring at the geometric oil depictions of powerful female figures. If I had the money Darcy does, I would buy the painting of the huntress Diana.

My chest tightens.

I never did ask to see his art collection.

I leave the gallery quickly before I lose control of my emotions.

After ten minutes calming myself in a public restroom, I head over to Ripley Lofts to explore the various small galleries. Ripley Lofts is one of my favorite places to look at art, an old hardware store converted into galleries, workspaces, and small lofts for artists. There is a wide array of spaces, from pristine to grungy, where I can easily immerse myself in each creator's vision. I love the variety; it feels organic.

At the top of the stairs, I enter a particularly grungy gallery called "The Hole." I try to keep my mind open even though I find the name stupid. I study a line of skateboard decks airbrushed with superhero vixens. It's not my taste, but the technique is good.

I pass through the next hall and immediately notice a familiar set of paintings toward the back wall, a rocket ship in front of an orange amongst others.

Geoff Whitney laughs with the people around him. His hair is pulled into an insignificant knot on the top of his head. A pre-man bun. I hesitate but walk toward him after he catches my eye.

"Little Liz!" he exclaims. He hugs me as if we're long-lost friends. The stench of pot hangs around him.

"Hey, Geoff. I didn't realize you were showing art here."

He appraises me with a smirk. "My friend Carter is renting this space. You remember Carter? He designs skateboard decks."

"He's good at it," I reply.

"Bummer my new stuff isn't out." He sweeps his arm behind him. "You probably have all these paintings memorized."

I shrug. "They're like old friends."

Geoff gives me an approving look.

"Do you want some wine?"

He points at a table of Two-Buck Chuck and a stack of short plastic cups. "Sure."

I end up hanging around longer than I planned. Geoff stays by my side and brushes his arm against me, and a familiar, uncomfortable feeling churns. I briefly wonder why Darcy told me to stay away from him. I ignore my feeling of unease and decide that I can be friends with Geoff if I want to be. Fuck Darcy and all of his assumptions. He thinks having a kid together is a good idea? Obviously, his judgment is faulty. Plus, Geoff is an artist. He could introduce me to the community in Seattle. It's in this frame of mind that I agree to go back with Geoff to his apartment to see his new work.

Geoff lives in a studio apartment on the edge of Capitol Hill near the point where gentrified and sketchy cross. A shiny new home is gated off next to a line of decrepit triplexes with peeling paint and yard couches. Geoff's studio is the upper floor of one of the triplexes. I feel like the stairs up the side of the house could collapse at any moment.

"Welcome to my villa," he says as he holds the front door for me.

The studio is almost bare.

A futon mattress with no frame sits in the corner with rumpled sheets and a serape twisted in the mess. A cardboard box is placed next to it to act as a side table, with a fancy glass-blown bong on top. Art supplies litter the far corner next to a large pile of canvases. Magazine cutouts of random pictures are taped on the wall around the pile: a cow, an umbrella, a pile of money.

I wander to the corner and look back at Geoff in expectation.

"Is this your new work?"

Geoff acknowledges me slyly and flips through the canvases to slide one out.

"This one," he says. "It's the beginning of my new series."

He leans the canvas against the wall and steps back.

It's appalling. A stenciled, spray-painted portrait of a familiar-looking girl in a lewd pose with neon pink genitals. She looks to the side with her legs spread and her arms braced on either side of her. Small neon green psychedelic flowers adorn her body.

"Is this Lydia?" I ask, stepping back from the painting.

"Good model, isn't she?" Geoff replies. "She isn't afraid to try anything." He pauses and turns toward me. "I'm looking for more girls to pose; I haven't been able to convince Katrina yet." He lets his gaze drift down my figure. "You interested?"

"Oh, uh, no…it' not really my thing." I shift my weight uncomfortably. Seeing my young cousin like that makes me feel vaguely sick.

"You're hot. You would look really good up there," he replies, stepping closer to me.

His mouth is close to my ear, but it doesn't feel right. It's not the same as Darcy's.

Darcy. Oh God, he was probably right about Geoff. I shudder and put some distance between us.

"I saw Darcy recently," I say casually, attempting to take the focus off myself.

"Did he still have a stick up his ass?" Geoff scowls.

"No, he was really nice actually. And…he seemed worried about you. Maybe you should talk to him?" I know I'm stretching the truth, but I'm desperate to keep the conversation on something Geoff would find unsexy.

"Darcy is only worried about the family name. He could care less about me," Geoff scoffs. "Let's not talk about him right now. Let's talk about you, Liz."

He examines me with a slow grin.

"Honestly, Geoff, it's not my thing," I force out casually. "Maybe I should go."

"Stay and hang out," he urges in response. "No model talk, I promise."

A forceful knock at the door startles both of us.

"God dammit," Geoff mutters. "I forgot."

"Forgot what?"

"Who else? Our best friend." He pulls open the front door and Darcy enters. Our eyes immediately lock, and a wave of shame overcomes me.

"Darcy!"

"Lizzie? What the hell are you doing here?"

I look between him and Geoff, not sure what to say. Geoff starts laughing.

"Am I stealing your lady?" he taunts.

"Fuck off," Darcy grinds out. He doesn't take his eyes from me. "Lizzie, what's going on?" He looks hurt and angry. I bite my lip and hug my arms around my waist.

"I was just, umm…" I gesture to the painting propped behind me. "Geoff was showing me his new work."

Darcy glances at the obscene painting of Lydia and doesn't hide his expression of disgust.

"It isn't Darcy's taste," Geoff says sarcastically.

"As much as I love looking at your"—Darcy indicates the painting with a wave—"you have an appointment with your parole officer."

"Hang on a sec." Geoff disappears to his kitchen, leaving Darcy and me alone.

"Need a ride home?" Darcy asks tiredly.

"Don't worry about it." I look at my feet and wish I could disappear. I take a fortifying breath and look back at Darcy. "For what it's worth, I did only come to see Geoff's work. We've been here fifteen minutes, if that."

Darcy holds eye contact with me but doesn't respond. I can't look away.

Geoff walks back to the living room with a plastic bladder full of yellow liquid.

"Let's get this over with," he says cheerfully.

Darcy breaks our eye contact and scrubs his face. "Jesus, Geoff, hide that so I can at least pretend I don't know about it."

Geoff shrugs and picks up a messenger bag. "Be a gentleman, will ya, Darce, and take Little Liz to the light rail." He slips the bladder in the bag and winks at me.

"Can I call you an Uber?" Darcy asks. "We'll wait with you."

I agree and wait with Darcy and Geoff by the curb during the most uncomfortable five minutes of my life.

I try to ignore my unsettled feelings on my ride home and try to quell the questions racing in my head.

Darcy and Geoff are talking now?

Geoff thinks he stole me from Darcy?

Geoff is on parole?

I arrive home to Jane in sweatpants drinking wine and watching reality TV with a half-eaten pizza from Pagliacci's.

"Lizzie! I was wondering when you would get home," she greets me.

"I thought I'd check out First Thursday," I reply. I sit by Jane on the couch and lay my head on her shoulder.

"How was your day?" I ask.

Jane shrugs. "They've assigned me a partner for some of my tougher cases." She sighs. "My boss suggested it may help me toughen up."

"Like a mentor?" I ask. I reach for Jane's glass of wine and take a generous sip. I pass it back to her, and she finishes off the glass.

"Maybe. I dunno." She sighs again and leans back. She stares at me and frowns. "I wish I didn't have to work so much. I've missed you. I guess you've found a bunch of new friends now though since I can never hang out."

Her statement causes my throat to burn. I blink and swallow, willing myself not to cry. Bad decisions don't warrant tears.

"Maybe we need to make more sister dates," I suggest. My voice is mercifully even. At least I think it is. Jane turns toward me and frowns.

"Is something wrong?" she asks.

Sometimes I forget how well my sister can read my moods.

I shake my head and try to reply, but instead I feel the tears building. Jane reaches out to rub my arms with a questioning expression. I can hardly control the tide of emotion, and I reach out for my big sister. She hugs me, and I cry into her shoulder.

"I'm—I'm sorry," I muffle into her shoulder. "I didn't—couldn't…" My emotions strangle my words, and Jane rubs my back.

"Are you ready to tell me about Darcy yet?" she asks gently.

"You figured it out?" I sniff. I sloppily run my arm across my wet face.

"I could tell Darcy didn't come over just because of your jacket," she clarifies. "And I also knew you wouldn't say anything about him till you felt certain."

Her observation is like a blow. I thought I was protecting Jane by keeping the thing with Darcy a secret. Then she wouldn't have to think about Chip and could move on. Some deeper, more vulnerable part of myself realizes that I kept the relationship a secret because I never quite believed he was really into me. If no one knew we were seeing each other, no one could judge me when I got dumped. I had enough of that with Ian and my former friends.

Numbly, I begin to tell Jane the history of how Darcy and I started hooking up. That leads to what happened the other night—the night of Plan B and the horrible fight that followed the next morning.

Jane stares, astonished, when I mention the part where he suggests we have a kid together.

"What! You haven't even been seeing each other that long!" she exclaims.

"I know! And there's so much I want to do before I start a family," I add. "I had to leave after that."

Jane nods in agreement. "It was unreasonable for him to put those expectations on you." She pauses and looks at me curiously and then shakes her head.

"What is it?"

Jane bites her lip. "I don't know if I should say."

"Just tell me."

"Well…" She hesitates. "What if he didn't want to have a baby, per se, but liked the idea once the possibility came about? He did say he loves you."

I shake my head.

"Jane, he doesn't know me. We didn't exactly talk all that much during this month of hooking up."

Jane shrugs. "I think you know each other better than you will admit."

"It doesn't matter anyway. That door has been closed."

"Is that what you want?" Her tone is soft and understanding.

"Yes. It's time for me to focus on my career anyway."

"You're sure?" Jane questions.

"Yes," I reply with more confidence than I feel.

Jane enfolds me in a warm hug. "I support you," she says. "No matter what path you chose."

I CAN'T SLEEP AGAIN.

I keep thinking about seeing Darcy at Geoff's, and my mind whirls with possibilities.

I can't think of a reason Geoff would be on parole since pot is legal in Washington. Maybe he was caught doing something heavier. Or maybe it's something worse since Darcy told me to stay away from him.

Part of me wishes I could talk to Darcy and clear up his disappointment in me. But what would that accomplish? I'm still not ready for the life he wants. As much as it hurts, it's not the right time for us.

I shift in bed, and the rustle of my sheets is impossibly loud against the silence of our apartment. If I strain my ears, I can hear the drizzle outside. Aunt Mai warned me that, once the rain started in the fall, we wouldn't see the sun for nine months. Seattle has two seasons: a short mild summer with one week of heat and an almost endless stretch of overcast gray with two days of snow in the winter. I have a Happy Lamp and vitamin D stashed in the closet that I'll have to bring out soon.

I sigh and reach for my phone. I can't will myself to be tired, so I start scrolling through Snapchat. Lydia posts constantly, her comments carefree and her face always gorgeous, but she's clearly desperate for attention. Katrina posts nearly as often, but for some reason it doesn't grate on me as much. Maybe because she isn't family, but I suspect it has more to do with the fact that she isn't trying to get her followers to praise her every move. For someone with such attentive parents, Lydia seems to need a lot of peer approval. Maybe that's why I get along so well with Katrina and can only handle Lydia in small doses.

My phone dings, and an email notification pops up. I hate the notification tags on my phone; they remind me of unfinished business. I click on the mail icon and refresh my messages.

I can hardly believe the bold name above my unread email. **Fitzwilliam Darcy.** The subject line is empty and below I see the beginning of his message: *"Dear Lizzie, I hope it's okay that I got your email address from Freddy. I know you don't..."*

I hold my breath and open the message.

Dear Lizzie,

I hope it's okay that I got your email address from Freddy. I know you don't want to hear from me right now, but I hope you will forgive me on this one occasion. I promise not to bother you again.

I realized when I saw you at Geoff's that I was pretty vague when I told you to stay away from him. Looking back, I should have told you why so you wouldn't hang out with him anymore. Of course, you are free to do whatever you want, and I know you will do what you feel is right, but I couldn't feel at ease until I told you the about our history. God only knows what Geoff told you about me, but you have to know why I keep him at arm's length and why you shouldn't get mixed up with him.

Geoff and I grew up together. Our dads were close—partners in technology—and our families often spent time together. My dad was Geoff's godfather and his dad mine. It was almost like they were brothers.

Our families often vacationed together up in Whistler. When my sister, Georgie, was in preschool and Geoff and I were in high school, we took a road trip up there for one of our ski trips. It started snowing when we were on our way, but my dad was a good driver, and Geoff's dad insisted he could handle the weather just as well. My dad made it to the lodge fine with Geoff, Georgie, and me. My mom rode with Geoff's parents in the other car so she could plan meals with Geoff's mom.

I remember when we arrived at the lodge that we waited for hours for the other car to arrive. Dad made a few calls while we waited and tried to make it seem normal, but Geoff and I could tell something wasn't right. Turns out that Geoff's dad took a wide turn on a mountain pass and slammed into a tree. No one in the car made it. It was the most difficult period of my life.

I won't go into the details of what followed. It's not a time I like to think about. My Dad took guardianship of Geoff, and we remained close. He got in trouble a lot at school, but I looked past it because I understood the pain.

Looking back, I probably forgave him more than I should have.

As you know, my Dad passed away from colon cancer two years ago. He left most of his assets to Georgie and me along with his shares in PMB. He also arranged a generous trust for Geoff, a combination of his inheritance from his family and some funds from ours. I never minded Geoff's tendency toward laziness until he blew through the entire trust in a year. He came to me after that and asked if there was anything left for him. There was: a sum of money available only for college tuition. Dad wanted Geoff to get a degree, but Geoff wasn't interested. He said he was inspired by my mom (she painted under the name Anne Fitzwilliam, if you've heard of her) and was going to be an artist. I thought I'd give him a chance, so I gave him the amount set aside for the tuition so he could promote his portfolio.

He came back again six months later asking for more. I can't imagine what he spent the money on. He told me that he needed more exposure, that no one seemed to like his paintings. I decided to help him promote them, and that's when I discovered that his portfolio was only five paintings and he hadn't sent it out to any galleries. At that point, I got angry and told him I wasn't giving him anything else unless he tried. Then we stopped talking.

I wish I could say that was the last time I heard from him. Unfortunately, he reemerged in my life some time later in a way I wish I could forget.

Freddy's parents took custody of my sister after our dad died and enrolled her at Eastside Prep. She did well there for the most part. She was probably too interested in being popular like most kids her age, but it didn't seem alarming to any of us. That is, until the school found a stash of Molly in her locker.

What came after that was an investigation from the school that revealed that Georgie had been passing along Molly and various prescription pills to her friends from an "unknown source." She was suspended and threatened with expulsion. My aunt and uncle were able to keep her in school with a generous donation, and they wore down Georgie until she finally admitted that the dealer was Geoff. It was his answer to help her popularity and help him make money.

I know my sister isn't entirely innocent in the matter, but I can't help but blame Geoff. He's an adult, and she's still a kid. I didn't think too much about the fact that Geoff liked minor recreational drugs and easy money till he threatened Georgie's future. I still don't feel like I can forgive him.

Of course, I can't get the guy out of my life. Last month, he called me after getting arrested for a DUI, and I bailed him out even though I probably shouldn't have. Since I don't trust him not to skip out, I've been taking him to his parole appointments until his license is reinstated, which is why you saw me last night. I guess I hope he will make something of himself, but I still find it hard to trust him. And even if he hasn't done anything shady with you yet, I would suggest you not trust him. He's capable of a lot of manipulation to get what he wants.

There's another thing that's been weighing on my mind, and since you probably will never talk to me again after this, I will absolve myself here. I hope you can forgive me, but I guess I will have to live with the fact that I'll never know.

I've known Chip a long time, as you know. He's one of the most welcoming guys out there and very easy to get along with. He can also be pretty insecure. When he was dating Jane, he constantly questioned why she was into him. When she started working more, his anxiety got worse.

I'm sorry to say that I couldn't forget what you mentioned when we were driving to the winery—that Jane followed your mom's life path for her faithfully. As Chip became more anxious, I started watching her more. While I could tell she liked Chip, it seemed clear she was more interested in her career. After his birthday party and their fight, he asked me for advice. I never should have interfered, but I did. I told him that I didn't think she had enough time for a boyfriend, and he listened to me. It didn't occur to me to feel bad about my advice until you told me she was heartbroken. I'm sorry. You can tell Jane that I'm sorry too, if you feel like it's right to bring it up.

Anyway, I guess those are my last thoughts to you. I wish that I hadn't been carried away the other morning, and I can't really explain what I was thinking except that it felt right at the time. I'm not usually so spontaneous, but I've never met anyone else like you. I hope you know how special you are.

Take care of yourself, Lizzie.

All the best,
Darcy

I stare at the message, numb. The words are plain, but I can't grasp any sort of feeling through the cold distance of technology. Instead, I feel a hollow ache somewhere outside myself. I know I should feel something, but I can't connect to an emotion.

I can see myself and all my decisions with hard realism.

Here I am, hurtling into adulthood, confident in my own sophomoric wisdom, yet stagnant and still challenging the world to *not* be impressed with me.

But who am I, seriously?

I hardly know.

Chapter Fourteen

Jane and I started sleeping in her room after we learned about our parents' divorce. We would huddle together under her *Little House on the Prairie* quilt and read *The Baby-Sitters Club*, play M.A.S.H., or make paper fortune-tellers. We would forget about the fighting, forget that Mom spent most days in her room while Dad would angrily tell her to stop neglecting us. Imagination helped us escape with each other.

A small root of fear started then for me. Mom would instruct us on how to find the right sort of husband. She would tell us about the warning signs she missed. "I know you girls won't make the same mistake I did," she would sniff as she dabbed her red-rimmed eyes. "You will never allow yourself to be deceived like this." Her confidence in our ability not to make her same mistakes was overwhelming. It made me afraid I would mess up.

Dutiful Jane watched her stoically, nodding in agreement. I could see her silent vow to succeed where Mom failed. My reaction was different. I resented Mom for blaming Dad. I vowed not to follow her rules for the "perfect husband" and instead to decide on my own. For different reasons, both Jane and I held an unspoken vow never to repeat our parents' mistakes. Much to my chagrin, however, I did find an inkling of truth in Mom's anxiety for Jane and me: it's easy to be deceived in relationships.

True to the course our mother laid out, Jane had a healthy mix of nice boyfriends who she would date and break up with at the appropriate times, like when going off to college or moving away. She's still Facebook friends with them all. The only one she ever loved was Joey in eleventh grade, but she guarded her heart well with him because she knew high school relationships never last. None of Jane's relationships died in flames like mine did. Well, until Chip, that is, who derailed all of her plans.

My first boyfriend was Tyler Chamberlin in tenth grade. We met in art class, and I was immediately interested by his ability to effortlessly draw human portraits. The fact that he dressed in black skinny jeans, wore eyeliner, and smoked cloves only served to increase the infatuation.

One day, I stayed after school to try and finish a large-scale portrait of a circus clown I had started. The perspective was off and I kept adding layer after layer of acrylics to make it better.

Tyler hung around the room silently. I was acutely aware of his presence but too intimidated to say anything. Instead, I kept on painting and hoping something decent would emerge.

Mrs. Jenkins, the art teacher, wandered in and out of the room. She had the oldies station on her radio. I remember clearly "Do Wah Diddy Diddy" accompanying our creations.

The third time Mrs. Jenkins left the room, Tyler spoke up. "Your hair is crazy. Like Medusa."

I turned around and stared at him. True, my hair was shorter at the time and caused my curls to poof out, but to be compared to a mythical monster!

"I'm not saying you're ugly or anything, just that your hair moves a lot. Like snakes."

"Is that a compliment?" I replied incredulously, wondering if I should convince Mom to let me get my hair relaxed.

"Yeah, it is. It means you're unique."

His soulful blue eyes rimmed in kohl were steadily fixed on me. When I glanced down at his sketchpad, I gasped.

"Is that *me*?" He looked momentarily embarrassed and then proud as I studied his drawing. "That's amazing," I breathed.

I think I must have fed Tyler's ego. We spent two years together in high school with me obsessively encouraging his drawing skills and learning the clumsy art of virginal physical exploration. The first time we had sex was incredibly disappointing. And it was so close to when I left for Stanford that we didn't have much time to make it better. Until I met Ian, I thought all sex was lying still for two minutes while guys moved and shuddered. The only thing I could say about my physical relationship with Tyler is that it got better when we were brave enough to buy a bottle of KY from the drugstore.

I had known who Ian was since freshman year at Stanford, but it wasn't until we were together in Prague in the fall semester in my junior year that I really got to know him.

By that time, I had realized my eye for art was more that of a critic than an artist. This conclusion increased my confidence. Ian was the darling of the art department. He could draw, paint, sculpt, and weld. His creations were enormous and detailed. His mind worked a mile a minute. I wanted to latch onto his energy and watch it burn from inception to creation.

We met while taking "Critical Approaches to Contemporary Art." We sat by each other in the salmon-colored classroom with uncomfortable office chairs and a misplaced chandelier. Ian would watch me take notes. He asked if I wanted to help him study for the first exam.

"I'm not cut out for this lecture/test format," he claimed. "I need to create to learn."

I met him in his room that evening, and we became distracted by creating various cocktails with Becherovka. "The Elixir of Life," the Czechs called it. I remember giggling and trying to focus on my blurry notes. The heady cloud of alcohol hung over me, and I swayed with self-induced vertigo.

From that moment on, we were inseparable. Despite his self-absorption and insomnia, I thought I loved Ian. He taught me that sex could be enjoyable. He told me my encouragement inspired him, but he also would pick fights and disappear for days at a time in the artist studio.

I can see now that first Tyler and then Ian fed into the sort of image I wanted to present to the world. I was artistic and unique. I could be an influencer. In a way, I used them to define myself. But Darcy—well, things with him have always been different. Instead of looking at him like a means to the completion of my self-image, being with him was all about being *with* him, even if it was just physical. His image doesn't fit into the image I've created for myself. In fact, he's probably more a type of guy my mom would choose for me. Maybe that's why I never took him seriously—because I didn't want to take my mom's advice about men seriously.

IN THE MIDNIGHT HAZE OF MY BEDROOM, I READ THROUGH DARCY'S EMAIL again. I'm ashamed that I didn't see through Geoff. I wonder what Darcy saw in me and how he could come to feel so much without me even catching on. Maybe I wouldn't let myself see it. I hate to admit that he affected me so deeply, but I can't help but realize that he's always been intriguing to me, even when I thought I didn't like him. Almost like the kid who pulls the pigtails of the girl he doesn't know he likes. Willful blindness, I guess, helped me ignore what I was starting to feel: I care about Darcy.

I wish I were angrier with Darcy so I could forget how awful this feels. Don't get me wrong, I'm still pissed that he advised Chip to dump Jane. But then again, I did joke that Jane was following our mom's life path. He didn't know Jane or me well enough to know not to take what I said seriously. And Chip didn't have to follow his advice either; his jealousy and insecurity were not cool at all, and to blame them on Jane? She doesn't deserve to be treated like that.

The thought of not seeing Darcy anymore and not being with him again is painful. And I hate that I hurt him. But I've seen what happens when a couple tries to fit together like two puzzle pieces from different puzzles, and it just doesn't work. It will always be forced and never feel right. It can't work when we're on such different paths. I'd have to be a different person, one I'm not ready to be now, if ever. And I won't give up my sense of self for anyone. I don't want a relationship that ends in resentment.

I call in sick to work Friday morning. I imagine Darcy has told Freddy about everything that happened and I don't want to face him. The cocoon of my bedding provides the empty comfort of denial.

At two, I finally drag myself out of bed and shower. I read Darcy's email again while I sit on the couch in silence. My feelings continue to fluctuate between depression, anger, confusion, and resignation.

I continue to scroll through the now familiar words and linger on a sentence toward the end. *"I hope you know how special you are."*

I don't know how to feel about this. Why couldn't he have just asked me out on a real date? Then I wouldn't have been so blindsided.

I exhale heavily, scroll to my contact list, and press the "call" button.

The phone is answered after one ring.

"Lizzie!"

"Hi, Daddy."

"To what do I owe this pleasure?"

I swallow the lump in my throat. "Just thinking about you. How's Dave?"

"Oh, the same," he replies dismissively. "He just joined the American

Numismatic Association and he's been busy with all his coin friends."

My answering laugh sounds hollow.

"How's the rainy city?" Dad asks.

"Just starting to rain regularly." I stare out at the dreary sky. "Mai bought me a Happy Lamp."

"Smart woman. Seasonal Affective Disorder is very common in the Pacific Northwest."

"Yeah…" We lapse into silence.

"You feeling a little SAD, pumpkin?"

"I don't think so," I brood. "It hasn't been rainy long enough."

"You sound low," he presses.

"Maybe just a little confused," I admit. I pause and take a breath. "When did you know Dave was the right guy for you?"

"Ah…matters of the heart aren't always the easiest thing to understand." He pauses thoughtfully. "When I met Dave, I wasn't ready for a relationship, you know. It was before the divorce was even finalized."

"But he was your friend until you were ready," I finish for him. I know this story.

"Yes, but more than that. We fell in love through our friendship. It wasn't the work of a single moment. It was the foundation of friendship and patience with each other. Dave had given up on me because I had so much going on at the time with the divorce and Yiayia's health. It wasn't until years later when he was my closest friend and I was comfortable enough in my own skin that we recognized we had fallen in love."

"Before you were together, did you ever think about him that way?"

"Oh, occasionally. But it wasn't the right time."

"What if you think you've met the right person but it's the wrong time?"

"I don't know, pumpkin. Why don't you tell me about it?"

I sniffle. "I—I can't. I'm not ready to."

My mind flashes to the earnest expression in Darcy's eyes when he declared *"I'm in love with you."*

Dad's sigh is audible.

"Did you skip work today?" he asks knowingly.

"Maybe," I admit in a small voice.

"Are you free next weekend?"

"Why?" I ask suspiciously.

"I'm buying you a plane ticket. I need some time with my girl."

THE PLANE ARRIVES AT O'HARE AT FIVE IN THE EVENING THE FOLLOWING Friday. I still feel like I'm on Pacific Time. This is the second Friday I've missed work, but I decide the financial sacrifice is worth it. Being around Freddy is embarrassing right now, and just seeing him reminds me too much of Darcy.

I find Dad hanging outside of baggage claim searching the crowd for me. When he spots me, his face brightens, and I feel a rush of affection. I try not to jostle my fellow travelers as I hurry over.

"Daddy!"

"Hey, pumpkin."

We hug, and he kisses the top of my head. His familiar smell of mint and clean laundry reminds me of a happy, pre-divorce childhood. I let the nostalgia embrace me.

"How's my girl?" he asks, pulling back from our hug. I'm too happy to let the misery of the past weeks overwhelm me. I laugh instead.

"Barely squeaking by, but putting in a good effort!"

He laughs. "That's the Venetidis spirit."

He takes the handle of my bag and wheels it toward the exit.

"Dave is making paella for dinner, and we got some wine from Trader Joe's. Buy three, get one free! So we bought eight bottles. I think we can spare one for you." He winks.

"Which one of you will surrender your fourth bottle? I know you can't survive without your standard sixteen glasses of wine a day."

"Dave, of course! You know how he likes to impress you."

After spending months in the mountainous Seattle landscape, I can't help but notice that Chicago looks starkly flat, and it's almost a shock not to see visible mountains on the horizon. The closely constructed stone houses feel historical in comparison to the rows of new construction I'm used to. Dad lives in Ravenswood with his husband Dave on the top floor of the triplex he inherited when Yiayia died. It's a three-bedroom apartment with an office and guest room. The guest room was meant to be my room all those years ago, and it's still decorated in the taste of my sixteen-year-old self with robin's egg blue polka-dot wallpaper and posters of my favorite bands from back then: Arcade Fire, Metric, Grizzly Bear. That was when my main goal was to be an indie music tastemaker and Dad took the time to find out who I liked best.

I linger only a moment in my room and head to the kitchen where Dave is cooking and listening to U2. Dad says Dave is "typical '90s cool" with his pierced ear, low ponytail, and affection for blue-tinted lenses. When I ask Dad what he is, he laughs and says, "failed English professor?" with a bit of uncertainty. I can see where he gets the notion: Dad is still good looking with olive-toned skin and a face lined with handsome distinction. His coffee-colored curls are mixed with grey, and he perches bifocals on his nose when he reads. He also favors tweed jackets with elbow patches. But he isn't in academia. Dad is an accident attorney who advertises on afternoon TV for new clients. He has the type of corny local commercials most people make fun of, including himself. I know he wishes he had worked harder and followed a more challenging path in law, but he claims he only wanted to start his life over once. The divorce was enough of an upheaval.

"Elizabeth!" Dave greets when I enter the kitchen. I approach him and he air kisses close to my cheek. "Aren't you a vision! Nik, she is your spitting image." Dave glances between us affectionately.

I grin at him. "It smells terrific in here."

"What a sweet girl," Dave says. "I'm so glad you came to visit."

I love seeing Dad and Dave together. Their affection for each other and toward me is a haven. *An invincible love*, I called it when I made a toast at their wedding last year. Dave cried when I said that.

"Your father will likely commandeer all of your time this weekend, so let's make the most of dinner tonight," Dave continues. "I want to hear all about your new life in Seattle and how Jane is doing."

Dave's comments remind me of what I left behind in Seattle. How Darcy couldn't look me in the eye when we waited for the Uber outside Geoff's apartment. That train of thought immediately leads to Darcy's email and the mess of guilt, sadness, and anger I feel.

I shake off my feelings.

"I can't wait," I say with enthusiasm.

I settle on the couch with Dad until Dave calls us to dinner.

"What's the story with our Venetidis girls?" Dave smiles over his glass of wine.

I hope my returning smile is bright enough. "I wish it was more interesting.

I've been cataloging items for Rose & Hunts for the last few months, but it's only temporary. I'll have to find a new job next month. Jane is working hard at a law firm. Probably working too hard," I say ruefully.

"Our steady Jane," Dave says fondly.

"Jane is dependable and very hard working. I do wish she hadn't gone into law though," Dad says quietly.

I look at him in question.

"Family law may be too much for her tender heart," he explains.

I consider her struggles over the last few months. The long days. The tough clients. The partner brought on to "help" her. I picture her face, and I see clearly that she's been deflating. I blamed it on the break-up with Chip, but could it be something more?

"She seems to be doing okay," I say hesitantly. "But we don't talk too much about the details."

"I need to check in with you girls more," Dad replies with a shake of the head.

"Daddy," I say, scooting close to him, "I'm glad you brought me out to see you. Spending time with you is just what I needed."

Dad puts his arm around my shoulder and kisses the top of my head.

"I'm glad too, pumpkin."

Saturday afternoon, Dad takes me to the Art Institute of Chicago. We go to Greek Island for dinner, a Venetidis Chicago staple. Dad claims it's the next best cooking in the city next to our Yiayia's. I order moussaka, and we split grilled pita and a bottle of white wine.

Our food reawakens vague memories of Yiayia's thick accent and humid kitchen. I'm reminded of my early childhood when we would visit her and she would cook for days, speaking to us almost entirely in Greek while Dad translated. Early on in my life, Dad had aspirations that Jane and I would be bilingual, but eventually gave up. Mom said it made her feel left out when she couldn't understand what we were saying to one another.

"So, pumpkin, what's the story?" Dad asks. He mops up some fava with half a pita and watches me expectantly.

"Ready to jump right into it, are you?" I ask, averting my eyes. Dad inches the wine glass closer to me.

"Is Seattle not working out like you thought?"

I shrug and take a sip of wine. "It is hard to find a job," I confess. "But even the most boring temp job imaginable pays the bills at least."

"And what would you do if you could pick your dream job?" Dad inquires. "Maybe I can help you find something out here?"

I feel a pang of guilt when he says this. I really should spend more time with my dad.

We both already know the answer to his question, but it indicates that I once had a direction for my life. Perhaps I should follow it before I wander too far off course.

"Honestly? I still want to curate art. It's just...I guess...well, I'm nervous about getting started." I don't want to mention Ian's comment that I lost my touch. I wish it wasn't so easy to believe him.

"And you know how to get started?"

I shrug evasively, but my stomach still flutters. Am I ready to truly follow this path?

"Lizzie?"

"You know I would need to get my master's," I reply in resignation.

"So why don't you?"

"I dunno," I reply honestly. "I guess I got too scared of failing. But I should probably go back unless I want to get stuck in some passionless job."

"The Art Institute has a good program, you know," Dad suggests.

I chuckle softly in response. "You just want me to be your neighbor."

"Guilty," Dad concedes cheerfully. "And I know a place you can live rent-free out here."

I shake my head and stare down at my half-eaten plate of food. "Jane and I are on a lease," I say quietly, knowing it's a thin excuse. Our lease would be up by then, I think.

"All right, all right, I won't pressure you," Dad replies in gentle resignation. He pauses in thought. "So, what are the steps to get from point A to point B?"

"Well, there's the financial side," I reply, looking back to Dad. "I mean, how will I support myself if I'm going to school full time?"

"Well," Dad begins, "you should have some sort of job. But it doesn't necessarily have to be full time if you have the right support."

"Dad..." I shake my head. "I can do this—"

"Lizzie, Dave and I don't mind helping you if you are being productive," Dad interrupts. "Let us help you. We helped Jane with law school, you know. And I should have been around for you more anyway. I'm the one who chose to leave California after the divorce."

We look at each other, and I recognize regret in his expression. He did choose to move away, but Jane and I never blamed him. I missed him fiercely, but Yiayia was sick, and Mom was unbearable; he had to leave.

Dad shakes his head, as if banishing the remorse, and his expression lightens. "Where would you want to work while getting your master's?"

"A gallery?" I answer uncertainly.

"That would be where you would eventually end up, right?"

"Likely, yes," I reply with a half shrug.

"So, go stalk your favorite galleries and look for part-time jobs or paid internships. Make friends with all the curators you admire." Dad gazes at me proudly. "I know you have it in you."

I roll my eyes. "You make it sound so easy."

"It's not easy." Dad raises his eyebrows and fixes me with a sober expression. "But you will do the hard work. Harvest that determination of yours."

I remember that determination. I feel a nervous tremor in the pit of my stomach. "You really think I can do this?"

"You have to try," Dad replies with a fierceness I haven't seen in him before. "Following the easy path often leads to a life full of regrets."

"Rent in Seattle is really expensive," I press. "I don't think I could ask that of you."

"Why don't you try?"

We stare at each other for a moment in silence. Dad's expression convinces me of his faith in me, and for the first time, I feel absolutely certain that I can do this and it will be okay, even if I fail. He wants to do this for me. I haven't felt this secure in a while.

I take a breath. "Dad, if I go to grad school, will you help me with rent?"

"I would be happy to," he answers with a large smile.

I'm overcome with gratitude, and I blink away the threat of tears quickly. "Thank you," I respond quietly.

We pause at this point, Dad watching me thoughtfully.

"So, now that we've addressed the career dilemma," Dad says slowly, "what about that thing you called me about last week?"

My mind snaps immediately to attention.

"Daddy..." I start, but he raises his eyebrows in silent reproach. "It's stupid," I deflect.

"Not if it made you call out of work and call me in tears."

I shake my head stubbornly. Dad examines me closely.

"Let's start with his name."

I cross my arms and lean back in my chair petulantly. Dad watches me in expectation.

"He hates his first name, so everyone calls him by his last name," I say quietly.

"And those names would be?" He watches me over the rim of his wine glass and takes a sip.

"Fitzwilliam Darcy."

Dad chokes on his wine and sets it down a little too forcefully.

"*The* Fitzwilliam Darcy?" he says when he's regained his breath.

"I didn't know he was 'the' anything, but his dad was George Darcy if that's what you mean."

"Everyone knows he controls the major shares of PMB. That guy must be loaded." He stares at me in wonder and then smiles ruefully. "Don't tell your mother."

"Trust me, I won't."

"So," Dad says carefully, "he broke your heart?"

I don't reply at first. Am I heartbroken? It kind of feels that way.

"Maybe. I don't know. It's more complicated than that."

Dad doesn't reply, just waits for me to continue. I sigh in resignation. At this point, it's better if he knows the whole story, no matter how uncomfortable it makes me.

I steel myself and begin.

"Jane and I met Darcy and his friend Chip at a bar my first night in town. Jane and Chip started dating, so we all hung out a lot, but then they broke up, so I figured I wouldn't see Darcy again," I say in a rush. "But"—I pause and attempt to slow down my story—"it turns out, his aunt is the CEO of the place I'm working, so I ran into him again at a company barbecue."

Dad nods but doesn't reply. He sips his wine and waits for me to continue.

"We, um..." I cringe and look away. "We started hanging out and, uh, things happened, and I had to take Plan B." The heat of embarrassment shrouds my face. I tap my fingers against the table but don't look up at Dad.

"Did you go to the doctor after that?" Dad asks quietly. I shake my head, and he exhales through his nose. "Okay, so you *will* go get tested when you get home," he says decisively.

I nod my assent but don't say anything.

"And how did this heartbreak come about?" he presses.

"Um, this is embarrassing."

"Pretend I'm Jane, then. What did you tell her?"

I close my eyes so I don't see him watching me. I picture Jane's sympathetic face while she let me cry on her shoulder. "I thought we were just casual for the month we were hanging out. We would just go to his place and, um, you know—but when I had to take the Plan B, he got really serious and suggested that I not take it and move in with him."

"He wanted to have a baby with you?"

I open my eyes. Dad stares at me in disbelief.

"He told me he loved me. Then I took the pill and ended things."

"Good," Dad replies firmly.

"I did the right thing?"

"In this situation, yes, I believe you did. Did you both clarify what you wanted from the relationship?"

"Kind of, but not really," I admit. My throat feels tight again. "We were too emotional to talk about it fully."

"And you haven't talked to him since then?"

I shrug. I don't know if I should count the run in with Geoff.

"He wrote me an email," I say softly.

"Elizabeth," Dad says in his stern lawyer voice. "You are twenty-two years old; you are smart enough to know when a situation needs closure."

I can feel the tears welling in my eyes, and I look away.

"I'm not ready to talk to him yet. I can't—" My heart twists, and I fall back on the familiar thought I told myself after Darcy and I first met. "I think I'm just too young for him."

Dad reaches across the table and lays his hand on mine.

"Learn from your father's mistakes," he states seriously. "A lot of heartache can happen if you aren't honest with yourself, and resentment will build if you aren't honest with others. Even if it's over, you have to find closure, or else your feelings will fester." He takes a fortifying breath and rubs the side of my hand. "Once upon a time, your mother was my closest friend. It's my fault she will hate me the rest of her life."

"That's not true—"

"You know how well Gardiners hold a grudge. And I did lie to her for fourteen years."

I don't reply to this. I never looked at their relationship this way. I feel a foreign sympathy for my mom. Dad's expression is humbler than I've ever seen before. I had no idea the guilt he felt.

"Promise me, Elizabeth, that you will talk to this boy one more time. You don't have to do it tomorrow, but eventually. Talk things through when you aren't in the heat of emotion."

"I promise," I reply softly.

And I really do.

I may not be ready to face Darcy again, but I can push past that and talk to him—soon. Dad is right: I will always feel unsettled unless I try.

Chapter Fifteen

The plane lands to a startlingly sunny October day. I wait out on the curb for Charlotte in the sharp fall air, squinting against the brightness as I search for her car. After seeing Dad, I'm anxious to start down my new path. And check on Jane.

I think of my sister and her encouraging smile when I told her dad was flying me out for a weekend visit. She could tell I needed this time away to figure things out. But there was some sort of emptiness bracketing the edges of her perfect lips with that smile—a wistfulness I failed to recognize at the time.

Coming home also means that I will have to woman up and talk to Darcy at some point, but the thought of him makes me uneasy still, maybe because the outcome is less predictable. I always know with Jane that everything will work out between us. With Darcy, I can't be that certain. A chasm of misunderstanding stretches between us, and I don't know if the hand I offer to the other side will lead to rejection.

I re-read my last text conversation with Darcy while I stand by the curb.

Darcy: What are you doing tonight?

Me: You

But if I don't try, would it be the same as failing? That evening outside Geoff's feels like it happened months ago, but how long has it been? Two weeks?

I wonder if Darcy hates me.

If I'm going to be proactive about anything, it seems easiest at this point to focus on a new gallery job and grad school applications. I'm certain I must have missed the deadline to start in the spring quarter, but I can apply for next fall.

There's so much to do.

Almost there!

A message from Charlotte flashes on my screen. I text back a thumbs-up emoji, put my phone away, and decide to think about Darcy later.

Crossing my arms, I scan the crawl of airport traffic again. A car I don't recognize pulls up near me, and Charlotte leaps out.

Colin emerges from the driver's seat to get my bag while Charlotte hugs me.

"How was your trip?" she asks breathlessly. Her cheeks glow happily. I didn't imagine Charlotte would bring Colin with her when she volunteered to pick me up, but I guess that's a thing that couples do.

"Great!" I reply, happy to see her. I wave towards Colin, and he nods back as he loads my bag into the trunk.

We quickly get caught up in the chaos of Seattle gridlock. "I haven't seen my dad in a long time," I explain as Colin attempts to merge gracefully into the mess of vehicles. "Sorry I arrived during rush hour."

Colin shrugs. "It's no trouble. It's not like I'm not used to commuting through traffic from Kent to downtown."

"You should move to the city," Charlotte suggests. "I don't see you ever leaving Rose & Hunts, so you might as well be closer to work." She speaks familiarly, as if they've had this discussion a hundred times before.

"Living with my parents saves so much money though." His reply sounds like he's not totally convinced in the assertion. Maybe Charlotte is wearing him down.

"If you get that promotion, you should consider it," Charlotte presses. "Anyway," she turns around to look at me, "what did you do in Chicago?"

I fixate on Colin and Charlotte's woven fingers pressed together comfortably. I haven't noticed how content she is till now. My selfish tunnel vision has affected more people than Jane. I shake the guilty feelings out of my system to reply.

"It was a standard visit," I say, dragging my attention to Charlotte's face. "Went to the Art Institute and drank a lot of wine."

"So your dad is why you're such a wino?" Charlotte teases.

I laugh. "I guess. He did give my first glass of wine at fifteen, even though it was watered down."

"Seriously?" Colin replies. I can see his raised eyebrows in the rear-view mirror.

I shrug. "Drinking doesn't have the stigma in Greek culture that it has in the U.S., especially if you're with your parents."

"Weird." Colin frowns. I try not to roll my eyes, and Charlotte moves to the next topic quickly.

We reach the freeway after twenty minutes of god-awful congestion. The road is still unbearably slow, and Colin turns on dubstep to fill the silence. I lean back and play with my phone to pass the time. It's too tempting not to look at Darcy's texts again. I cross my legs and will the unsettled butterflies to fly away. I'll ask Jane's advice about him once I make sure she's okay.

Colin and Charlotte drop me off at the curb in front of my building. The sunset brushes the horizon in burnt orange. Commuters rush home purposefully, some looking haggard after dreary fall days in their cubicles. The lucky ones have that air of satisfaction after completing another fulfilling day. That's the type of person I hope to be.

I open the door to a dark apartment. Jane must be working late again. I switch on the lights and drag my suitcase in noisily through the door. I hear a stirring from the couch.

"Jane?"

Jane sits up, her eyes red and bleary. She's still in her work clothes, but her hair is matted and her eyeliner smudged. Her clothes are wrinkled too, and I wonder how long she's been lying on our couch in the dark.

"What's going on?" I prop my suitcase against the wall and approach the couch. I sit down next to her and take her hand.

"Welcome home," she murmurs weakly. She glances up with a weak smile and trains her eyes on the wall beyond me.

"Are you okay?"

Jane presses her free fingers to her forehead. I wonder if she's going to cry. I let go of her hand and wrap my arms around her.

"What's wrong?" I whisper.

"Work," she exhales. "I haven't won any cases," she nearly whispers. "My boss—he said that even though I'm hard working, he doesn't think I have it in me. I'm too sympathetic to the other side."

She stares up at me, her eyes glimmering with unshed tears.

"They let me go." She shudders and breathes in deeply. "I'm a failure."

I press her into a hug. She bears down on my shoulder, and I can feel her swallowing her grief. Jane hates showing weakness.

Dad was right, and he wasn't even here. If only I had paid attention to how Jane was feeling this entire time. I was too busy focusing on how she seemed to be doing everything right, just like Mom always wanted, that I failed to see her struggle.

I'm struck by a powerful realization.

Jane is just like me.

She isn't the golden child. She is no more Mom's favorite than I am Dad's. We both want to avoid our parents' mistakes, but we go about it differently. I want to do it my own way. My big sister, on the other hand, trusts Mom's advice for happiness in life and does her best to follow what she believes is right. Deep down, though, we are still two Venetidis girls searching for purpose.

I pull back from Jane and grip her shoulders.

"You're not a failure," I say firmly. "You were just too focused on the job you thought you should have, and maybe it just wasn't right for you and your talents."

"But what am I supposed to do now? All this debt and education is meaningless if I'm not a lawyer."

I rub her shoulders. "I don't know, Janey."

"I don't think I can do it again. I'm just not cut out for the workload and negativity. There's so much suffering." She shudders. "I see it every day, the fighting parents and their confused kids. Some of them want to work together, but for the most part—" She rubs the heel of her hand against her eye. "I thought I could make a difference."

I search her face and think about how to help her. We've always been each other's safety nets in times of crisis. This is why we moved to Seattle together. This is how we have survived so far.

"What if you asked Uncle Eddie for advice? Or Dad? Dad really helped me figure some stuff out this weekend."

"I'm so embarrassed," Jane sniffles.

"They won't care. None of us do." I rub her back. "We just want you to be happy. Call Uncle Eddie," I urge. "You aren't alone, and you'll worry and worry if you don't think of a plan."

Jane meets my eyes. "You're right." She leans to hug me again. "Oh,

Lizzie, I've missed you. I've missed everyone. This job has been so lonely." She shakes her head. "I feel so lost."

"You'll figure it out, Janey." We both will.

AFTER WORK ON TUESDAY, I DECIDE TO GO TO CAFÉ LONGUE AND JOB search. I have less than a month till my contract ends at Rose & Hunts. Katrina makes me a free latte, and I start refining my resume and ranking the galleries in the area by my favorites.

It's quiet in the café. Katrina approaches my table with a slice of coffee cake and takes a seat across from me.

"Hey Lizzie, do you have a minute to talk?" She slides the cake to me and smiles nervously.

"Sure." I close my laptop and look up at her. "What's up?"

Katrina sighs. "It's about Lydia."

I'm on my guard instantly. "What's going on?" I ask with trepidation.

"The thing is, her partying has been getting a little crazy, especially after she started spending so much time with Geoff and his friends."

"You guys need to stop hanging out with Geoff," I reply with concern. "I told Lydia he's a creep. Did you see that painting he did of her? And he's on parole!"

Lydia and I, in fact, had an argument about Geoff last night. I told her she should take a break from him, and she told me to stop acting like her mom. Then I told her that I heard he's on parole, and she shot back with "you can't trust what you hear from Darcy."

"How do you know I heard it from Darcy?" I replied, annoyed.

"Geoff thinks you guys were, like, banging or something. I know alllll about how Darcy saw you when you were at Geoff's."

"Okay, so, Darcy saw me at Geoff's when he was *picking him up to see his parole officer.*"

"That's what Darcy told *you*," Lydia replied. "They were really meeting with lawyers to talk about Geoff's inheritance."

How can Lydia even trust Geoff? And what would he even do if she had a seizure around him? The thought makes me shudder.

"Well, I'm usually out with her, so I can keep an eye on her to make sure she doesn't get too out of control, even when we're with Geoff." I start to protest, but Katrina keeps talking. "I think it would be good if you had a spare key though, just as a back-up, you know? You and Jane can keep it in case of emergency. I mean, sometimes I want to drink when we're out too and, like, I know I shouldn't, but—I don't know—it's hard not to want to be part of the group."

"So instead of staying away from this creeper, you're asking for an on-call babysitter?"

"You and Jane are responsible," she explains with a blush.

"But you and Lydia are both capable of making good decisions," I protest.

"Yeah, but you know what Lydia's like when she's partying," Katrina replies.

"What she should really do is stop drinking," I observe in frustration. Convincing her to stop, though—that's another battle.

Katrina slumps. "Lydia will do what she wants," she mutters.

Don't I know it. "Maybe if we stop going out with her, it'll lose the appeal?" I suggest.

"I wish." Katrina laughs tonelessly. "Lydia likes Geoff and his friends. The least I can do is make sure she isn't alone." She stares at me with eyes round in worry.

I try again. "Maybe I should talk to her parents?"

Katrina immediately protests. "You know how overprotective her mom is. She'd probably take her out of school."

"Maybe that would be better at this point."

"Please, Lizzie. Just try it out with us. You can hang onto our spare key, and I'll only call if we're really stuck somewhere, I promise. I doubt we'll even have to call you, but I like knowing we have someone to turn to—someone who will make sure we're safe."

It was never a question of whether I would agree. I wish Lydia were smarter, but I could never leave her on her own. "I can hang onto your spare key, but if she gets any worse, I'm calling my aunt."

Katrina grins at me in relief. "Thank you, thank you, thank you!"

"I still think you should try to convince her to go out less. And try to keep her away from Geoff; she wouldn't listen to me."

"I promise I'll try." She gives me a set of keys dangling from a chain shaped like a flip-flop. "I should get back to work," Katrina says cheerfully.

I watch her with a bad feeling in my stomach. Why does it seem like this plan won't work?

I've been attending regular art walks since I moved to Seattle to keep up my interest in art, and I began frequenting a set of galleries that have since become my favorites. I decided to start applying to these galleries even though they currently don't list any job openings. Dad's encouragement helped make me brave; the promise of a future fuels my stubborn determination. If this goal is helping distract me from some uncomfortable unsettled feelings about other parts of my life, all the better.

And so, late one Saturday morning, I set off in one of Jane's professional outfits to meet the curators of my favorite galleries, hoping my boldness will gain me some positive connections. I start my day downtown, at the waterfront near Pike Place and move south toward Pioneer Square.

I start out small, identifying the head curators and asking about the gallery. As the morning passes, my courage increases, and I even ask one curator for coffee so I can pick her brain. By the time I reach D.B. Shaw, my favorite, I am a little tired but cheerful. Still no real job prospects, but at least I'm establishing a network.

D.B. Shaw still has the same paintings hanging up that I remember from First Thursday, the geometric depictions of powerful women. The faces are striking: strong angular features suspended by spider webs of crisp lines. My gaze is entranced momentarily till I force myself to the front desk. I smile warmly at the girl on the phone. She smiles back and holds up her finger.

"Can I help you?" she asks after she hangs up.

"Yes, is Diane Reynolds available?" I got the head curator's name from the gallery's website and already sent her an email with my résumé.

"Let me see if she's in."

The girl picks up the phone again and props it on her shoulder. I try not to watch her expectantly as she murmurs into the receiver.

"Your name?" the girl says, cupping the receiver.

"Elizabeth Venetidis. I emailed her a few days ago. I would love to learn more about this gallery if she has the time."

The receptionist says a few more things into the phone. "Five minutes," she says after she hangs up.

I thank her and begin to examine the paintings around me again. My palms are damp against my folder of résumés, and I take a deep breath to quell my nerves.

A woman emerges from the back room a few minutes later and glances around the room. "Miss?" the girl at the front desk calls. I step forward, smile confidently, and hold out my hand.

"Ms. Reynolds?" I say to the older woman.

"Yes?" she shakes my hand and holds eye contact with me curiously. She wears an airy dress designed to conceal rather than show her figure. Her hair is in a long frizzy braid streaked with grey. Her oversized dangly earrings look handmade, wood ovals with brightly painted tribal designs. Her complexion is make-up free, healthy, and well moisturized.

"Hi, I'm Elizabeth Venetidis. I sent you my résumé earlier this week, and I wanted to follow up in person. I'm a huge fan of your gallery. I realize you may not be hiring at the moment, but I would love a moment of your time to learn about how you select your art. I love this collection you have right now." I indicate the geometric paintings around me and smile nervously.

"Elizabeth," Diane replies thoughtfully. She has a friendly glint in her eye, and I relax slightly. "I recall your résumé. Come to my office and have a cup of tea with me."

I follow her to the back of the gallery and to a small office in the corner. The walls are overwhelmingly crowded with eclectic paintings, but the room is otherwise orderly and clean. Diane turns on an electric kettle and settles behind her desk. She indicates the chair on the other side, and I sit.

"So. What brings you into our gallery?"

"D.B. Shaw is one of the best galleries I've come across since moving to Seattle. I come here often, and if there is any opportunity, I'd love to be part of it."

I'm left in suspense after the kettle boils. Diane asks me what kind of tea I'd like, and I say green because she's already holding the box. She pushes a mug across to me and seats herself at her desk again.

"I do remember your résumé," she says after taking a sip of tea. "Recent Stanford grad, semester in Prague with special interest in art nouveau. Interned at the Franklin Gallery in San Francisco. Not a bad start." She frowns slightly and peers at me closely. "No master's degree though. All of our curators require an MA."

I eagerly nod my acknowledgment. "I agree. I plan to remedy that next fall, but in the meantime, I am interested in any exposure in the field. I'll be your janitor if this gallery needs one!" I laugh anxiously.

Diane's eyes twinkle, and she chuckles. "I like your enthusiasm, Elizabeth.

Tell me, what were your duties at this internship of yours? And what have you been up to these past five months since you graduated?"

After twenty minutes of talking to Diane, it dawns on me that she is interviewing me. I'm not sure what for, but the thought excites me. After I finish telling her about how I kept myself motivated during my stint at Rose & Hunts, she starts drumming her fingers on her desk.

"Well, kiddo, you're in luck. Ashley, at the front desk, just gave her two weeks yesterday. We need a gallery assistant."

I could leap across the desk and kiss Diane Reynolds. Instead, I squeak out "Really?"

Diane laughs again, suddenly more relaxed than she was during our earlier conversation.

"Imagine," she says, "we didn't even have to put up a job posting! What a sweet bit of serendipity."

"Thank you," I reply, still slightly stunned.

"I'd like you to start before the upcoming preview for our high-value patrons. That way Ashley can show you the ropes and hand off her duties to you so that you don't feel too overwhelmed during the preview. When can you start?"

"I have a week left on my contract at Rose & Hunts," I reply apologetically.

"Next week then." She gives me her card, and we both stand.

"Thank you so much, Ms. Reynolds."

"Diane," she corrects.

"Diane," I repeat confidently.

Diane walks me out to the front of the gallery. "I have a good feeling about you," she states with an affirming handshake.

I have a good feeling about her too. Everything about D.B. Shaw inspires me. After this one weekend afternoon, I suddenly don't feel so lost anymore.

Chapter Sixteen

It's our final week at Rose & Hunts, and our group gets together for lunch one last time at Lambert's, a nearby seafood restaurant on the waterfront. Lunch is loud and slightly chaotic, but I'm glad it was planned. It will be good to have a chance to say goodbye to everyone who shared the stifling boredom of the past three months. Miserable camaraderie is still camaraderie.

I decide to sit by Freddy since it's been a while since we've talked. Granted, I *have* been avoiding him, but Freddy is my friend, and I want to say goodbye and thank him.

Problem is, I don't really know how to start a conversation with Freddy right now. I'm pretty sure he knows everything about Darcy and me, and I'm...well...embarrassed.

I swallow my discomfort and approach the empty seat by him.

"Is this seat taken?"

"It is now," he says with a smile.

I settle down next to him and immediately pick up the menu. Freddy leans back and looks around at his group of peons.

"Are you gonna miss us?" I ask awkwardly. "I don't know how you'll get through the day without Todd and Julie."

Freddy snickers and shakes his head. "Nah. Some of these folks will come around again anyway when we have another catalog-tagging project. The serial contractors." He indicates Debra, a middle-aged woman with unnaturally red hair and thick clear-rimmed glasses. "Todd and Julie can go off into the sunset, though."

I laugh but don't know how to reply. I play with the edge of the menu.

"How's—"

"I hear—"

We start at the same time. I smile and say, "You first."

"I hear you have a new job already. Impressive!"

"Thanks," I reply. "I actually got myself a gallery job. It's not much—being a gallery assistant is pretty much a party planner meets receptionist—but it's a start!"

"That's great," Freddy replies enthusiastically. "Dar— I heard that you want to be a curator."

I nod. "It's the goal. And I've finally accepted the fact I need to get my master's if I want to achieve it, so I'm applying to schools too."

"I knew you were meant for more than a job like this."

I laugh and shrug my shoulders. "Maybe."

We lapse into silence, and I contemplate asking about Darcy. Would it be weird? Freddy *did* pass along my email address. I drum my fingers on the table.

"You look like you're doing better," Freddy observes softly. I shrug.

"It was good to visit my dad," I agree in the same low tone.

Freddy holds my eye contact in sympathy, and I look away.

"How is he?" I ask finally, unable to make eye contact with Freddy.

"I was afraid you would ask that," Freddy responds. "Look, I really don't want to get in the middle of it, but I do feel a sense of obligation since I told you to talk to him…" He pauses for a long moment. "He just needs time," he says vaguely.

"Oh," I reply, disappointed. "You think he'll be okay?"

"Sure," Freddy says too quickly. I frown at him, and he sighs. "I can't say I totally understand what happened between you two aside from a whole pile of miscommunication, but I do think he's bouncing back. I have confidence."

Does that mean Darcy is getting over me? And if so, shouldn't that make me relieved instead of dejected?

BY THE FIRST OF NOVEMBER, THE SKY HAS COMFORTABLY SETTLED INTO A dreariness that Mai and Eddie claim will last until March. Along with the overcast skies, spitting rain, and wind, the sun sets so early it's hard to imagine I'm ever awake during daylight. I read somewhere that Scandinavian countries help keep their winter depression at bay by using copious candles, so I've lined our apartment with dollar store votives and cheap tea lights.

Taking Eddie's advice, Jane recently started studying to be a mediator. With this goal in mind, she has a new confidence about her, something I haven't seen since we moved to Seattle. Jane has the unique ability to encourage cooperation, and I'm positive her peacemaking nature will pay off in this role. Plus, Eddie said he would refer clients to her.

My first days at D. B. Shaw are overwhelming, mostly because we are on the brink of the preview show. Planning the event along with the daily administrative duties has given me a lot of details to take in. I'm grateful Diane is giving me this time to shadow Ashley; there's so much to learn.

On Tuesday, Ashley trains me on the internal RSVP system we use and instructs me to follow up with the "No Replies" so we can provide a final head count to the caterers by Thursday. I methodically click my way down the list, one by one sending a personal email to each "No Reply." I've barely made it past the Cs when I am suddenly arrested by a name.

Fitzwilliam Darcy.

How strange it is to send him a professional email when the last I heard from him was that email. I must be staring at the screen too long because Ashley looks over my shoulder.

"Oh yeah," she says, pointing to his name. "We have a lot of well-known patrons. Of course, it doesn't hurt that Diane was best friends with Anne Darcy back in the day."

I look over at Ashley in surprise.

"Was she?"

Ashley laughs. "Totally! Diane looooves to talk about their adventures too! They apparently did some wild things in their youth."

I don't reply, but my heart starts to race. Will I see him again? Would he think I found a job here, at the gallery of his mother's best friend, on purpose? I feel my cheeks flush.

"Don't worry about it!" Ashley pats my arm. "Mr. Darcy's really cool and low-key. I know it's intimidating to meet people you usually only read about, but he's chill."

"Do you think he'll come?"

Ashley shrugs. "Depends. He skips more events than he attends, so I wouldn't count on it."

"Oh."

She laughs. "I know, he's hot, right? Well, don't be too disappointed—Alex Santiago is on the 'yes' list, so you will at least meet one local celebrity."

I stare back at his name and almost ask Ashley to email him for me so my name doesn't show up in his inbox, but then I remember that I'm sending these emails from the gallery, not my personal account. I exhale shakily.

"You got this?" Ashley asks, straightening her posture.

I square my shoulders and smile at her.

"Yep, I should be done soon."

Ashley nods in approval and plops down in a chair to play a game on her phone. She's instructing me, but she's slowly getting more and more checked out. Not that I blame her. I understand short-timers' syndrome too well.

I finish sending out the emails and see that I've already gotten a few replies. *Fitzwilliam Darcy sends his regrets.*

I'm not sure if I'm disappointed or relieved.

SATURDAY IS MORE CHAOTIC THAN I IMAGINED. I'M SO BUSY COORDINATING the caterers, supporting the artist on preview, and running out on random errands, I have hardly enough time to get myself ready. Earlier in the week, Ashley advised me to find myself a standard little black dress and comfortable heels for gallery events. Tonight, we nearly match as we position ourselves by the front doors to welcome the patrons like uniformed greeters.

I start to feel more confident after greeting the fourth patron. I am harnessing the strength Dad believes I have. I got this. If Dad were standing next to me, he would be humming the *Rocky* theme song in my ear.

I am turned away from the line slightly, answering general questions from one of the patrons when I hear a familiar voice:

"Hey Ashley, I know I sent my regrets, but I was hoping you wouldn't mind squeezing me in."

I spin around and lock eyes with Darcy. For the next heartbeat, we stand transfixed. Darcy's face seems to have drained of color. Embarrassed, I start to turn back to the patron, but he interrupts my deferment.

"Lizzie." His tone is assertive, yet it caresses my name in a way that almost hurts. When I look up at him, I see a sweep of pink across his cheeks. My face is warm too.

"Hello, Darcy," I say as calmly as I can. Behind me, I hear the patron excuse himself, so Darcy and I are left to converse.

"Do you work here now?" I recognize his tone as one of interest, though I never placed it as such before. Before, I thought his questions were merely a play at politeness, but I failed to grasp the sincerity. I smile nervously.

"Um, yes, actually. It's my first week."

His eyes meet mine, and I feel like the wind has been knocked out of me. What was I thinking before, shutting him out like I did? I regret the path of false intimacy I unknowingly led him through. Of course, I didn't realize I was shutting him out at the time. I thought I was being worldly.

He places his hand on my shoulder and says earnestly, "I'm so glad for you."

His touch is warm, and I can't seem to reply. Ashley approaches us then, apparently unable to quell her curiosity.

"You two know each other?" She glances pointedly at the line and back to us.

"Oh, yes," I start to stammer. Darcy squeezes my shoulder and drops his hand.

"I'll catch you inside," he says.

I try not to watch after him, but I can't let go of the haze surrounding me. Should I hope? Do I *want* to hope?

Darcy finds me after I've made the necessary greetings to the incoming patrons. Ashley instructs me to mingle with the patrons and make myself available for questions. It's also up to me to keep a sharp eye on the artwork to make sure no one harms anything.

I've just placed a red dot next to a painting when I spy him approaching me with his habitual determination. I hold my posture professionally erect as he approaches.

"You're in your element," he comments when he reaches me.

I smile. "Thanks."

"How are you?" He looks down at me uncertainly and rubs the back of his neck.

"Good!" I try not to wince at my jittery enthusiasm. How can he be so civil, so kind to me, after I stomped all over his heart? "I, um, I got lucky finding this job," I start to babble. "They hadn't even gotten around to posting it when I came in with my résumé. I was so lucky."

"And tenacious," Darcy adds. "Not everyone is brave enough to put themselves out there like that."

Embarrassed, I start to protest, and he laughs.

"You're exaggerating," I say, poking my finger at his chest. His eyes dance when they catch mine, and he shakes his head as if to say, *You're not fooling me.*

How has this feeling between us changed so drastically over the course of a silent month? I never would have imagined after leaving him outside of Geoff's apartment that we would be laughing and kind of flirting. I would have expected animosity from him. But even though there is tension between us, it isn't the bad kind. Uncertain, yes, but not uneasy.

"Anything you're interested in?" I ask Darcy. "Diane tells me you're one of our frequent buyers."

Darcy shrugs and looks around. "Which one do you like?"

"Professionally, I find great merit in all these paintings. And they're going fast." I indicate the red dot I just placed next to a painting of a Viking ship propped up in a stark field.

"But you do have a personal opinion," he presses. His eyes dare me.

I nod my head toward a wall to the left. "Follow me."

I stop in front of a painting of a cityscape with a large pastoral scene interrupting the chaos, like a bubble of solitude amongst the clutter. The oil strokes are impossibly detailed and accurate.

"This one struck me," I say seriously. "Miller is showing us the peace among the noise. Like this unachievable sort of sanctuary is attainable."

We stare at the painting in silence. I can feel his quick glances at me and back to the painting.

"You know, my mother painted pastoral landscapes," he says quietly while we both continue to stare at the painting. "Mostly of her childhood home in England. It was demolished when I was young—got too dilapidated. But her paintings made it look like the most serene place in the world."

I look over at him and he back at me. More information about the Darcy I'd like to know. How much there is to learn about him.

"Is she the reason you started collecting art?"

He shrugs and looks back at the painting again. "I'm just building on her collection. I thought if it continued to grow after her death, it would be like she lives on. Maybe it's silly, but it's a comforting sentiment to hold onto."

"That's not silly," I reply solemnly. I feel like I should take his hand and reassure him, but I'm also not sure I'm allowed to, and not just because of my job. This isn't a topic we can bring up anyway—not here. Our fragile conversation is framed by our past experience.

Not that I will shy away from transparency. Not this time. Not anymore.

Darcy looks at me again and smiles. I smile back, and it's not awkward. We may not be speaking, but the warmth of his expression assures me.

"What are you doing after this?" he asks finally.

"Going home. I'll be working till midnight." I shrug. "Why?"

"If you aren't too tired, can I take you to 13 Coins? I mean, I know it'll be late, but—"

"Sure," I interrupt. "I'd like that."

HE WAITS FOR ME OUTSIDE OF THE GALLERY UNDER THE OVERHANG. I CAN see his breath when I step outside into the drizzle, and I shiver.

"Are you sure it isn't too late?" I ask when I reach him.

"Not at all." He watches me lock the front door and pull out an umbrella.

"You really aren't from here," he laughs as he indicates the umbrella. "No native would be caught dead with one of those."

"Keeping this under control takes too much work," I say, waving at my hair. "I am not getting it wet."

He nods to his car down the sidewalk. "Shall we?"

We walk next to each other, shoulders close but not touching. It would only take an inch to bump into each other, but we move with separate anticipation. When we reach his car, he opens the door for me and takes my umbrella to shake out the raindrops as I slide into the seat.

I feel happy. I am happy. I can't stop the corners of my mouth from lifting.

"What?" he says, looking down at me.

"Get in before you get too wet," I laugh.

It's humid in the car, and the windows fog from the rain. The clouded interior envelopes us in a surreal sense of intimacy. Darcy turns on the ignition and allows the glass to clear.

Depeche Mode plays over the speakers, and I wonder fleetingly if Darcy's favorite music genre is New Wave. I add it to my mental list of questions to ask about him. We hardly talk on the drive over.

Darcy opens my door for me when we arrive at 13 Coins, one of the few twenty-four-hour restaurants in the city. The inside thrums with nightlife. Crowds of city dwellers laugh and absorb their drunkenness with fancy egg dishes or grab one last drink before calling it a night. Darcy gently bumps his shoulder against mine as we wait for a table, and I lean into him.

His attention causes a rush of emotion I can't quite name. Anticipation, maybe, but also something more akin to hope.

Are we on the same page now? What is our page?

Once seated, we smile nervously, and I wonder what we should make of this night. I take a careful sip of water and smooth the tablecloth to distract myself.

Darcy clears his throat. "I think it's really great that you're working for Diane."

I look up, and we catch eyes. My heart races. I swallow another sip of water. Composure, Lizzy, composure.

"Thank you. I hear she was good friends with your mother."

"She was," Darcy confirms. I feel a clinch of longing in my heart as I recall his tender kisses and our quiet nights eating Thai food in bed.

"A very good friend," he replies. Then he adds, almost to himself, "Out of all the galleries in the city, you found hers. I pretty much grew up there."

"Diane said it was serendipity that I happened to show up when she needed a new assistant."

We continue to hold eye contact, and I wonder how things between us can feel so different now. The space between us is wide open with possibilities, but I can't be sure.

My fingers itch to slide across the table and hold his hand, but I don't want to break this delicate spell. There's hope here, and I don't want to crush it.

The server comes to take our drink orders, and Darcy chuckles when I order pink wine. "Still your favorite?" he asks, and I blush.

"So, uh, how's Jane?" Darcy asks when we have the table to ourselves again.

"Good, actually!" I reply. "It was tough for a while, you know. She missed Chip, and then she lost her job."

"I'm sorry to hear that," Darcy says with a frown.

"Yeah, well, I think it was for the best. She's studying to be a certified mediator now. I think she'll do better at that." I hesitate and then ask the real question pressing on my mind. "How have you been?"

"Um, all right," Darcy replies uncomfortably. "It wasn't easy, the—" He makes a vague gesture between us.

"No, it wasn't," I agree. "We did that whole thing ass backwards, didn't we?"

The tension cracks a little, and we both relax.

"Yeah, that's one way to put it." He hesitates a moment and then reaches across the table. The pressure of his touch is feather light but so tender I can barely breathe. I swallow and meet his eyes again.

"I'm really glad I saw you tonight," he says.

"Me too," I whisper back.

We order food, and he stretches his foot under the table. I bump mine against his purposefully. We continue our casual conversation with our feet touching.

"So," I lean across the table slightly. "Tell me about yourself."

"What do you mean?" His expression is bright, and he leans closer to me.

I straighten my posture and bump my foot against his again.

"I realized recently that I never found out where you went to college or what you studied, for instance."

He leans back, watching me, and sips his drink. "It's nothing exciting," he replies. "I studied economics at CalTech. Now I spend all my time watching stocks and investing in startups—pretty much what my dad wanted me to do."

"Is that what *you* wanted to do?"

Darcy shrugs. "It wasn't a hard path to follow. But it also doesn't feel very important. It's just—what I was supposed to do, I guess."

Our feet are still connected under the table, and I shift mine against his.

"No one expects you to save the world," I say gently. "I'm sure your backing means a lot to those startups."

"That's what's great about you. You find the best side of everything."

I snort and shake my head. "That's not always true." I think of how badly I misinterpreted him before.

"Yet you remain optimistic. And you stay true to yourself," he says. "It's inspiring."

I shake my head again but don't reply.

"I'm serious. It's so easy to do what's expected of you. I elected to follow in my dad's footsteps because he wanted me to. I often wonder whether I would have chosen something different if I hadn't had those expectations." His expression is rueful, and I tilt my head in agreement. "But *you* found what you wanted, and now you're going after it." He says this last sentence with a fixed stare that is almost startling.

I clear my throat. "And what do you want?" I ask, trying to keep my voice from wavering.

He doesn't reply right away. Our food is brought, and he continues to watch me carefully, contemplating his answer.

"I thought I knew, but so much has happened..." He flashes me a significant look. "But right now? I just want to be around you."

I reach across the table and pick some imaginary lint off his sleeve.

"Well, I can help with that," I say archly.

"Can you?" His eyes have a vivid expression.

"All you have to do is ask."

Darcy pauses and stares at me thoughtfully. "Do you want to see my mom's art?" he asks suddenly.

"Sure?" I'm confused by the change in topic.

"It's at my dad's house. We still own it, Georgie and me, but no one lives there. We maintain it, though, so you don't have to worry about it being creepy or anything."

"I would love to see your mom's art." I reply and imagine when he will take me there.

"Okay, let me just get the check."

"Now?"

"Why not?"

It's almost 2:00 a.m., last call for all the bars, when we pass through the Capitol Hill nightlife to the stately Montlake neighborhood. The houses are beautiful here, pillars of old Seattle money from families like the Nordstroms. It hardly feels like we're in the heart of the city when we reach the winding roads shrouded by trees. Darcy pulls into a long driveway in front of an old large mansion with white pillars.

"I didn't know houses like this existed in Seattle," I say in wonder as he pulls on the parking brake. He shrugs modestly.

Darcy helps me out of the car, and I cling to his arm. There are hardly any lights about, and I tighten my grip.

"Sorry it's so dark," he murmurs. "We usually don't have the lights on unless we know people are coming over."

We climb up the stone steps to the front door. He unlocks it and flips on the lights. I squint against the brightness as he rushes to punch off the alarm.

"This is where you grew up?" I say when I can finally take in the large front foyer with smooth wooden flooring, an understated Persian rug, and a beautiful landscape hung by the staircase.

"I know," he says. "It's a lot."

"I wouldn't say that," I counter. "It's nothing like Cathy's house. Large, certainly, but charming too."

He touches my cheek, and my throat sticks in anticipation. He drops his arm slowly and takes my hand.

"C'mon."

We wander down the hall to a study and then to a door in the back corner that could be a closet. But Darcy leads me through, and I gasp.

The walls are filled with paintings of unusual landscapes. The colors are vibrant and purposefully complementary, the paint strokes wide and graceful.

"Did you mother like Van Gogh?" I ask, turning in a circle to observe more.

"Van Gogh, Picasso, Matisse, all those artists who turned realism on its head."

"These are beautiful," I remark, still in awe.

"I can't tell you what it means—" His eyes are shiny for just a moment. He takes my hand again, and we turn back to gaze at a wall of paintings.

"I could never do anything like this. Georgie can, though it's more of a hobby for her. Still, it's nice to have something tangible like this left of my mother."

I lean my head against his shoulder. He reaches his arm around me and pulls me closer.

"Thank you for showing them to me," I whisper.

We turn to each other then and I wonder if he's going to kiss me. Maybe we should talk about us, but it doesn't seem like quite the right moment.

He doesn't kiss me. Instead, he smiles with a soft hope that I recognize as if it's my own.

I examine the paintings for a long time, long enough that my feet become sore and I have to take off my shoes. Then we end up lying in the middle of the floor, sprawled on the rug and talking about anything we can think of till our voices grow hoarse. Our conversation grows deep, and I learn about the pressure of the expectations placed on him since his dad died. I tell him about my recent grad school application and the fear that I "lost my spark," as Ian put it. He carefully asks me about Ian, and I tell him about my last semester of school and how hard it was to feel so alone.

"I don't understand how all of your friends could turn on you like that,"

Darcy says. "You're the type of person who's so easy to like. People could have hung out with you and your ex separately."

"You haven't seen Ian's work," I reply. "He's one of those artists who has that *thing*, you know? It's such a small community, and no one wants to lose him as a connection."

Darcy scoffed. "People can be selfish idiots."

He tells me about his most recent ex after that—about how she didn't understand how it was a challenge for him to devote the time she wanted to her when he was grieving his dad. He broke up with her as they disintegrated into arguments that she wasn't getting enough attention. I realize we both understand what true loneliness feels like.

Morning light is creeping up the walls and steeping the room golden as we drift off to sleep at dawn with our fingers entwined. His soft snores are achingly familiar, but the chaste touch of his hand and the wide expanse of everything I'm learning about him hold a beautiful promise. My eyes grow heavy, my hand tightens on his, and I smile.

Chapter Seventeen

wake up curled around Darcy's side, my cheek pressed to his chest. I open my eyes slowly to see him gazing down at me.

"Morning," he says. His voice is scratchy, but tender and well remembered.

"Morning," I reply contentedly. His fingers graze my ribs. "What time is it?" I ask, taking the time to look around the room. The hazy glow of an overcast Sunday morning filters through the windows. Darcy pulls me closer so he can look at his watch.

"Almost eight."

"Hmmmm." I burrow my face in his chest and close my eyes. "Still early then." I can feel the warmth of his breath on my forehead. The brief graze of his lips.

I'm not ready to leave this spot yet. Not ready to break this embrace and the intimacy. But the cramp in my side reminds me that we are sleeping on the floor, and I shift.

"Are you uncomfortable?" Darcy asks when I move again.

"No," I reply stubbornly.

I can feel his chuckle beneath my cheek. "Two hours of sleep on the floor and you aren't even a little stiff?"

I shrug and close my eyes again. "I have my favorite pillow," I murmur.

"Lizzie," he exhales. I reach my arm across his chest.

"We can lie down some place more comfortable," he suggests. "There are, in fact, beds in this house."

"Mmmm," I reply.

"I can show you my old room. Only to sleep, I promise."

"Whatever you want," I mumble tiredly. "Just to sleep."

"I promise," he repeats.

He laughs and smoothes my hair when I sit up.

"It's crazy, isn't it?" I say, running my palm down the back of my head.

"Yeah," he replies affectionately. "Crazy bedhead."

He helps me to my feet, and I go to pick up my shoes in the corner of the room. He touches my hair again before leading me out of the gallery and up the stairs. The second floor has more doors than I care to count, and I wonder how many bedrooms are in this house. We reach a door, and he pushes it open.

"Here we are," he says.

His old room is neat, with a blue plaid bedspread and posters of Van Gogh's Starry Night, the Smiths, and Mount Rainier. A bulletin board displays an outdated cat calendar.

"You really do love cats!"

"It was a gift from Georgie. Misty is her cat, but I took her when Georgie moved in with our aunt and uncle. Aunt Vivian is allergic."

"And here I thought you were a crazy cat person," I reply in mock disappointment.

"I'll have to find a way to redeem myself," he replies.

I look over at him smiling down at me. I want to stretch up and kiss him, but I keep myself in check. There will be enough time for that later. After we've talked about us.

He leads me to his bed and the soft mattress is heavenly. I lean against the pillows and sigh, and Darcy sinks down next to me. We don't get under the covers, but I roll over, back to the familiar nook of his shoulder, and close my eyes again.

"Do you have any place to be today?" he mumbles, his voice growing tired again.

"No," I murmur back. I can feel the heaviness of sleep pressing my eyelids. "Wait, yes," I say, gaining a bit of consciousness. "I have brunch with my aunt and uncle at noon."

"I'll set an alarm," he says, and I feel him fumbling for his phone.

It doesn't take long for his breathing to grow steady as we catch a few more precious hours of sleep.

I'M MOMENTARILY CONFUSED WHEN I HEAR AN INCESSANT ROOSTER CROWing till I come to my senses enough to realize Darcy's alarm is going off. I groan and gracelessly detangle myself from his embrace.

"So tired," I grumble.

"Yeah," he agrees, still sprawled on his back. His clothes are more rumpled than I've ever seen them. He discarded his button-up shirt at some point and was just wearing his undershirt and slacks. I stare down at his chest, remembering our uncontainable attraction. I want to run my hand over his muscles, but I don't.

I need coffee.

I shift forward and rub my eyes. Darcy sits up too, reaching for his shirt while I adjust the top of my dress. I run my tongue over my unbrushed teeth and reach for my uncomfortable tights in a ball on the floor.

"Um, can I use your bathroom?" I ask.

"Sure, it's two doors down. To your left."

"Thanks."

I pad down the hall to the bathroom and close the door. I glance in the mirror and make a face at my insane hair. I think I have a hair tie in my purse. I roll my tights back on and then lean over the sink to rub my fingers against my gross teeth. This will have to do. It's probably a good thing that my morning breath will keep me from doing anything impulsive.

When I get back to his room, Darcy is already putting his shoes on. I decide to wait to slip my heels on till we're almost out the door.

"Do you need coffee?" he asks as I scoop up my purse from the corner.

"Am I that obvious?"

"Maybe."

"Well, I would never say no to caffeine, especially on so little sleep." I pull a hair tie from my bag and coil my hair into a bun.

"Let's stop by Victrola on our way to your place," he suggests.

I nod in agreement. Anything to prolong our time together.

We dawdle in the coffee shop, and Darcy takes the side streets home. It's full morning now, with weekend joggers in their fluorescent jackets streaking down the sidewalk and hungover partiers from last night sipping their huge coffees while wearing unnecessary sunglasses in the overcast daylight.

When we reach the back alley behind my apartment, neither of us moves when Darcy turns off the ignition. I look up at him, the question poised but stuck in my throat.

What are we doing?

Darcy lets his fingertips drift down my cheek. My eyes flutter closed then open again. He stares at me intently but doesn't move. It's as if we're replaying that first scene in his car where he kissed me and this thing between us was unleashed in an untamed and destructive manner. I decide to take the initiative.

"This evening after I get home, will you come over? I think—I *know* we need to…" My heart pounds, and I swallow. Why is it so hard to say the words?

Our hands link across the console. I stare down at them and then, gathering courage, look straight into Darcy's eyes.

"Let's be honest with each other, okay? Let's talk about what this means. I want to be on the same page."

Darcy nods once and smiles, looking slightly nervous. Our grip tightens as if in fear that we'll lose this thing we have. Maybe we will. The thought is heartbreaking, but it would be even worse to venture in again without understanding each other.

"I'll text you later," he says quietly.

Gently, I lean across the console to kiss his cheek. I keep the contact light, a brush of the lips really. He looks back at me, dazed, but doesn't move.

"Later," I confirm.

I exit his car shrouded by the dreary late morning haze. Rain starts to spit as I make my way to the back entrance. I turn to wave to Darcy before I enter the building. He waves back and waits, presumably to watch me enter.

I feel half in a dream as I ascend the staircase. When I enter the apartment, I see the couch has been pushed back and Jane has set up her yoga mat. She is perched gracefully in crow's pose. She gently moves out of the position as I close the door behind me.

"Lizzie!" She stretches quickly, from her toes upward then pauses the audio on her phone. "Were you out all night?"

I shrug, and then I can barely contain my smile. Jane raises her eyebrows and scans my rumpled appearance.

"You'll never guess," I say, my grin growing.

"I know that look," Jane squeals. She drags me over to sit on our couch, shoved back against the bay window.

"You know how people always say Seattle feels like a small town, but we never believed them? Well, you'll never guess who was a long-time friend with my boss at the gallery."

"Who?"

"Darcy's mother. Did you know he pretty much grew up there? I had no idea!"

Jane's face falls a little, and I imagine she's recalling my earlier heartache. Still, she doesn't interrupt, just watches me expectantly.

I clear my throat. "So, he was there, last night. And it was really nice to see him. He was kind, very attentive. And, considering our last interaction..." I trail off.

"So," Jane surmises carefully, "you were with Darcy all night?" I can tell she wants to ask if I slept with him. I shake my head to try and help her understand.

"I was with him, but not like you think. We went to 13 Coins; then he showed me his mom's artwork. It's *amazing*. Then we talked all night till we fell asleep. That's all. Just talked until we couldn't keep our eyes open anymore."

"Really?"

"He's coming over tonight. Is that okay?"

"It is if that's what you want," Jane says carefully. "But, Lizzie, remember what he asked of you before? What if he still wants to settle down right away?"

I shrink somewhat. "I thought of that too. It would hurt, I think, but at least it would be honest. We would know exactly where the other person stands. No more surprise punches to the gut."

"You never said, but what *do* you want from Darcy?"

I straighten my posture confidently. "I'm twenty-two. I'm not ready for marriage and kids yet. But what I would like is a boyfriend. A serious one. One who could maybe grow to be something more in time, but also someone who doesn't pressure me to hurry up or figure out my life when I've only barely started. I still need freedom. I want to be myself with someone who is himself, but we are together. Does that make sense?"

Jane looks at me, eyes bright. "It's what I want too, I think," she admits. "Mom wants me to get married and have kids in the next few years, but I want what you're describing. I want to be myself first."

I reach over and hug my sister. She's a little sweaty from yoga, but I don't care.

She pulls back and checks the time on her phone.

"We should get ready for brunch."

JANE DRIVES US TO EDDIE AND MAI'S HOUSE IN THE SUNSET HILL AREA OF Ballard. Their house almost has a view of Puget Sound and is within walking distance of the park that overlooks the marina. I'm glad Jane is driving; her newer VW Passat doesn't stick out in the affluent neighborhood as much as my beat-up Corolla would.

Mai has prepared an excellent spread: a waffle buffet, eggs Benedict, and a constant stream of coffee. The food Mai makes is usually good, but this is better than usual. It makes me wonder if they are breaking bad news or if Mai's pregnancy has caused particularly decadent food cravings.

I glance at Jane as she praises the meal, but she doesn't appear to have my same suspicions. I try to give her a look, but she returns my silent question with her own inquiring expression. I sigh and Eddie, perhaps noticing our unspoken conversation, clears his throat.

"Well, girls, we had ulterior motives for this brunch." He glances at Mai, and she smiles serenely at us with that unique maternal glow that can only be gained naturally, no matter how many moisturizers one uses. Her eyes glitter happily. Eddie rubs her back.

"The baby is coming soon," he continues, "so we're making the family rounds while we still have the time."

"Meaning?" I say, looking between them.

"We're spending Thanksgiving with my family," Mai states. "I know we had planned to have you girls over, but I hope you understand. You know how my parents hate to travel."

It's true that Jane and I only met the Nguyens once for Eddie and Mai's wedding. That day was a strange clash of wills between our Grandma Agatha and Mai's mother. Mom, Jane, and I spent most of the day trying to stay out of their way while Mai attempted to smooth the waters.

"I thought your family didn't celebrate Thanksgiving," Jane remarks. "Not that we mind. Lizzie and I have enough friends around to find some place to go."

Mai smiles. "They usually don't care about it, but Eddie has time off, and we can still spend the day together at the restaurant." She rests her palms over her rounded belly and reclines slightly. "Besides, we probably won't see them again till this little guy is ready to travel."

"And we still have Christmas," Eddie adds. "Your Mom will be coming up for that."

"What about Lydia?" Jane asks.

"She already told us she has plans," Mai replies with a fond shake of her head. "I can't keep track of all her friends!"

"Lydia's always been popular," Jane agrees. I nod absently, still feeling unsettled by my conversations with Lydia and Katrina the other day. I haven't heard from Lydia since our argument.

I change the subject away from her. "You went through a lot of trouble to tell us this," I say, indicating the generous spread.

Mai, always the people pleaser, blushes. "We wanted you to still feel special to us."

"Oh, Aunt Mai," Jane says, moving to hug her. "You always make us feel special."

"I'll take any of your unnecessary culinary bribery though," I tease.

Eddie laughs. "Don't let her fool you—she's been eating breakfast food for the last month straight."

"I'm not complaining."

Jane's phone buzzes. She glances at her text messages and frowns.

"What is it?" I say to her.

"Nothing," she replies, slipping her phone back in her purse. "Anyway, I'm not complaining either," she continues. "This meal was *amazing*."

"I'm glad you girls are okay with the change in plans," Mai says.

"Like Uncle Eddie said, we have Christmas. And any other weekend we want," I affirm. Regardless, Jane and I still have each other for the holiday. The two of us will never be alone.

JANE IS QUIET AS WE DRIVE HOME. I ASK HER IF IT'S ABOUT THE MYSTERIOUS text message, but she evades my question, saying she's just thinking about some errands she needs to take care of. We ride home without talking, covering the silence with the radio.

I check my own phone. Darcy hasn't texted me yet, but it hasn't been that long. I wonder if I should say something to him first. I want to, and we aren't playing games this time around, so I send him a picture of an awkward fat orange cat inserted into the Mona Lisa. His reply is almost instant.

How was brunch?

Good, I reply. *My very pregnant aunt made us a feast. I would show you a picture, but I don't want you to get jealous.*

Too late, he texts back. *I had Cheerios when I got home.*

Poor Darcy, I reply with a string of crying emojis.

Jane, perhaps noticing my attention to my phone, asks if I'm texting Darcy.

"Yeah," I reply absently.

"Did you guys happen to talk about me last night?" she asks hesitantly.

I shrug. "He asked how you were doing."

"Oh," she replies. She looks forward and stares at the stoplight.

"Is this about that mysterious text you got earlier?"

She grips the steering wheel. "It was Chip. He says he wants to talk to me."

"What?" I exclaim. "Are you serious?"

"What could have brought this on?" she asks as if I have the answers.

"I did mention you missed him at some point, but that wouldn't be enough to—"

"You told Darcy I missed Chip?" Jane interrupts.

"Not like that," I say. "I mentioned that the other job was hard on you and you missed Chip, but you're doing better now."

"So he only texted me because Darcy told him I'm no longer at the firm," she concludes.

"I don't know, Jane. I really don't. Darcy is coming over tonight, so maybe we can ask him what he said."

"I don't want to be jerked around," Jane declares fiercely. "I tried *so* hard to make it work with him."

"I know you did," I reply soothingly. I can see the glimmer of tears in Jane's eyes. I rub her shoulder.

"What did he want from me?" she says, her voice growing stronger. "For me to give up my career?"

"It wasn't fair," I say.

"It was selfish," she says, her expression resolute. The statement hangs in the air as we approach our apartment.

"So, will you ignore the text?"

Jane slumps after she turns off the car. "I don't know," she mutters. "I still have feelings for him. I can't help it."

"I know what you mean," I reply honestly. I can compare it to my...thing with Darcy, but how much more does Jane hurt having experienced a real, defined relationship with Chip—a relationship she had future plans for?

"I'll have to think about it," Jane says, shaking off her melancholy. "I hope you don't mind if I make myself scarce tonight. And"—she hesitates as if she feels guilty for asking—"can you guys not talk about me and Chip? Please?"

"You don't want to know what Darcy said?"

"I do," she replies. "But not till after I know my mind about this."

I nod in assent. I glance down at my phone with mixed feelings. I feel guilty interfering with Jane and guiltier still that the excitement of my text flirtation with Darcy can distract me from her pain.

I guess the reality is that Chip will be around as Darcy and I try dating. This thought casts a bittersweet twinge on my burgeoning happiness. If only Chip could get his act together then it would be perfect. If only.

Chapter Eighteen

Darcy arrives early. It doesn't take long for Jane to excuse herself, claiming she is reading up for a conflict-coaching seminar she's attending soon. After she leaves, I stand across from Darcy, awkward, wondering how we should start this conversation. It was easy enough to flirt and text about nothing all day long, but now that we're face to face, the reality of being on the precipice of this thing with him is dizzying.

"Um—"

"Have you—?"

We both start and then laugh.

"You first," I say.

"Have you eaten?" Darcy asks. "We could pick something up, maybe? It's starting to snow, but it's pretty light. It probably won't stick."

"Follow me," I reply, leading Darcy into the kitchen. I pull out a drawer of take-out menus. "Jane and I have been collecting these. Not all the good places let you order online."

Darcy stands close to me as we shuffle through the menus, and our shoulders inadvertently brush. My face is hot.

"How about this?"

Darcy holds out a menu, and I move closer to him to read it. I can't ignore how conscious I feel standing so close, no matter how innocent the contact. Every moment and whisper of skin holds both memory and possibility.

"Sure. We can walk there even."

As we walk out of my apartment building, Darcy reaches for my hand. We catch eyes and he smiles somewhat nervously. My pulse is racing, and I smile back, tightening our grasp. We walk hand-in-hand to a mom-and-pop burger joint around the corner.

In line, we laugh about the milkshake flavors and try to outdo one another with strange combinations. Hesitantly, he tucks my hair behind my ear when we talk. I rub my thumb over his knuckles in response, marveling over how easy it is to be with him.

When we reach my apartment again, we settle onto the couch to eat. Darcy glances at me, perhaps with the same thought I have: *we should talk, we should talk, we should talk.* Our knees are close enough to touch. An impulse—or habit, perhaps—urges me to lean over and kiss him. But I don't. I know if we start, we won't stop—even with Jane in the other room.

"So," I say earnestly.

"So," he repeats.

"I'm having a good time with you," I say. Darcy reaches to tuck my hair behind my ear.

"Me too." He pauses and then changes the subject. "I still can't get over the fact you're working for Diane," he says, shaking his head.

"Shows how much we really knew about each other before," I reply ruefully. "I didn't even know your mom was an artist."

"We know more about each other now," he says earnestly.

"Last night was the longest conversation we've ever had."

"I think it's the longest conversation I've ever had, period," Darcy agrees warmly. He has the greatest smile. I try not to let it distract me as I bring us back to the real reason why we're here, talking.

"I think we need to say what hasn't been said yet. I mean, we've never been good at being direct, have we? We should get it over with. Talk it out. I don't know how to say this without sounding awkward, so I will just sound… whatever," I babble, gesturing between us. "What we're doing—what's between…us. This is—"

"A second chance?" he finishes with a hint of anxiety in his expression.

"And you are—?"

"Taking it slow," he completes more confidently.

I laugh. "So what you're saying, in Mad Libs format, is that we have a second chance to take things slowly and do this right." I hesitate before addressing what's pressing against the potential of the moment and what threatens our fragile understanding. "With no baby talk. I'm only twenty-two,

Darcy. I'm not ready for that, with you or with anyone."

We both flinch, remembering that horrible argument.

"Lizzie…" He cradles my cheek. "I promise not to ask you for what you're not ready for. I'm still ashamed of that suggestion."

"I believe you," I say softly.

"Right now, let's just have long dates and good conversations. I want to learn everything about you."

"Me too," I say. "I've made up so much about you in my head that I need to replace with reality."

"Real is good," he says, and slowly, carefully, he leans forward to touch his lips to mine. It's so sweet, yet familiar and electric. I want to deepen the kiss, but I don't want to change the moment from what it is. Darcy pulls back gently, runs his thumb across my lips.

"I guess we'll have to get better about talking about things if we're going to try this out," I say carefully.

"You're right," he says firmly. "I know I assumed too much before. I was so caught up in it all, you know? I just wanted you so much and didn't want to lose you. I've never felt so…so passionate."

I glance up at him at this admission and see he's slightly flushed. I wonder if he's embarrassed.

In the spirit of being real, I say honestly, "The thing is, I didn't know you even liked me beyond sex. I thought that was all we were to each other."

"I can't tell you how much I regret that," he says with a frown. "How delusional was I? Thinking that we were dating when we never went anywhere with each other. I guess the time we spent together felt domestic, like we had skipped the dating bullshit and gone right into a relationship. It didn't even cross my mind that it could only seem like hooking up to you."

"The email you sent did help me understand you better," I admit. "But if we decide to, you know, *be* together, I need to *know* you."

"I promise to answer every question you ask me," he replies, seeming somewhat nervous. "And…I would love to introduce you to my sister when she comes home for Thanksgiving.

I look up at him, a smile playing across my lips. "Okay…I'd like that. If you're sure."

Darcy grins. "Absolutely," he says. "I know your sister, so you should meet mine."

I start to clean up, and Darcy follows me into the kitchen. He stands so close that it's hard to concentrate.

"Look," he says, indicating the window.

Outside, the snow is falling thickly now. I walk over to the window and glance down at the dusting on the sidewalk. Being from California, I've rarely seen snow. Likely, this will melt by tomorrow, but right now I appreciate the novelty. Darcy comes up behind me and leans his chin on my head while his arms wrap around my waist.

"I always have mixed feelings when it snows," he says quietly.

I turn around in the circle of his arms. "Because of your mom? And Geoff's parents?"

He nods, and his eyes drift to the window. "It's still beautiful, though. As long as I don't have to drive in it."

"I'm glad we're inside," I say. I lead him to the couch. He pulls me close.

"You're so cozy," he says, pressing his face to my shoulder. I make a noise in agreement and kiss his forehead. He lifts his face and kisses the corner of my mouth.

We're still not ready to go beyond chaste kisses. I think we can both feel it, and maybe we're both still a little gun shy, considering how things went before. In light of the falling snow, I suggest that he wait till morning to drive home. By unspoken agreement, we don't fully undress before going to sleep. I wear leggings and a sweatshirt and Darcy keeps on his jeans and undershirt. I hope he isn't too uncomfortable, but he doesn't seem to mind when he crawls into the bed and pulls me into an embrace. For the second time, I fall asleep in his arms. It feels more intimate than all that time we spent hooking up—and scarier. The vulnerability of hope.

I WAKE UP TO MY PHONE BUZZING ON MY BEDSIDE TABLE. GROGGILY, I reach over to silence it without picking up the call. It's probably a telemarketer from the east coast at this hour. I burrow back into the warm circle of Darcy's arms and start to drift off. Minutes later, my phone starts up again.

"Who keeps calling you?" Darcy says sleepily.

"Who knows." It's too cold outside of my covers, and I don't want to move but reluctantly decide to sit up and check my missed calls.

I glance at the screen and see six missed calls from an unknown number and a voicemail. I hit the button to check the message.

"Hey, Lizzie, it's Katrina." Her tone is urgent and panicked. "I hope you wake up soon…Lydia and I are detained at the police station in Capitol Hill. I'll explain more later. *Please* come and bring Lydia's meds. *Please hurry*."

I pull the phone away from my ear and stare at the screen in shock.

"Hey," Darcy says gently, touching my arm. "What is it?"

I wordlessly turn my speakerphone on and play the message again. He listens with a concerned expression.

"Why in the world are they detained?" I say after the message ends.

"Do you want me to drive you?" he asks worriedly. I glance outside at the snowy road and cringe.

"But the weather," I start to protest.

"I can handle it," he says confidently. "Your cousin needs her medication, right?"

Numbly, I nod and go to find a pair of jeans to change into. The phone buzzes again while I'm getting dressed.

"Hello?"

"Lizzie! Thank God!"

"Katrina!" I put my phone on speaker so I can put on my shoes. I look over at Darcy who's buttoning his shirt. "What's going on? You're in jail?"

"I can't even—it's been the worst—" she stammers tearfully. "So, what happened was we were all out at Bright Bay when Lydia and Geoff got into a drunk argument with Marianne and this gross guy she's been hooking up with. Geoff even broke the guy's nose! I tried to stop it, but they called the cops anyway, and they brought all of us in. I lost my purse, and I'm afraid Lydia will have a seizure if she doesn't take her meds soon. She's already missed a dose!"

"I'm coming, don't worry," I say soothingly. "I'm heading out right now."

"I don't know what we would do without you to help," Katrina replies, her voice shaking. "Please come quickly."

"I will," I say. I hang up and turn to a stern-faced Darcy.

"They're with Geoff?" he asks stonily.

I swallow and blink quickly. "I tried to warn them about him." I can feel the tears rising, and I'm so ashamed. I should have tried harder to convince Lydia. She may be headstrong, but she's like my younger sister. I *know* she knows I want the best for her.

"We should go," Darcy says without emotion.

We don't talk as we head to his car. I send Jane a quick text letting her know where I am and pray we get Lydia her meds in time.

We drive to Katrina and Lydia's apartment in silence. Once parked outside, I tell Darcy to wait, and I try not to skid on the ice as I hurry up the steps and fling open the door to their apartment. I barely pause to note the mess that litters the apartment as I rush to the bathroom to locate Lydia's meds. They're in the vanity where Katrina said they usually are, and I race back down to the waiting car.

Darcy drives in cold silence toward downtown. I can't tell if he's upset at me for letting my friends still hang out with scumbag Geoff, or if his ire is reserved for Geoff alone. Either way, I'm ashamed. We were in such a good place tonight, but I can only imagine he's now questioning why he'd want to be with me. I keep bringing Geoff back into his life in complicated and uncomfortable ways, and that's the last thing I want to remind him of. Oh God, I hope Lydia's okay. I feel so much guilt and worry that it's hard to keep my mind straight. I wish Darcy would say something. The longer he stays quiet, the more I feel I'm losing him. I know we said we would try and talk more openly, but his silence is increasing my fear. I blink back my tears and stare out the window. Jesus fucking Christ. At least Katrina knows how to hold Lydia if she does have a seizure. Worst case scenario, Katrina will keep Lydia safe. She has to.

The station is bustling with energy when we enter. I approach the front desk uncertainly, and Darcy follows behind me.

"Hi," I say nervously to the desk sergeant. "I'm here to see Katrina Mori and Lydia Phillips? I have Lydia's medication. She has epilepsy and has already missed a dose."

"We need a doctor's order to administer her medication," the sergeant says briskly.

"How do I do that?" I ask, my concern spiking. "She needs it now. Can we call someone? Her doctor, maybe?"

"One sec," the desk sergeant says, and she picks up the phone.

Darcy is still grave and silent. I wish I knew what he was thinking.

Another officer appears a moment later and asks if I would like to talk to Lydia and Katrina. I agree, and he leads me back to their holding cell, but Darcy doesn't follow. I turn around quickly to look at him, but he is talking to the desk sergeant. I hear a commotion as the officer and I approach the cells. The officer makes a call on his radio as he picks up his pace, and I struggle to keep up with him.

We arrive at a holding cell in chaos. Katrina is cradling Lydia's head while her limbs jerk wildly. A smear of blood streaks the knee of Katrina's jeans.

"She hit her head," Katrina says with wide eyes. She turns her head toward the officer. "She needs to go to the hospital. Please!"

"Someone is on the way," the officer replies crisply. I'm gripping Lydia's pills, unsure what to do as her jerking slows to a stop. Katrina strokes her head and whispers soothing words. Lydia emits a low groan as she comes out of her trance-like state, turns on her side, and vomits. The rest of the women in the cell start to curse at her, and I stare transfixed at the scene, unsure what to do.

"We're transferring her to Swedish," the officer says. "You two can meet her there. We are releasing you, Ms. Mori, and Ms. Phillips as well. We have some paperwork for you to complete before you can go. Ms. Phillips can complete hers once she's released from the hospital."

We follow the stretcher out as they transfer Lydia to a waiting ambulance. Katrina sniffles next to me.

"How did you get here?" she asks. We both know my crappy car wouldn't be able to handle the snow.

"Darcy," I say absently. "He's still out front, I think."

I'm led to the front waiting room while Katrina is taken back for paperwork. Darcy isn't there, and I turn around, wondering where he could be.

"Your friend went back to see Geoff Whitney," the desk sergeant tells me.

I slump into a plastic chair and pull out my phone. The florescent lights sting my eyes.

Lydia had a seizure and hit her head. She was taken to the hospital, I text Darcy.

A few minutes later, he emerges with an officer I don't recognize. He walks straight over to me and sits down.

"Is she okay?" he asks.

I shrug miserably. "We're supposed to meet her there. They let both girls go."

"I'll take you, but then I have to come back here. There are things to take care of," he says grimly.

I nod and feel my eyes start to brim. He cups my cheek and kisses my forehead lightly.

"I'm sure she'll be okay," he says softly.

I am ashamed at the moment because all I can think about is how my irresponsible cousin ruined my time with Darcy. I'm in danger of resenting her for it, but I also feel guilty that I'm upset with her. She has a head injury, for God's sake. But I hate that Darcy and I are sitting in this dirty, artificially lit police station instead of lying in my bed, and Darcy keeps looking at me with an inscrutable expression that makes me desperately uneasy instead of the sweet, hopeful one he gave me earlier.

Katrina joins us a moment later, and Darcy leads us to his car. The car is silent on the way to the hospital. Darcy pulls up to the emergency door, and Katrina exits when I tell her I'll meet her inside.

Darcy looks as uncertain as I feel. I reach out for him tentatively then pause and let my hand fall away.

"I'll let you know when we hear news," I whisper. I want to beg him to stay, tell him that I need him with me, that all I want is his comfort, and that I don't want him to go. But he draws his lips in a thin line and nods.

Then he reaches over and pulls me into a long desperate kiss that is in no way comforting. It almost feels like goodbye. I pull back to search his face, but his expression is unreadable.

"I'll call you later," he says, and I nod.

"Bye," I say weakly.

Chapter Nineteen

find Katrina sitting in the waiting area of the emergency room, staring at her shoes.

"They won't let anyone go back yet," she tells me when I take a seat beside her.

Seattle doesn't do well with snow, and the packed waiting room shows it. Thankfully, it stopped snowing sometime during the night. The roads, however, are still frozen and are apparently treacherous, according to the TV droning in the corner. I press my eyes closed and hope that Darcy doesn't encounter anything dangerous while he's driving.

I'm not sure what to say. Katrina absently swings her leg and knots her fingers, her expression taut as a rubber band about to snap. I understand the feeling of anxiety but try not to show it. As long as Lydia's safe, it will all be fine. I realize I should call Aunt Penny and Uncle Rob, but reason it's too early. Then I snap out of it and realize they need to know what's going on right now.

It takes a few rings before Aunt Penny picks up. I must have woken her, and I feel vaguely guilty for making a call no parent wants to get in the middle of the night.

"Hello?" she says sleepily.

"Aunt Penny, it's Lizzie," I say. "I, um…Lydia is in the hospital. She hit her head, but I think she's okay."

"Lyddie's hurt?" Aunt Penny asks. I can hear the panic rising in her voice. "Why hasn't the hospital called us yet?"

"We just got here. They'll probably call you soon, but I thought you would want to know—"

"Yes! Yes, thanks for calling. I'll have Rob get us plane tickets. Do Eddie and Mai know? Am I the first person you called?"

"Yeah, I haven't talked—"

"Check in with me after you see her, will you? Oh, my poor baby," she wails. "Which hospital are you at? What happened? Give me all the details you can!"

I have to take a moment to breathe after I hang up with Penny. I think I've been acting on autopilot since Katrina's call and doing what needs to be done. Talking to my aunt makes this feel a lot more real. I wish Darcy were here. I glance at my phone and don't see any texts or missed calls. Not that I expected any. If Darcy is stuck taking care of that tool Geoff, I imagine he'll have a lot of crap to deal with after he leaves the police station.

I don't know what to do with myself while we wait. I pick up a year-old *Celebrity* magazine and flip through the pages absently. My eyes catch on an article titled "Inside the Met Gala," and I pause when I see a familiar face among the famous. The caption reads: *Chloe Fairchild in Christian Dior, Fitzwilliam Darcy, and Jay Zimmerman.* I stare.

Most of the time I forget that Darcy has these connections and that he's well known because of his father. True, his presence appears unremarkable next to the mumblecore indie darlings Chloe Fairchild and Jay Zimmerman, but I'm suddenly reminded how far apart our worlds can be. These are the types of acquaintances he has.

I close the magazine and toss it on the table.

"I wonder when we can go see Lydia," Katrina says anxiously. She picks up the magazine I discarded and flips through the pages.

"Hey, look!" she says, indicating the picture of Darcy.

"I just saw that."

"Sometimes I forget how well known he is with how Geoff talks about him."

"I don't want to hear about Geoff," I grumble.

"What's wrong with Geoff?"

"Are you kidding me?" I stare back at Katrina's innocent eyes. She's way too trusting. I shake my head. "Can you honestly say he isn't the reason we're in this mess?"

Katrina slumps. "Lydia loves him," she says weakly.

"He's not worth it," I shoot back.

We wait around for another half hour, and the sun continues to crawl across the sky. The city comes to life outside with people wandering up and down the sidewalk. The snow is melting now, causing rivulets of water to stream down the pavement.

"Want to find coffee?" I ask Katrina. She agrees, and we follow the signs in the hospital toward the entrance where we locate a coffee cart with a discouragingly long line. I glance at my phone. Still nothing.

I hope everything's okay, I text Darcy.

"So, are you, like, *with* Darcy now?" Katrina asks while we wait in line.

"I think so," I say, feeling odd. We decided we were starting over last night, but this morning I'm feeling so insecure I wonder if it's actually real.

"Since when?"

I shrug. "It's new. We're not official or anything yet. Last night was only our first—or maybe second—date, if you could call it that."

"Jesus, really? Thanks for answering my calls. I probably would have ignored them."

"I'm glad I didn't," I say as we reach the front of the line. I order a huge Americano and try not to think about Darcy.

Katrina checks back in with the receptionist when we get back to the waiting room and asks if we can see Lydia yet. I sip my coffee and watch another pair of people sitting in our vacated seats. A girl slouches with her shoeless foot propped on a chair reading the *Celebrity* magazine. I shift my feet uncomfortably.

Five minutes later, a nurse brings us to a small examination room. Lydia is pale, hooked up to an IV with a large bandage around her head. She is gazing blankly at the wall but turns and smiles wanly when we enter.

"They said they want to observe me," she says hoarsely. "You never know with head injuries."

It's shocking to see Lydia this way—so solemn and still. I'm used to her exuberance, her overwhelming nature. There is no familiar grin gracing her features, just a vacant, resigned expression.

Katrina quickly pulls a chair close to her bedside. "I'm so glad you're okay," she says tearfully. I blink back my own tears but try to remain strong. I've seen Lydia have seizures before, but she's never hurt herself like this. I pull another chair up close to her and reach for her hand.

"Did you call my parents?" Lydia replies dully. I nod. "Thought so," Lydia mumbles. Her hand sits limply under mine. Next to me, Katrina absently rubs the blood streak on her jeans. Lydia watches the movement and grimaces.

I'm not sure what to say, so I stupidly ask Lydia how she's feeling.

"Tired. Sore." Then she adds, "I hope Geoff is okay."

"We left him with Darcy," Katrina says, glancing at me for help.

"Fat lot of good that will do him," Lydia grumbles.

"Darcy came with me," I reply sharply. I produce Lydia's medication and set it on a nearby tray table. Lydia looks confused.

"Lizzie and Darcy are dating," Katrina explains.

"Oh," Lydia says, looking away from me. "To each their own, I guess."

Her flat tone hurts. I mean, if she loves Geoff and believes the lies he's been telling her about him, I can see *why* she wouldn't like Darcy, but it still rankles. I should have tried to talk to her more about Geoff's selfishness and how dangerous he could be. Maybe I could have convinced her to dump him before all this happened. My throat burns in guilt and disappointment.

"I should call Jane and Eddie and Mai," I say. Lydia frowns but doesn't reply. "Maybe we can bring some stuff for you—your own pillow or something to read if it doesn't bother your head?"

Lydia stares dazedly at the wall again and then looks at me with unfocused eyes. "Can you bring back Blankie?" Her youth and her fear are apparent in that request. I promise to be back soon.

I quickly walk back to the waiting room, anxious to get everything for Lydia and to talk to Darcy. I call him to check in, but it goes straight to voicemail.

"Hey, it's me," I say. "Lydia is okay, so I'm heading home for a bit. Call me later? When you're done with Geoff, I guess? I hope you're doing all right. It's been a rough night…" I swallow thickly. "I, uh, I can't wait to see you."

I hang up quickly and then call Jane.

"Lizzie?" she says groggily.

"Jane! Did you see my text?"

"No, you woke me up."

"Listen, everything is fine. It's kind of a long story, but I'm at the Swedish Hospital on First Hill with Lydia. She had a seizure and hit her head, so she's under observation, but she's fine. Everything is…fine."

"Lydia hit her head?" Jane repeats, more awake.

"I'm taking an Uber home, and then we can bring her some stuff, okay?

She asked for her Blankie, and I thought we could bring her some magazines or something."

"Text me a list," Jane replies, sounding much more in control than I feel. "I can bring her things. You sit with Lydia till I get there, and then go home to rest."

"I don't mind…" I say, aware that the occupation of taking care of Lydia will relieve my anxiety.

"I want to help, Lizzie," Jane says. "Have you called Eddie and Mai yet? They'll want to know."

"Just Aunt Penny." I'm starting to feel tired when I recall all that's happened so far this morning. "I think she and Rob are looking for plane tickets."

"Listen, just sit with Lydia till I can get there, and send me a list. I'll be there as soon as I can."

"But Jane, how will you get into their apartment? I have their spare key with me."

"I'll come by and get it then," she says firmly. "Leave it to me."

I call Uncle Eddie then return to Lydia's room. She's listening to Katrina talk about one of their friends from school who just got a bad haircut. Lydia doesn't really respond with much interest. I scoot up my chair close to her and let her know Jane will bring Blankie soon.

"Lizzie…" Lydia hesitates and plays with her hospital bracelet. "Have you heard from Darcy at all since we left the police station? I'm just wondering how Geoff is doing." She fixes her large blue eyes on me imploringly.

"I haven't yet, but I'm sure I will soon," I reply soothingly. Inside, I'm not so sure. The morning is growing later, and I haven't had so much as a text from Darcy. I mean, I know he was taking care of legal stuff, but he hasn't even let me know he's all right. I wonder how he's handling driving in the snow.

After stopping by to get the key and going to get Lydia's stuff, Jane replaces me an hour and a half later. I decide to call an Uber even though she offered to let me drive her car home. I'm feeling too overcome to drive right now, let alone on unsalted slushy roads.

ONCE I GET HOME, I HEAD STRAIGHT BACK TO MY ROOM AND COLLAPSE, exhausted, onto the bed. I pull the pillow Darcy used close then numbly stare at the ceiling until I drift off to sleep.

I wake up hours later, and still there's nothing from Darcy.

I wonder if I should check in with Freddy. What if something happened to Darcy in the snow? What could he be doing?

Why won't he just call me?

After an internal debate that goes on a little too long, I tell myself to suck it up and just call him again. After last night and the talk we had, he can't just suddenly reject me, right? That's not him. And if the phone rings again and doesn't go straight to voicemail, it probably just means he's stuck in some legalish meeting. He's safe, I assure myself.

I scroll to his number and press call again.

It rings once and then I hear a hushed "Lizzie" on the other end. I sit up quickly and a wave of vertigo hits me.

"Darcy!" I exclaim. "Oh my God, I've been so worried!"

"Sorry," he whispers back. "I'm at my lawyer's. Hang on—" I hear a rustling, and a moment later he says my name again but at a normal volume.

"You should have texted me, just so I'd know you're alive. Are you okay? Where have you been?" I know I sound frantic, but I can't help it. I've been holding this in all day.

"I'm sorry, Lizzie. I had to arrange details with my lawyer and Geoff's parole officer…this whole day has been a mess. And"—he hesitates—"I thought you needed time with your cousin."

"That doesn't mean I don't want you to check in. I was so worried that something had happened to you!"

"Oh God, I'm *so* sorry, Lizzie—"

I exhale and rub the heel of my hand against my throbbing eyes. Remorse creeps in; it sounds like he had a worse day than I did. "When do you think you'll be done?" I ask, softening my tone.

"I'm not sure yet," he replies. "We haven't decided whether I'm going to post bail for him or not. If I do, I'll probably have to take Geoff to my place to keep an eye on him." The sigh that follows is wrapped in infinite disappointment, and I wonder how much more of Geoff Whitney Darcy can take.

"You'll let me know when you're done, right?" I say gently.

"If you want me to," he replies.

"I do. I do want you to. Call me when you're done. I think we could both use each other's company."

"Okay."

"Good luck. And I'm sorry too. I shouldn't have gotten so crazy."

"Thanks," he replies. He pauses and then says, "I'll see you soon. I promise."

"You better," I tease.

We hang up, and I throw myself back on my pillows in frustrated relief. He doesn't hate me. He really is taking care of things with Geoff. I only wish he were here now to assure me that everything is going to be okay.

I MAKE MYSELF MORE COFFEE AFTER I FINALLY SHOWER AND DRESS FOR THE day. I spend the afternoon distracting myself on the internet when a turn of the lock and the jingle of Jane's keys causes me to jump.

"How's Lydia?" I ask immediately, forgetting to greet her as she walks through the door.

"Better, I think. Eddie and Mai are with her now. The hospital is scheduling some tests for tomorrow after Penny and Rob get here. It seems like her seizures have been getting worse, so she's been referred to a specialist."

"Probably for the best," I reply.

"I wish it didn't come to this, but…maybe Lydia needs to be home for a while. Aunt Penny makes her take care of herself." She hesitates for a second. "Lizzie, when you see Darcy next, will you thank him for us?"

"Sure." My throat constricts, and I swallow.

"Not just for helping this morning," Jane continues. "For calling his uncle too."

"What do you mean?" I reply, confused. "What about his uncle?"

Jane looks surprised. "Oh, I thought you knew!" she exclaims. "His uncle, Dr. Fitzwilliam, is a neurologist. He's the specialist Lydia was referred to. He came to the hospital today because Darcy called him."

"He didn't mention it," I say, thinking back on our earlier conversation. He didn't even allude to it. I wonder why he didn't tell me? I can't help but feel amazed at everything he's done for my family today. God, I want to see him right now. My eyes burn with tears; I can't believe how generous he is. Here I was annoyed that I hadn't heard from him, and all that time, he was taking care of my wayward cousin. It's hard to believe I deserve him.

THE CUT OF LIGHT THAT STREAMS INTO MY ROOM ROUSES ME. I ROLL OVER on my side and see it's Darcy. He's still in his clothes from last night. He sits on the edge of my bed and looks down at me, his features etched in exhaustion.

"Hey," he says softly. "Jane let me in."

"No bail?"

He shakes his head. "Not this time." He rubs his eyes and drops his hand dejectedly. "I'm so sick of his bullshit," he whispers. I sit up and draw his jacket off his arms. He shrugs it off and turns around to face me.

"Lizzie, I'm sorry—I'm not used to—I figured it would be easier if I kept my distance while you were taking care of your cousin."

"You are so stupid," I say, leaning in and kissing him lightly. "But I forgive you. It sounds like you really saved the day. Although, next time, keep me informed. And maybe let me help." I wonder if he will bring up his uncle so I can thank him. Maybe I should bring it up.

He looks at me softly and strokes my cheek. He holds my gaze in unspoken admiration. I feel myself blush and lean in to kiss him again. Darcy pulls back and kicks off his shoes.

"C'mere," he says. He lies down and pulls me against his chest. I can feel him breathing against my hair, his body molded against mine in a tight spoon.

"What am I going to do with you?" I say, rubbing my thumb over his knuckles.

"Keep me, I hope," he sleepily replies in my ear.

Like there's any doubt.

DARCY AND I LIE IN BED FOR HOURS THAT AFTERNOON—SOMETIMES SLEEPing, sometimes talking, always touching. He tells me about his awful day and how painful it was to see Geoff, who didn't even seem to care that Darcy was trying to help him.

"Why do you do it? Why bother when he doesn't appreciate it?" I ask. I trail my fingers up and down his arm, and he breathes into my hair.

"He's my responsibility," Darcy replies stoically. I shift to my side so I can make eye contact with him.

"No, he isn't. He's his own responsibility."

"But I've protected him from trouble for so long. I never let him learn his lesson. And your cousin—I hope everything goes okay for Lydia."

"I would say you've done your duty and more, at this point. Lydia is lucky you called your uncle on her behalf. Jane told me," I say before he can interrupt me. "Thank you."

"It's the least I could do," he says seriously. "When I called my uncle,

I wasn't thinking of Lydia; I was thinking of you. I wanted to relieve your worry."

I laugh humorlessly. "Oh, the irony. While you were doing that, I was nearly hysterical with worry for you," I say wryly. "Proof of my unpredictability, I guess."

He looks at me intently. "Most of the time, your unpredictability is a pleasant surprise. You'll say something or do something I don't expect, but it's a breath of fresh air." I feel myself flush and he continues, "I wish I could have guessed you would be upset though."

"I think," I start slowly, "that we have a bad habit of assuming what the other person is thinking." I can see it clearly now, how Darcy came to his conclusion and tried to work in my best interest. It probably worked well for him in the past with the people he's known his whole life to just jump into action to help them. But I am someone new. *We* are something new.

His mouth twists in an ironic smile. "That has seemed to get us into trouble before."

"So, we will try to do better at it then? Asking or telling each other what we want?"

"That's probably the smartest approach."

"And...you want to try? With me? With us?"

"Yes," he states matter-of-factly.

"Good," I say snuggling closer to him. "Because I like being with you. In fact, I love it."

And I love you. The realization isn't as surprising as I thought it would be. I guess it's been coming on so gradually that I hardly know when it began. And this situation, this emergency, nudged it to the forefront of my mind. I touch his cheek softly. He smiles at me then, erasing all the weariness in his expression. I beam back at him.

"What's going on in there?" He taps my head gently.

"Nothing really. I'm just relieved. And happy to be with you."

"Me too."

They're the best, most honest words we've said.

Chapter Twenty

Darcy and I text constantly now—about the most mundane things, really, but I can't help what my face does whenever I get a message from him. Sometimes he sends me weird observations from around town.

A lady tried to sell me a shoplifted dress today. I told her it wasn't my style.

Not fancy enough for you? I respond, grinning stupidly at my screen.

You know me, he replies. *I can't accept anything less than a full ball gown.*

I appreciate his wry jokes and remember how dry his sense of humor was even at the cabin. It's almost like I forgot who he was when we were caught up in the fog of sex. Or maybe I just didn't really know him till now.

It's a standard overcast Seattle day today, but the clouds are gathered in ominous dark puff balls, not the standard watercolor grey cover I've grown used to. It's Ashley's last day of work, and Diane wants to take her to lunch with all the employees.

I snap a picture of the sky on our way to the sushi place around the corner. It looks like there's a face in the clouds.

The face of God? I text to Darcy along with the picture. *Or some alien observer?*

"Hey, space cadet!" Ashley says, tapping my shoulder. "We're here."

I quickly slip my phone into my purse and follow the rest of the group in.

Along with Diane, there are four other curators in the gallery. Theodore, a dapper gentleman with a large assortment of bow ties, is the newest of the bunch, hired two years ago. Rosa and Danielle were hired around the same time, in the early 2000s, to contribute to the then-expanding gallery.

Marjorie, however, has been with the gallery almost as long as Diane. She's in her early sixties, a little reclusive but brilliant. Diane has mentioned offhand that Marjorie will probably retire in the next five years. I take this as a suggestion to get myself ready to curate by then. At least, I hope that's what she's suggesting.

Ashley shares the details of her new position in New York as assistant to a smallish upscale fashion designer. My phone buzzes again, and I check it.

Creepy. I hope it's not the all-seeing eye of the Illuminati. You're not in on any conspiracies, are you?

I feel the corners of my mouth turning up when I text back.

Who, me? I'm as innocent as a lamb.

"Who do you keep texting?" Ashley asks when there's a lull in the conversation.

"No one," I say quickly, slipping my phone into my purse again.

"Yeah, right," she teases. "You are *so* infatuated."

"Oooo, it's a boy!" Danielle says excitedly. "Let me live vicariously through you. I haven't dated in ten years."

"Who is he?" Rosa prods. I wrinkle my brow and glance around the table. Diane watches me with serene interest. Danielle looks desperate for details.

"Um, just this guy," I say. "We sort of dated before and we're trying again. That's all."

"What's his name?" Danielle asks eagerly. I shift uncomfortably. They all know who Darcy is, and I can't help but feel embarrassed. I look over at Ashley with a silent plea for her intervention.

"Oh my God," Ashley says with dawning comprehension. She looks around the table in conspiracy. "I know who it is. Unbelievable!"

"Ashley…" I start, but she's no help. She looks at the group smugly.

"Lizzie here is holding out on us. Our new girl is dating Fitzwilliam Darcy."

The group stares at me in disbelief. Danielle mutters "holy shit" under her breath. Rosa elbows her to stay quiet.

I swallow. "I—um, he showed me his mom's art a few weeks ago," I say, desperate to change the subject. "It's beautiful. Did she ever show at the gallery?"

Diane appraises me for a moment and then nods her head at Marjorie. "She was Marjorie's first acquisition," she says. "Back in '78." Her expression is neutral, and I wonder if she's considering whether I'm good enough for

Darcy. I catch a knowing gleam in her eye and exhale the breath I didn't know I was holding. Theodore leans in toward me.

"She's got her eye on you now," he warns with a wink.

Even though Darcy and I are gradually becoming more comfortable with our budding relationship, I still occasionally question what's actually going on between us. Like the other night, when we went out and afterwards had our first make-out session since we started over. I think he felt as nervous as I did about going too far too fast. We're probably both in danger of overthinking this. It was the most awkward we've been with each other, complete with hitting our teeth together and too much space between our bodies to be comfortable. I guess we're due for a talk. He's all but said the words that he's committed to me, and I've implied the same, but neither of us has felt brave enough to broach the subject. This subtle uncertainty is probably why I feel jittery as I wait for Darcy and his sister at the coffee shop on Saturday morning.

I've chosen an armchair in the corner by a large picture window so I can people watch. I sip my large latte carefully; it's still hot enough to burn my tongue.

I've barely gotten comfortable when I see Darcy enter with a teenage girl in tow. I wave in greeting, and he nods in response as they make their way to my corner. Seeing Darcy with Georgie is almost striking. They are both tall and lean with a similar aquiline nose. But where his features look handsome and defined, hers are sharp and athletic. Georgie is tall and almost boyishly built with angular features and bluntly bobbed dark hair that makes her neck appear even longer than it is. Despite her androgynous features, she is dressed in stylish jeans and a feminine chiffon blouse. Her handbag is large and designer. She looks like she should be at Fashion Week.

I rise as they approach, and Darcy kisses my cheek. I blush and look at Georgie. She catches my eye, smiles, and looks at her feet.

"Lizzie, this is my sister. Georgie, this is Lizzie." Darcy is clearly anxious and hopeful for a friendship to flourish between us.

"It's so nice to meet you," Georgie says in a sweet, soft voice.

"You too!" I reply cheerily. I reach out to pull her over to the chair across from me. She looks back at Darcy in amused alarm and sits down.

"Let me get drinks," Darcy says. "You want anything else?" He indicates my latte. I shake my head and wink at him.

"So, when did you get into town?" I ask Georgie while we wait for Darcy to rejoin us.

"Actually, we just came straight from the airport."

"Seriously?" I glance over at Darcy at the register. "I hope you aren't too tired!"

"I'm fine," she says quietly before chewing her lip. It's clear to me that Georgie is incredibly shy. She keeps peeking over at Darcy and looks relieved when he returns with coffees.

"You dragged your sister here from the airport!" I exclaim when he settles into an empty armchair.

Darcy shrugs, looking sheepish. "Georgie was excited to meet you."

A deep blush blooms on Georgie's cheeks, and she smacks Darcy's arm. "Will!" she exclaims. Then she looks at me almost apologetically. "I've heard a lot about you."

"Really?" It's my turn to feel embarrassed, but I try to rise above it. "Well, now we can both satisfy our curiosities."

A small glance of understanding passes between us, an acknowledgment of our eagerness to be friends.

I ask Georgie about her art and mention my position at D.B. Shaw. Darcy contributes here and there but is generally satisfied to sit back and listen.

"How long are you in town for?" I ask Georgie when we've exhausted the topic of thrift-store kitsch art.

"Till Saturday. Oh! We should go to the Antique Mall if you aren't too busy," she says, her animation growing. "They have great weird stuff."

"That sounds fun," I reply enthusiastically. "Jane, my sister, and I are pretty free this week."

"Oh?" Georgie replies. "What are your Thanksgiving plans?"

I shrug and laugh. "Microwave turkey dinners and reality TV? We'd go to my aunt and uncle's, but they're out of town."

Georgie turns a pleading expression on Darcy, her large brown eyes puppy-dog round.

He rolls his eyes and shakes his head. "You don't have to look at me like that, Georgie." He turns to me. "I was going to ask if you and Jane would like to come to our family's for dinner. If you want to, that is."

I hesitate. "Are you sure it wouldn't be an imposition?"

"Of course not!" Georgie exclaims.

"I would love for you to come," Darcy says seriously.

"I'll ask Jane," I say.

Earl and Vivian Fitzwilliam live deep in Sammamish, an area in the Seattle suburbs that feels rural with its long spans of evergreens interrupted only by the occasional field or horse in pasture.

"Are you sure we're going the right way?" Jane asks, glancing down at the route on her phone.

I pick up her phone. "Yeah, unless Google is leading us on a merry chase."

"This is really out there."

"Only forty-five minutes," I qualify. I haven't been able to voice to Jane how nervous I am to spend the holiday with Darcy's family. It feels like a big step for a relationship that is just "starting over."

We continue to drive on, scanning the unfamiliar terrain till the voice from the map app jars us. *In one and a half miles, turn right.*

We take a few more confusing turns until we emerge from a wooded lane to find an iron gate. Behind it stands a wide stone mansion, almost like a modern lodge, with crisp manicured hedges offset by rugged boulders and massive evergreens.

"It looks like 'Alone in the Wilderness' for rich people," I remark as we edge toward the gate

"Do we just drive up?" Jane looks at me nervously.

"Looks like it."

Jane approaches the buzzer and says, "Um, hi, it's Jane and Lizzie Venetidis. Darcy's friends?"

The reply is almost instant. "Welcome! Park anywhere in the east driveway," a friendly female voice says.

Jane and I exchange another glance and then roll down the pristine pavement to the east driveway; we consult the compass on the phone to make sure we're right. I'm relieved when I see Darcy's Tesla among the other line of cars.

"How do I look?" I ask when I emerge from the car. I smooth my palms down the front of my velvet skirt.

"Perfect," Jane assures me.

We are greeted by a beaming older woman who immediately reaches to embrace us and introduces herself as Vivian Fitzwilliam. "I feel like I know you girls already!" she says. "From Fitzwilliam, and, you know, Chip on occasion. Come, come sit with us! The boys are watching football, so you can visit with the ladies!"

She leads us through the marble entry, through the kitchen, to an attached open-concept sitting room. I notice Cathy de Boer perched on a chair, drinking a white wine, and smile in recognition. She barely acknowledges me and takes another sip. I guess she doesn't remember me.

Georgie has an apron on, and she is chopping vegetables with another woman I don't recognize.

"Hi Georgie," I exclaim, making my way toward her. Georgie looks like she doesn't know what to do with her knife and then awkwardly sets it down. I give her a sincere but slightly uncomfortable hug. "Georgie, this is my sister Jane. Jane, Georgie."

"And you already know Cathy, Lizzie; but Jane, meet Earl's sister. And this is Marissa, Vince's wife."

I'm surprised Vivian knows about the connection between Cathy and me considering Cathy's non-greeting. Jane and I exchange pleasantries with the rest of the group.

Vivian directs us where to put our things and offers us wine. We engage in small talk about the weather, the drive out, and our families' plans for the holidays among other things. We've been chatting for a few minutes when Cathy joins the conversation.

"So, Lizzie, was it? You were one of those girls Colin wanted my company to hire for our latest project if I remember correctly."

Surprised, I turn toward her. I assume a confident expression and glance around the room. "Yes, he recommended my friend Charlotte and me. We had both recently graduated and were looking to do something more than make coffee."

Cathy sniffs, and I hear her murmur "quite young" under her breath.

"Was my Freddy your supervisor, then?" Vivian asks, glossing over any tension in the room.

"He was! We became pretty good friends, actually."

"You have a lot of *friends*, don't you?" Cathy replies coolly. She sizes me up, and I feel my cheeks start to heat.

"I'd like to think so," I reply evenly.

"Colin, Freddy, and…Fitzwilliam. But Fitzwilliam invited you."

"I invited them," Georgie interrupts softly. All eyes turn to her, and she looks at Vivian awkwardly. "I, um, they didn't have any place to go."

"And the more the merrier, I say," Vivian concludes. "Georgie, why don't you let your brother know his guests are here?"

Georgie departs, cheeks flushed, and leaves us to the awkward silence. I take a generous sip of wine.

"So," Vivian says with forced cheer, "what are you doing now that you're no longer at Rose & Hunts?"

This leads to a discussion about D. B. Shaw and Diane Reynolds. We are just about to talk about my art history degree when Darcy enters, Freddy in tow.

"Lizzie!" Freddy exclaims. He hugs me and then tousles my hair. I roll my eyes, and he moves on to introduce himself to Jane. Darcy catches my eye.

"Hey," he says quietly.

"Hey."

He reaches for me, and his touch is so warm and distracting that I barely remember where I am.

"I'm glad you made it," he says.

"Me too," I reply.

I feel the shroud of our own little world around us, remembering the date Darcy took me on last night. At first, we had decided we were going to wait till today to see each other, but then we were both texting and watching TV separately when I mentioned I couldn't wait to see him.

Me either, he replied. And then, after a minute, he texted: *Why don't we get dinner?*

He took me out to a kitchsy Italian restaurant in Wallingford, and we shared a carafe of wine. Later, after he took me home, we ended up making out far longer than we intended. When I felt his fingers skim the sensitive skin of my stomach, I pulled back abruptly.

"Sorry," he said, panting. We could both feel the danger of losing ourselves fully to the moment. We still hadn't defined the pace of our new relationship except that we were "taking it slow." I sat up and smoothed my hair.

"I—I guess we should talk about how long we want to wait until we—" I gestured between us.

Darcy smiled ruefully. "Right now, you could say almost anything to convince me not to wait, but—"

"—we're still getting to know each other," I finished for him.

"Exactly," he agreed.

"I don't think it needs a timeline," I said slowly. "But maybe let's talk about it beforehand? Like, make sure we both feel ready? I don't want to make the same mistakes we did last time."

He decided to leave shortly after that, but not without a long kiss by the front door. It's easy to be caught up in how soft his lips are and how great it will be when we both feel ready to take our relationship to the next level.

Staring at him, I'm struck with how I love just to be around him. His thumbs skim my knuckles and I long to curl into him—to finish what we started last night. He searches my face and smoothes my hair behind my ear. We're being *that* couple, the kind who can't look at anyone else, and yet I can't bring myself to be bothered by it.

"Lizzie, you gotta see this," Freddy says, interrupting our spell. "My dad and Vince are deep-frying the turkey this year."

He leads us to the back of the house then downstairs through a large wood-paneled TV room with a pool table to a back patio. In the center of the backyard, we watch as an older man in a chili-pepper apron and black rubber gloves slowly pulls a turkey out of a large metal pot—Doctor Fitzwilliam, I assume. A younger man, who must be Vince, checks the temperature. They let the turkey hang for a while, shaking off the excess oil. Darcy slips his arm around my waist.

"Dad loves to show off," Freddy remarks. "Be sure to tell him how delicious it is."

I absently rub Darcy's back but continue to watch the two men as they carefully transport the turkey to a paper towel-lined pan.

"Deep-fried turkey will be a first for me," Jane remarks.

"I bet Dad will make Vince dispose of the oil. He knows how much Vince hates doing that," Freddy says.

Darcy snorts. "And other dirty work," he adds sarcastically.

We all turn back to the house when Freddy says he wants to see the football score.

"So, you've been watching the game while the women cook upstairs," I say, glancing from Darcy to Freddy. "How *typical*."

"The older Fitzwilliams haven't gotten over traditional gender roles." Freddy winks. "But we can stay out of that generation's hair for a while."

"We should find a way to rescue Georgie," Darcy adds as we reenter the house.

Freddy motions for us to follow him up to a wet bar. He nods to Jane with a grin. "What's your poison?" he asks her affably.

She laughs. "Whatever you make best."

Darcy draws me away from the wet bar, just so we're slightly out of earshot.

"I don't think we have pink wine on hand," he says softly.

"I'll survive."

We sit down on the couch and wait for Jane and Freddy to bring drinks over. Darcy's arm is draped around me, and at this moment, I want to exhale in relief and pleasure. Never in my life has something felt so *right*. We all end up staying out of the way in the downstairs sitting room until we're called to dinner. Georgie joins us under the pretense of helping her Uncle Earl with the turkey. The five of us are easy company; Jane seems comfortable, and Georgie is more animated than she's ever been before around me.

"So this is where the fun crowd has disappeared to," Marissa says as she comes in with an expression of mock annoyance. "Dinner's ready."

We follow Marissa upstairs to the formal dining room, elegantly arranged with a large spread of food interspersed with autumnal flower centerpieces. The lights are low, and the room glows. I take a seat between Jane and Darcy. Darcy grasps my hand under the table, and I catch his eye warmly.

Cathy, it seems, has decided to place herself directly across from me. She watches my interaction with Darcy with pursed lips. I wish I knew why she doesn't like me.

Despite Cathy's disconcerting attention, I find myself enjoying Thanksgiving with the Fitzwilliams. Darcy and I can barely stop ourselves from touching each other, whether it be the small touch of an arm or sitting close enough that our legs press against the other's. We are on the precipice of this understanding; I feel it so certainly. The next time we are alone, we will hash it all out: what we are to each other, what we want right now and in the future…all those important adult things you discuss when entering a romantic relationship. In high school, we called this the DTR—the "define the relationship" talk. Once the DTR was complete, you could proudly call your crush "boyfriend." This is what we will be to each other soon, I realize. Boyfriend and girlfriend. Lizzie and Darcy. A defined couple.

This understanding produces a mixture of anxiety and anticipation that, despite my confidence in the outcome, causes an unsettled swoop of nerves that almost makes me dizzy. I reach for my drink to settle myself and accidentally knock it over.

"Oh!"

"Lizzie, your skirt!" Jane exclaims.

Red wine drips down the table and pools onto my lap. The deep color seeps into the cranberry-colored fabric. I glance around for a paper napkin instead of the finely folded cloth ones Vivian has put out.

"I don't want to ruin your rug—" I glance around the table, and Darcy leaps up.

"Paper towels," he declares before briskly walking from the room.

Jane is examining my skirt. "We can salvage it. It's close to the same color," she says soothingly.

My face is warm. "I'm so sorry," I say to Vivian, who waves it away.

Darcy returns a moment later with a roll of paper towels that Jane snatches from him to help me.

"Here, let's clean this up in the bathroom," Jane says. "Where's the nearest one?"

"Around the hall to the left," Vivian answers Jane.

Jane and I carefully hurry to the bathroom where we set about the task of cleaning the wine off my skirt.

I shake my head in embarrassment when we close the door.

"I guess no day can go perfectly," I say ruefully as I take off my skirt to clean it more easily.

"This is just a minor annoyance. It's going fine," Jane replies reassuringly. She has a knowing glint in her eyes, and my face warms again for a different reason.

"I'm glad we came, though," I say as I dab a damp paper towel against the fabric. "I think it's going well, don't you?"

Jane smiles. "I bet you five dollars you will be officially together by the end of the evening."

"I think it will more likely be tomorrow," I reply dreamily. "We need to DTR without so many people around."

Jane bursts into laughter. "DTR! I haven't heard that term in forever!"

After a few minutes, it seems we've lifted the stain as much as possible.

"Not bad," I say as I examine the skirt.

Jane nods approvingly. "Let's get back. I'm ready for pie!"

I link my arm through Jane's, and we head back to the dining room feeling cheered. We're starting to round the corner when Jane stills me. I look at her curiously, and then I hear it.

"... could do so much better, Fitzwilliam. She's practically the same age as your little sister! You're nearly thirty years old! Stop playing around!"

I suck in my breath and blink my eyes quickly. The room is uncomfortably silent. I swallow uncomfortably and will myself not to cry. I vaguely register Jane slipping her arm around my shoulders and squeezing.

"I am serious, Cathy." His voice is quiet enough that I almost don't hear it. There is no mistaking his sternness, though. I release the breath caught in my chest.

"Can you imagine taking her to one of your investor dinners? No one would take her seriously! Nor you, by extension!"

"Cathy—" Vivian says, but Darcy interrupts her.

"You obviously don't want to understand me, but it doesn't matter. I won't change my mind. If you knew her like I did, or even how Freddy got to know her when she worked for you, you would realize that she's smart, interesting, caring, and kind. And driven. She walked right into D.B. Shaw and handed them her résumé without any job openings to speak of. Diane told me."

"Someone like Annalise would be more appropriate—"

"I think that's enough, Cathy," Earl says. "The girls are our guests, and we don't want them to hear anything."

The room sinks into silence again, and all I hear is the scraping of cutlery. I glance over at Jane, but we still hang back.

"The turkey turned out well," Marissa says neutrally.

"Dad's the expert," Vince replies in a similar tone.

We take this as our cue to enter. I try to pretend I didn't hear anything, but I can't bring myself to look at Cathy. I slide into the chair and turn toward Darcy.

"How's the stain?" he asks softly.

I hold his gaze for a long moment. I want to tell him I overheard what he said and let him know what it means to me. I settle for a kiss on his cheek and an expression that I hope communicates gratitude.

"It's fine. It's good. Thanks to your fast thinking with the paper towels," I say.

He nods and then leans in to murmur close to my ear. "I don't think I mentioned how pretty you look today and how glad I am that you're here."

If we weren't surrounded by people, I would kiss him.

"Do I get to see you tomorrow?" I ask.

Darcy smiles and tucks my hair behind my ear. "Absolutely," he says.

Chapter Twenty-One

Jane and I both sleep late the next morning. When we emerge, it's colder than expected for this time of year. We walk around the corner to get coffee and have to bundle up in woolen scarves and gloves. The air stings and carries the sharp aroma of frost even though the ground is bare.

On our way back home, coffee cups in hand, Jane raises the topic I've been dying to hear about but haven't wanted to bring up first.

"Chip is still texting me," she says. She says it without emotion, and I wonder how I should respond. I casually take a sip of coffee.

"Have you replied yet?"

Jane shakes her head and fixes her eyes on our shadows stretched in front of us.

"I still don't know what to think," she says finally. "But he hasn't stopped texting."

We walk in silence for a few more minutes until we reach our building and walk inside. I cast Jane a sidelong glance to ascertain her mood, but her expression remains blank.

"I think I should talk to him?" Her statement sounds like a question. Her fingers drum against her coffee cup.

"You do?" I reply carefully.

Jane looks away from me and stares uncertainly up the staircase. "I think I'll always wonder if I don't."

"And what if he wants to get back together?" I ask. Jane starts up the stairs and I hurry to catch up with her. "Jane?"

"I guess it depends on what he has to say." She opens the door to our apartment, and I follow in after her. I turn on the heater and watch her unwind the scarf from around her neck.

"You know, it really comes down to one thing," she says, finally making eye contact with me. "Does he want to be with me—the person who wants to have a career helping kids in broken homes? Is he willing to be patient and not grow resentful or jealous when I build my reputation as a mediator? It's more than me fitting into his life; he has to fit into mine too."

"You're right," I say. "And I think it's really brave of you to talk to him again."

Jane shakes her head modestly. "Brave, maybe. More likely masochistic," she says in a rueful tone, foreign to her normal sweet attitude.

"Don't doubt yourself." I squeeze her hand. "You've got this."

"I hope you're right," Jane says dejectedly. "I'm still so confused."

"But you know what you want," I affirm. "That's what counts. I know you'll stand your ground when it comes to your career. And your love life, for that matter."

"I don't know what I've done to deserve your confidence." Jane shakes her head and rubs her eyes.

"You've always been strong," I reply with a steady gaze. Jane smiles at me wanly. She's so much stronger now than she was before when she was so overwhelmed and uncertain in her life as a lawyer. I know Jane will get through this conversation with Chip and come out of it in control.

THE RESTAURANT CROWDS ARE THIN SINCE IT'S THE DAY AFTER THANKS-giving, which provides Darcy and me a certain privacy we normally wouldn't get on a Friday night. We don't stay out too late, however, since he had to get up early to take Georgie to the airport, so we end up going back to my apartment to "watch a movie." I suggested *Herb & Dorothy*, my favorite documentary, about an older couple, a mail sorter and a librarian, who spent most of their lives and income collecting art. We valiantly watch the entire thing without making out, even though the feeling of him pressed close to me is incredibly distracting. We've been fairly chaste thus far, but that feeling has been slowly shifting recently.

When the movie is over, I stare up at him in my dark living room. We don't talk, and I marvel over how much I love his face—the warm brown eyes, the finely sculpted cheekbones, the inviting lips. He touches my cheek lightly while I hold his gaze. I can barely draw in oxygen. The moment is spellbinding. He lifts his face and kisses the corner of my mouth. I wait for his next move. Then he kisses me deeply.

I feel the twinge of nostalgia as a familiar frisson jolts through me. We are so good together like this. When he touches me, it's as if I've suddenly been lit up after years of being in the dark and the light is so bright that it's almost overwhelming. No one has ever done this to me before.

He's shifted me so I'm sitting on top of him, knees planted next to his hips, and his fingertips drift up and down my spine while we kiss. I hear myself moan when he pushes against me.

I pull back quickly, panting. He tightens his hold on my waist and stares up at me. He blinks up at me quizzically.

"What's wrong?"

"So, you're like my boyfriend now?" I blurt breathily. He responds by laughing.

I climb off of him and cross my arms in a huff.

"Lizzie," he says, still sounding amused. I raise my eyebrows in challenge. "That's what this second chance is, right?"

"Except you didn't ask me. You just assumed again."

Darcy moves toward me and plays with our fingers for a silent moment until they are woven together in a strong grasp.

"All I want is to be with you," he says finally. "If *you* want to be with me. So, yes, I would like you to be my girlfriend."

I feel happiness shoot through me. "Good. Thank you. I *do* want to be with you," I say, punctuating each sentence with a kiss. "There, was that so hard?"

"No, it wasn't," he agrees.

He tugs our joined hands and starts guiding me toward my room. I try not to laugh at his eagerness.

We don't bother turning on the lights when we enter. As soon as the door is closed, he reaches under my sweater and pulls it over my head. He kisses me again and again till my lungs burn, and I'm being lowered gently onto my bed. I feel so much closer to him than I did all those other times. I reach up for him, and he lowers himself over me. I welcome the weight. He pulls back a moment, chest rising and falling, and stares down at me.

"This is real," he whispers in wonder.

"Yes," I reply softly. He undoes the buttons to my jeans and I lift my hips to help him slide them off. He removes his own sweater and jeans and hovers over me, touching my lips lightly at first and then increasing the pressure until we are kissing deeply again.

"Please," I whimper.

He kisses his way down my throat and removes my bra to swirl his tongue around my nipples. I'm so tightly wound I can't help dragging my fingernails up his sides. He moans against me, kissing down my stomach to my thighs and then to the apex between my legs. Oh God, he's good at this. The pressure builds, but I want him inside me, so I reach down to pull him back up to me. We kiss again and again and again. I can hear the soft drum of raindrops outside. After retrieving a condom, Darcy enters me smoothly, and I gasp in pleasure. He covers his mouth with mine, and I groan against him. The room is quiet aside from the creak of the bed and our urgent but muted moans. I'm so close. And I love him.

The erratic pivot of Darcy's hips signals his coming release. I reach between our bodies to touch myself and quicken my orgasm. He grips the back of my knees and pushes my legs up so he can drive deeper. I can feel the building tension. When I cry out, Darcy pushes into me with a shuddering thrust.

"Oh God," he says when he rolls off of me. He nestles me into his arms and kisses my forehead multiple times. He stops to stare in my eyes, his expression intent. "I—I want you to know that my feelings—what I said to you before—nothing's changed. I never stopped loving you."

I look up at him, my fingers drifting along his jawline. "I love you too," I say softly. We smile at each other and then start kissing again.

We make love twice that night before we fall asleep, and he rouses me early in the morning with intimate touches. We barely get out of bed all day.

Enough hours pass that I assume Darcy plans to stay over again until he rolls over on his side and stretches.

"I should feed Misty. And change."

I link my arms around his neck and press my face to his shoulder. He laughs.

"I like it here with you," I mumble against him.

"Come back with me then."

"Okay."

His palm drifts down my hip. "Bring some stuff for tomorrow," he murmurs in a low voice.

I look up at him happily; he doesn't have to ask me twice.

It's twilight by the time we drive at Darcy's townhouse. Misty is crazy for food when we walk in the door, and I drop my bag next to my shoes while Darcy goes to feed her.

Darcy's dining room table is set up like a makeshift desk and littered with papers. I wonder what he's been working on.

"Been busy?" I ask, indicating the mess.

"Oh, yeah, kind of," he says. "I was tapped to be a judge for *Directed Infinity*, and I'm reviewing pitches."

"Are you really?" I reply, interested. "I think Charlotte sent in a pitch."

"Don't tell me her project; I can't show favoritism," he says, joining me at the table.

"All I know is it's some sort of software. Charlotte said it's top secret." I rest my arms on his shoulders. "Look at you, making those start-up dreams come true," I say.

He shakes his head modestly and kisses me. "Do you want to order Thai?" he asks. I grin and nod.

An hour later, it's just like old times but better. We sit in his bed, lazily eating take-out with only the sheets as our cover. This time, I know what we are. The realization suddenly makes this ritual sweeter; all those times before were just a prelude to us now.

DESPITE THE FACT THAT I LOVE MY JOB, RETURNING TO WORK AFTER A long weekend is painful. Even more difficult is the distraction I feel with everything that's happened in the last seventy-two hours. I haven't been home since Saturday morning.

It was my first time commuting from Darcy's place to the gallery. I was able to sleep in some since he lives closer to downtown than I do, but leaving bed was still difficult, especially on a dark, rainy November morning with his warm body wrapped around me.

I promised him I'd come back after work. I suddenly realized that I'm becoming one of those girls who falls off the face of the earth when she gets a boyfriend. I used to make fun of girls like that—the ones who would disappear when they had a new guy to become absorbed in and would only emerge for the occasional girls' night out then leave early to go home to the boyfriend.

I know I'm absorbed. It's hard not to be at this stage of new love.

I'm so caught up that I practically float in through the gallery doors past Diane and Rosa to my desk. I know I have a ridiculous look on my face. I can feel it, but I can't bring myself to care. Love is overtaking the cynic in me.

"Good morning, Lizzie," Diane says.

"Morning!" I sing cheerfully.

Diane laughs. "You would think the sun was shining by the look on your face."

I shrug, and the corners of my mouth turn up. "I'm in a good mood."

"And how is Fitzwilliam?" Diane asks, raising an eyebrow.

"Great," I reply. I switch on the computer and smooth my hair after I sit down. "Never better."

Diane gives me an approving nod. "Glad to hear it," she replies.

To my later embarrassment, I act a little stupid all day with my secret texts to Darcy and my dreamy expression, but my colleagues seem understanding—today, at least. I'll have to get my head out of the clouds at some point.

I bus straight back to Darcy's place, and we stop by the market to buy groceries for dinner. He chops and I cook while we listen to *PBS Newshour* from the living room. I get a text from Jane as we're sitting down to dinner.

Just wanted to check in, it says.

I cringe as I reply. *Sorry!! I'm still at Darcy's. I should have told you my plans.*

It's fine, she replies. *I know what it's like ;).*

The emoticon doesn't soften my guilt.

"What is it?" Darcy asks, watching me.

"Jane's just checking in. I, uh, I think I'm neglecting her."

Darcy makes a pensive noise. "As much as I hate to say it, we don't need to spend *all* our time together."

"But I like spending all my time with you," I tease fondly.

He smiles and shakes his head. "We could always hang out in a group," he suggests. "Like we did this summer."

"You mean when Jane and Chip made out in front of us and Emmeline was catty to me?"

Darcy laughs. "Emmeline won't be there this time. And Jane and Chip are still working stuff out."

"Okay," I concede. "I guess we could plan a 'group hang,'" I say with exaggerated air quotes. Darcy laughs at me again and drags me over to his lap.

"You make me so happy," he says, kissing me softly.

In the end, we agree to spend the next night apart. And, much as I miss him, I am grateful for the time with Jane. She and I walk over to the sushi place a few blocks from our apartment, and she starts to tell me about Chip.

"He keeps asking me to hang out, but he isn't pressuring me for anything more," she says while we push through the entrance of Chiso. "And when we do hang out, we talk about *everything*. He seems really interested in my new job."

I meet her eyes and read the hope in her anxious expression.

"So what's next?" I ask.

Jane shrugs, and we silently follow the host back to a table.

"I know you must want something more if you're still hanging out with him," I say after we're seated.

"Maybe," Jane says. "We'll see."

Jane soon changes the subject, speculating about when Mai will have her baby and how it will be when our mom comes to town for Christmas.

"I bet she'll be distracted by the new baby," I say while we eat.

"*I* think she'll want to get to know Darcy," she replies.

I roll my eyes. "Can't I introduce him to Dad first?"

"Mom will love him," she affirms.

"That's because he's rich and famous," I snort.

"Or because he's good to you," Jane says seriously. "I know she comes on strong, but you know all she wants is for us to be happy."

"Yeah, yeah, I know," I grumble.

My mother may be annoying, but I do have to grudgingly admit she wants the best for me, even if she has tried to control the way I get there.

"Well, you'll have a lot to show for yourself when she comes into town," Jane says brightly. "Right on her timeline too!"

"Jane!" I exclaim. "I think that's the first sarcastic thing I've ever heard you say! Good for you."

Jane laughs and shakes her head. I've grown a lot over the past six months, but so has Jane. I can't help but feel proud of her.

It doesn't take long for Darcy and me to establish a pattern: two nights at my apartment, two nights at his house, and three apart. It's a nice arrangement, and it still gives me time to see my friends. Jane and I have also established a Wednesday evening yoga-and-dinner ritual that keeps us connected.

Jane and I are doing dishes, having completed our living room yoga and finished dinner. We made Mom's favorite Buddha Bowl recipe in Jane's recent campaign to live "cleaner" and go vegan. Chip's even started following her strict guidelines—I suppose in part to impress her. Despite his attention, they still aren't officially back together. Jane is making him prove himself.

"Lizzie," Jane says hesitantly, as she passes me a dish to dry, "what do you think about Chip?"

"What do you mean?" I towel off the plate and stack it on the shelf.

"Well, I haven't been making it easy on him. I mean, I told him he would have to hang out with me as friends for a while before I considered anything else."

"That was a smart decision," I say as neutrally as possible.

"But I have to admit...I still care for him...romantically."

"I know," I reply nonchalantly.

"You do?"

"You're testing his mettle for a reason."

"I guess I am," she replies thoughtfully, as if the idea hadn't occurred to her before.

"So?" I ask, taking a drinking glass from Jane.

"So, I guess it's time for me to put him out of his misery."

"He'll be relieved, I bet."

Jane's eyes sparkle at me. "You think?"

"The man's not on a raw vegan diet because he *enjoys* it, Jane."

Jane laughs happily and finds her phone. "I may be a while." She glows with hope as she drifts to her room.

Chapter Twenty-Two

I n early December, Darcy and I plan our first "group hang." We invite
Jane and Chip to Linda's for brunch and bottomless mimosas.

Jane and Chip are still careful around each other, but I can see Jane
slowly rebuilding her trust in him. And Chip is putting in an impressive
effort. He must really care about her.

Chip, of course, brings Winston along to our outing, and I can't help
but coo over his sweet face and wiggly Corgi butt.

"Well, boys," I say after we're seated at our table. "I hate to break it to
you, but Barbie Venetidis is coming to town next week."

"Lizzie!" Jane laughs.

"I'm just saying we should prepare them," I reply dryly.

Chip laughs but looks a little concerned. Darcy reaches to capture my hand.

"Just be thankful you're part of the 'successful life' checklist. That grants
you extra brownie points," I say, glancing between Chip and Darcy seriously.

"Any other suggestions?" Chip asks anxiously.

"Start your 401(k)," I tease him. "Brush up on fad diet knowledge. And
make sure you have a workout routine!"

Jane touches Chip's shoulder. "You don't need to do all that," she says
soothingly. "Lizzie is just joking."

Chip laughs nervously. Darcy leans close to my ear. "Should I take your
mother out on a run?" he asks, eyes bright.

I roll my eyes. "Try not to be *too* perfect," I reply. "Then she'll say I
don't deserve you."

"What a ridiculous idea," Darcy replies. "It's me who doesn't deserve you."

"Flattery will get you everywhere." I then kiss him in front of Chip and Jane. It's a good thing they're getting used to our behavior.

A few days before Mom arrives in town, Mai has her baby.

Jane and I visit them in the hospital as soon as we hear. Sweet little Noah is so tiny and perfect. Jane holds him first, nestling his small body in her arms.

"I've never held one so new before," she says softly. I look over her shoulder, and he blinks intently, staring up at us.

Jane then passes him to me, and I shift him in my arms.

"He's beautiful," I marvel, touching his tiny hand with my finger. He curls his own small fingers around mine with a gentle grip. I inhale his intoxicating baby smell and smile at Aunt Mai. She smiles back, her expression a mingling of joy and exhaustion. My mind skips back to the moment of that terrible fight Darcy and I had and what he had envisioned. Was it this? A flawless little creature so perfectly reflecting the image of both parents? The strong brow of my uncle and the delicate features of my aunt. Every detail of his being miniature and carefully formed.

Someday.

My heart is full of possibilities. It will be years till I'm ready to talk about a family with Darcy, but we can deepen our love in the meantime and explore that in the future. I've never felt so lucky.

In preparation for Mom's imminent arrival, Jane and I go shopping. In the long run, it won't matter; she will focus on our jobs, our bodies, our boyfriends…but we can't help it. She's built such a strong framework for our lives that the anticipation makes us want to show we're living up to her expectations.

I think, in time, I will be comfortable enough in my own decisions not to question myself when facing her judgment. I'm so used to her voice as almost my conscience, whether I agree with it or not. But now…now I understand my own inner voice. I'm nervous in a different way, I guess. I want her to approve my decisions, but for myself, not within the framework she's set out. I want her to be glad of where I am. There's a chance she could disapprove, and if that's the case, I hope I feel at peace.

Downtown is uncomfortably full of holiday shoppers. Street musicians crowd the corners with turned-up hats full of coins. Jane and I link arms so we don't get lost in the shuffle. It's dark already, the sun setting at barely past four, and lights twinkle on the bare trees lining the sidewalks. Even once inside the store, the crowd is elbow-close, and the generic Christmas music is nauseating.

"Please, let's get this done as soon as possible," I entreat Jane.

"Agreed," she says. "It is overwhelming out here!"

In fact, the amount of time Jane and I take to pick out clothes Mom will approve of is almost heroic. Jane examines a pair of pearl earrings, but I won't go that far. I refuse to cross the Stepford line.

We arrive home, exhausted and laden with shopping bags. Jane checks the mail on our way to the door.

"Something for you, Lizzie," she says, handing me a large envelope after I unlock the door.

I drop my shopping bags and turn the envelope over.

"It's from UW," I say, with a slight tremor in my voice. "A big envelope is a good sign, right?" I look up at Jane nervously and worry my bottom lip.

She smiles in assurance. "Only one way to find out."

I rip open the envelope and scan the letter on top of the packet inside.

Dear Elizabeth,

Congratulations! On behalf of the Admissions Committee, I am pleased to inform you that your application for admission to the School of Art, Art History, and Design has been approved...

My heart skips a beat, and I glance up at Jane in bewilderment. Seeing my expression, she instantly squeals and hugs me.

"You got in!" she surmises.

"I got in," I repeat. I can't stop grinning.

"I knew you would." She beams.

I feel in a daze. I sit down on the couch and then stand up again. "I don't know what to do with myself." I laugh.

Jane laughs too and hugs me again. "Call Dad, of course," she says. "He's the one who told you to apply in the first place."

I absently nod in agreement and gather up my admission packet as if it's some kind of precious treasure.

"He'll be so proud of you," Jane declares.

"I got in," I repeat, smiling at Jane again.

"Go call Dad," she replies, hugging me again. "I'm so proud of you!"

I meet her eyes, and I can see the tears gathered there. Jane has always been my biggest champion. I wish I knew how to tell her how I feel, how grateful I am for her and her unwavering support, but I can't seem to find the words. I hug her tightly then go call my dad.

I STAY OVER AT DARCY'S THE NIGHT BEFORE MOM ARRIVES. "IT'S THE CALM before the storm," I joke to him. I've mentioned to her that I have a boyfriend, but I haven't said who, hoping she either won't recognize his name or, if she does, she won't make a big deal out of it. So far, the pattern Darcy and I have set up is so normal that it's easy for me to forget about his money and occasional photo in *People*.

We settle into bed for the night with Misty sprawled between our legs. As has become habit, Darcy reaches for me, and we start gently kissing as soon as the lights are out.

I giggle when he moves his lips to my ear.

I laugh. "It tickles."

Darcy makes a noise somewhere between a laugh and a moan. I relish this time together. Our intimacy hasn't lost its addictive quality yet either. I hope it never does.

After we finish, I cuddle into the crook of his shoulder and stretch my legs across his. He lightly rubs my calf and kisses my forehead.

"Darcy?" I ask softly, looking up at his face. "Have you always gone by your last name?"

He doesn't respond right away, and I almost repeat myself before he answers.

"No. My family, you've probably noticed, call me Fitzwilliam." He makes a distasteful face, and I laugh.

"I did notice Diane calls you Fitzwilliam," I say.

"Yeah, she does." He hesitates and then continues. "My mother called me Will. Georgie still calls me that too, but only her. It's a…special nickname."

I search his eyes tenderly.

"You can call me Will too if you want," he says quietly.

"Will," I test the name on my tongue and then kiss him lightly. "I'll have to practice, I think."

I repeat the name again and rise up to my knees. I kiss his cheeks and jaw, down his neck, across his chest. He guides my knee to the other side of his hip and grips the swell of my backside.

"I love you, Will," I say as I lower myself onto him. He kisses me passionately and pushes upward. We both groan simultaneously then laugh.

"Lizzie," he says, as we increase our pace. "Elizabeth," he draws out my name. I throw my head back and lose myself in the sensation.

I come harder than I ever have before, crying out incoherently. His release follows mine as he pushes up and shudders. In the stillness that follows, the only sound is our breathing. He still grips my hips and then moves his touch up my sweaty back.

At this moment, I know that I will eventually marry Will Darcy. I can't imagine loving anyone else as much as I love him.

JANE AND I PICK UP MOM FROM THE AIRPORT ON FRIDAY AFTERNOON. She meets us at baggage claim, as fresh faced as Jane, wearing a fashionable Lululemon ensemble of heathered grey leggings and a cashmere zip-up hoodie.

"Girls!" she shrieks. She kisses both of us on the cheek, leaving bubblegum pink lip prints behind.

"Hi Mom!" Jane greets cheerfully, rubbing her cheek clean. "How was the flight?"

"Don't even ask," Mom replies, pushing her white-blonde hair over her shoulder. "I sat next to this"—she leans in conspiratorially and whispers—"very *large* man. I could hardly move my arms. *And* there was this loud child near me that made me wish for Xanax. I'm *so* glad to finally be here."

She looks between us brightly and rubs the lipstick off my cheek with her thumb.

"What would you say to a smoothie, girls? And a power walk before dark?"

I can't help but be amused at her boundless energy. Some things never change.

I sit in the back seat while Jane drives home. Mom prattles on about a new juice cleanse she'd like to try, and she turns around to examine me.

"You could use some more citrus, Lizzie. It helps with frizz." She pats the top of her head meaningfully. "It's a shame you got your father's hair. I could barely get a brush through it when you were young."

"I know," I reply, rolling my eyes.

She raises her eyebrows at me, silently telling me to stop challenging her. I look out the window.

"So, anyway," she says, "when do I get to meet your men? I'm *full* of curiosity!"

"We have reservations tomorrow night," Jane says. "At Canlis."

"It's fancy," I say, catching Mom's eye in the mirror while she reapplies her lipstick.

"Is it now?" she says, turning around happily. "I have just the dress to wear."

Jane shares a bed with me that night and gives Mom her room. At five in the morning, we are startled awake for a morning run.

"You've got to keep your figures up!" Mom sings, flipping the lights on. I groan and turn over, but Jane slides out of bed.

"The weekend is for sleep," I whine, burying my head under the pillow.

"Laziness gets you nowhere. Up, up, up!"

I miserably jog after Jane and Mom while the sun rises. I have the crazy impulse to call an Uber and go straight to Will's, just for some extra sleep. We jog all the way to the Ballard Locks and pause to stretch by the guardrails above the water. My lungs burn, and I take a huge gulp from my water bottle.

"A sea lion!" Jane exclaims, pointing over the body of water. The sea lion splashes above and below the water surface a few times before disappearing.

"Good eyes, sweetie," Mom praises.

The park is empty this morning, as if the whole city is still hibernating. The stillness around us is soothing. *Not as soothing as my bed right now*, I think sarcastically, but the tranquility does have an appeal, I suppose.

Mom props her leg up on the rail above the water and joins my stretching.

"So, tell me about this job, Lizzie," she says, examining me closely. Our breath fogs out in front of us as we pant.

"I'm a gallery assistant," I say simply. Mom gives me a look and motions for me to continue. "It's like a glorified receptionist. I help with the logistics of the gallery—scheduling, pick up, events…"

"And you're happy with this *job*?"

"Yes," I reply sharply, trying not to feel offended. "The head curator is grooming me to take over when one of the older curators retires. I just, um, need to get my master's first."

"Do you now?"

I bite my lip nervously and glance over at Jane. She nods at me in encouragement.

"I was accepted at UW next fall," I say carefully. "Dad's going to help me."

"Oh," she replies simply. She continues to stretch in silence. Jane and I exchange worried glances.

"Well," Mom says, regaining some of her pep. "It's only fair he help you since he helped Jane through law school. At least he's taking *some* responsibility for your education."

I don't know what to make of this comment, and by Jane's expression, neither does she. Is Mom happy about my job path? Or is she jealous that Dad is helping and not her? As much as I love her, I don't know that we'll ever totally understand each other.

THAT EVENING, WILL AND CHIP MEET AT OUR APARTMENT TO DRIVE US TO dinner. Chip nervously presents Mom with a bottle of wine while Will follows in after her.

"Mom, this is Chip," Jane says, "and Darcy."

"Fitzwilliam Darcy," she states, a little shocked. She turns her head toward me sharply. "What is this?"

"Darcy is my boyfriend."

She's silent for almost a full minute. Will looks a little sheepish and Chip lost. Jane, who has grasped Chip by the arm, starts drumming her fingers against him.

"Well, okay. Your boyfriend," Mom starts to say. "Your father was quite the innovator," she says, wagging her finger at Will. "You're a little famous!"

"Not by choice," Will replies uncomfortably. I try not to laugh.

"Darcy and Chip grew up together," I offer.

"Oh, Chip, thank you for the wine," she spins toward him and kisses his cheek. "He's cute, Jane." She winks.

"Mom," she whines, but she smiles anyway. Chip's face is red.

"Shall we?" Will says, gesturing toward the door.

"Oh, yes, Fitzwilliam Darcy, let me take your arm!" She adjusts the cleavage on her dress and drags him out the door. "Where in the world did you meet him?" she calls over her shoulder.

"At a bar, Mom," I reply, rolling my eyes.

"So normal!" she remarks.

"Of course it is," I say, slightly exasperated. Darcy glances over his shoulder at me, his eyes laughing. I press my temple and shake my head.

I hope Mom gets over *Fitzwilliam Darcy*, son of the legendary George Darcy, soon.

Much to my horror, my mother flirts with Will throughout dinner. When it is revealed that he picked out the restaurant, her effusions over the elegance are almost embarrassing. The only thing keeping me grounded is Will's hand in mine under the table while he graciously attempts to cover his embarrassment.

When Mom leaves to use the restroom, I slump in the chair with a long-suffering groan.

"It's not *that* bad," Jane says.

"Mom isn't hitting on *your* boyfriend," I quip, rubbing my eyes.

"Don't worry about it," Will says tenderly. He kisses my forehead and then my lips just as Mom is returning.

"I bet you two will be married in the year!" she declares as she takes her seat.

"Mom," I entreat, embarrassed. "I'm only twenty-two!"

She waves the protest away as if it's a non-concern. "I was pregnant with you at your age."

"No wonder you look like their sister," Chip says awkwardly.

"Oh!" Mom replies, clearly flattered. "Sisters! I prefer that to what they call me at work. What does MILF even mean? It sounds like it's short for Milfred."

I almost choke on my water.

"Mom!" I groan.

"It means Mom I'd Like to F—"

"That's okay, Chip," Jane interrupts. "We can tell her later."

"Mom I'd like to F—?" Mom repeats. She looks around the table, puzzled, until she finally figures it out. "Oh!" she declares. "Well, I don't mind being called *that*." She looks between Jane and me seriously. "Girls, this is why we keep up our figures. When you're my age, wouldn't you still want young men desiring you?"

"Oh my God," I say, rubbing my forehead.

"We do yoga on Wednesdays," Jane says weakly.

"Save me," I whisper to Will.

"It will be over soon," he whispers back.

I love my mother, but thank God she lives two states away.

Chapter Twenty-Three

Christmas seems to fly by with all of the family obligations and holiday parties. It's with a mix of relief and sadness that Jane and I take Mom to the airport the day after Christmas. Mom was sad to leave too but told us seriously that the gym gets the most business after the New Year. "It's all the resolutions," she explained for the hundredth time.

Mom has left, but Georgie is home for winter break and Emmeline is also in town for the holidays. Earlier in the year, she had convinced Chip to throw a New Year's Eve party at the Victory Room in the Queen Anne Plaza, which has an impressive view of the Space Needle. Jane privately mentioned that Emmeline planned it but made Chip pay. She looked slightly irritated when she revealed this detail.

"I think Emmeline is used to getting what she wants," I whisper.

"Maybe not everything." She glances over at Will, who is approaching us with two glasses of pink wine. I smile at him as he joins us.

In the spirit of New Year's Eve, we have all dressed to the nines. I am wearing a shimmery gold strapless dress and tall shoes that I know I will abandon at some point during the night. Will is wearing a tailored suit that makes me want to stroke his shoulders.

"I'm going to make you dance with me tonight," I say, accepting the glass of wine.

"You don't want to see that," he replies, laughing.

I raise my eyebrows flirtatiously. "Dancing is fun—when you have the right partner."

"Darcy!" Emmeline cries, joining our group. The music playing is upbeat but not dance worthy yet. Around us people mingle, drink, and snack on canapés. Emmeline touches Will's arm possessively.

"I've barely had a chance to see you since I've arrived back in town. How are you? And…" Here she winces and glances over at me. "And Lizzie, how are you?" Her tone holds a desperate sort of friendliness. I can see her struggle between jealousy and grace. She catches my eye worriedly, and it's then that I feel a little sorry for Emmeline. She may be ridiculously single-minded when it comes to Will, but it's this single-mindedness that's keeping her from finding a guy she could actually be with. I step forward and give her a hug I try not to make awkward.

"It's good to see you, Emmeline," I say sincerely. "I can't believe it's almost been six months since we were all together."

"Yes," Emmeline replies, surprised. "Time flies."

"Find me if 'Twist and Shout' comes on." I wink. "I think our dance needs a revival."

We exchange some idle chitchat while Emmeline's gaze lingers on Will's hand that rests on the small of my back. She soon makes an excuse to depart with Jane.

"You handled that well," Will says when we're alone.

"It's sad, really. She won't let herself look at anyone else."

"I know. I never knew how to get her to look somewhere else without saying something mean, so I just ignored it."

I raise my eyebrows at him. "What else could you do?"

A stupid pop song comes on, and I gaze up at Will.

"I have two left feet," he pleads.

"Just stand with me then." I laugh as I drag him to the dance floor.

Will looks incredibly awkward while I dance around him. I place his hands on my hips and shimmy. He laughs but looks a little lost. I decide to have mercy and lead him off the floor.

"You are hopeless," I say.

"You can't teach rhythm," he jokes self-consciously.

We keep to the sidelines for a while and enjoy our drinks. Chip and Jane are on the dance floor, seemingly in their own world. The sight of them warms my heart. They are happier now than they ever were before.

The music cuts out so we can begin our countdown. I turn to Will and think of everything we've been through. The heartache and love. And growth.

We still have a lot to work on. But we always will, won't we? There will always be challenges. The New Year will see a court hearing and possible rehab for Geoff but also a trip to Chicago where I'll introduce Will to my dad. Charlotte will compete on *Directed Infinity* with her cyber security software. Jane and Chip will continue to fall madly in love. Maybe Emmeline will even open herself up to someone new. Katrina will spend a semester abroad and stretch her wings beyond Lydia's influence. And then there's Lydia. I can't predict what's in store for her aside from her work with Doctor Fitzwilliam while she grieves her relationship with Geoff. It took time for her to understand that his feelings were much shallower than her own. His inevitable neglect after her time in the hospital was painful to watch, yet I have hope for things to come. She's even making the effort to get to know Will.

Will and I clasp hands as the countdown continues.

Five...four...three...two...one.

He kisses me warmly with a love that I never fathomed was within my grasp. I never predicted I would usher in the New Year this way. I never knew he was a possibility until I got to know who he really was.

I don't know a lot of things. But Fitzwilliam Darcy: him, I know.

Acknowledgements

There are so many people whose support and hard work have been invaluable throughout the process of completing *All the Things I Know*.

- My husband Ryan, who encouraged me to remain disciplined throughout the early stages of writing.

- My early readers: Ali Brown, Amy Walter, Brittany Roebke, Maria Palantini, and the folks at AHA for helping me whip my first draft into good shape.

- Meryton Press for taking on the book and especially Sarah Pesce, my awesome editor. This book wouldn't be what it is without you.

- My besties, the A-Team, who tolerated my incessant brainstorming throughout this process.

- And the rest of my family: Emme, Camille, Nick, Annie, Grandma, and everyone else. Thanks for always being my number one fans.

About the Author

Audrey Ryan is the nom de plume of Andrea Pangilinan: daydreamer, wife and step-mother, and obsessive story consumer. She studied writing in college, dreamt about becoming a novelist, and slowly forgot about it when real life took over. With a particular affection for contemporary retellings, adapting *Pride & Prejudice* to the modern day has always been a dream.

When she's not reading and writing, Andrea earns her living by marketing for the internet. She enjoys talking crazy to her weirdo cat, consuming copious amounts of wine and coffee with her girlfriends, and record shopping with her husband.

Oh yeah, and there's that small Jane Austen obsession. That doesn't take up any time at all.